CRIMSON TOBACCO BRIDES

BOOK 1

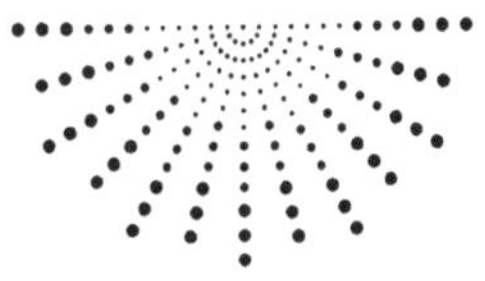

ID JOHNSON

For Ms. Gosch. You were so much nicer than your husband.

CONTENTS

1

LANDFALL

Sarah

DARK CLOUDS, SWOLLEN WITH RAIN, HANG OVER THE SAILS AND RIGGING of the *H.M.S. Waterlily*, the ship that has been my home for the last four and a half months. As much as I resent those clouds for the seasickness they promise in my future, I also welcome them. With their heavy covering overhead, I can stand on deck and enjoy the faint comfort of the salt air instead of hiding from the searing sun below.

Faint comfort truly is the best way to describe it. The deck rolls under my feet, sodden planks threatening to tip me end over end, sending legs and petticoats flying for the amusement of the cadre of sailors whose heavy, leering gazes only leave my shoulders to eye the other women aboard. In truth, I don't know whether such a simple act could knock me over anymore. Dark strength coils in my limbs, still unfamiliar to me. Sometimes, when my hand snaps out with unnatural speed, or I cross a room in a heartbeat instead of a few slow breaths, it feels as though someone—something else has taken control of my body. Four and a half months since we set sail in late Decem-

1

ber, and I am still no more used to my own abilities than I am the swaying of the sea.

"Land ho!" the youngest of the sailors bellows from the crow's nest.

A welter of activity begins around me—men shifting ropes, tying knots, talking to each other in brogues so thick my London-trained ears can barely believe they are speaking English. I peer at the gray horizon. After all the stories I've heard of the New World, I expect our arrival to be drenched in burning golden sunshine as we approach a coast so lush with life it calls to mind Eden more than anything that truly exists in our fallen world. But the sea ahead looks so much like the dove-colored waves I left behind, and I can barely pick out the vaguest humps of shadow on the horizon as land.

I blink quickly and turn away. Before that fateful ball, I wouldn't have been able to see a thing other than the fog, and we need to blend in if our plan is to be of any use at all. Better not to look, so no one has any cause to wonder what I am seeing.

Unfortunately, my gaze lands on Elizabeth, smiling coquettishly as she leans over the shoulder of Fergus, a fire-haired sailor she's decided to amuse herself with for the length of the trip. My heart beats a staccato rhythm against my breastbone, and I hurry across the deck toward her.

"Little sister?" I say as sweetly as I can manage around my fear. "Did you not hear the boy's cry? We approach land."

Elizabeth cuts the brilliant blue eyes she inherited from Father at me sharply, silently warning me to leave her be. I have been after her about Fergus almost since we set foot on the ship, and she's quite tired of hearing it. Surely, though, she understands whatever dalliance she struck up with him has to end before we reach the New World.

"Little sister?" Fergus says curiously, his Irish accent blurring most of the letters together into a single sound. "Forgive me, I assumed—"

He has assumed what nearly everyone assumes: that Elizabeth, with her dancing golden curls peeking out from her cap and her lilting laugh, is the heir to the Wentworth barony, and I am her dark younger sister, whom she brings around to be kind. It's a notion Elizabeth rarely troubles herself to correct. In truth, I have ceased trying years ago. I prefer to stand by her side rather than in the center of attention.

Elizabeth covers her mouth to hide a sweet laugh. "Lady Sarah has a year on me, it is true. Alas, she has the younger face."

"Now, I wouldn't say as such." Fergus grins at Elizabeth as if there's no one around to see the two of them, as if they do not both know Elizabeth's fate as soon as we disembark.

"We really must change," I insist. My voice sounds shrill to my own ears, and I almost wish to shake my head at myself as Elizabeth does.

"And in that year, she learned worry," Elizabeth says playfully. "I must indulge her, but this will not be our last goodbye.

"I'll wait for ye." Fergus winks—truly winks!—at Elizabeth before turning back to his work.

I slide my arm through Elizabeth's and begin walking toward the narrow trapdoor which will allow us below decks before she can risk her reputation any further. "What are you thinking? Any of these men could elect to stay in the colony once we reach it, and you would be ruined."

"Fergus has wives on two continents," she replies flippantly. "He doesn't wish to see me after this voyage any more than I wish to see him."

"An upstanding choice." My acerbic words taste bitter, but Elizabeth needs to understand. "Once we make land, we will be under intense scrutiny. No longer will there be all of London society to distract from us."

For all the good that does us, I think. Though I seem to be treating our escape with more of the gravity it deserves, I cannot lie to myself. I would have given almost anything to stay in lovely London, attending balls and sharpening my skills, rather than trudging out to the colonies. Even rumor can't disguise the hard work that awaits us on the other side of this journey. Our easy lives lie behind us. I can only hope to stop missing them someday.

"Jamestown is larger than ever," Elizabeth says as we squeeze our skirts through the hole in the deck. Privately, I thank the Lord that farthingales are no longer the style. We would never have been able to navigate the ship with cages around our hips. "I've heard the colonists number nearly a thousand."

"Far fewer than several hundred thousand." The steps of the ladder creak ominously under my embroidered leather shoes, a gift from Father at the last Christmas that didn't find us on a galley like this. "Elizabeth, our survival depends on carrying out these contracts."

"Do you think I don't know that?" Her voice slices through the gloom below decks more sharply than the guttering candle in the lantern. "Who secured us the contracts?"

"You did." I lift my skirts over a puddle my unluckily sharpened nose informs me is not seawater. "However—"

She stops abruptly in front of me, meets my gaze, and takes my shoulders in both her hands. "You trust me, don't you, Sarah?"

I take a deep breath. When I woke, scared, ill, and alone, on my first day in this new life, Elizabeth was the one beside me. When she confessed to me what she believed she had become however many days before, I didn't run. Growing up without a mother and with such an absent father as we had, we spent so long as each other's only companions. Though there are a few other women on the ship with similar contracts around their necks, we will soon be that again—alone together.

"More than another living soul," I admit. "Though perhaps I shouldn't say that now."

"Another unliving soul?" She laughs.

My skin crawls with gooseflesh at how easily she admits that, but I still let her slip her arm back through mine and lead me to the cabin we've been sharing with two other tobacco brides for the whole long trip from England. Our future awaits.

FERGUS HELPS ELIZABETH, NOW WEARING HER SECOND-FINEST GOWN, into one of the rowboats going to land with a sly smile. I pull my hood further over my head and pray the slowly lightening clouds linger long enough that we might get inside before we start to burn. The chiffon rimming Elizabeth's sleeves—and already melting in the salt air, as I told her it would—won't protect her a whit.

"One of you must deliver this to Sir Thomas Forrest, Esquire," the captain says sternly, studying each of us in turn as if trying to guess which woman wouldn't be silly enough to drop the wax-sealed scroll in his hand overboard on the short trip to shore.

"I'll safekeep it," Elizabeth offers brightly.

After another moment's hesitation, the captain relents. Elizabeth tucks the scroll inside her kirtle, tight against the under-bust corset she insisted the colonists would appreciate seeing. My nerves hum. Elizabeth took the scroll to quickly mark herself as important to Sir Thomas—but I trust her. Perhaps being important will grant us additional goodwill instead of just shining attention we can't bear up under.

The sailors lowered us to the surface of the sea with a splash, and we were free from the threat of Fergus. A pair of burly oarsmen rowed in long, powerful strokes. Jutting out from the riverbank was a dock much like those from home, but the closer we drew to the new world, the stranger it looked. There were no pebble beaches, only humps of grayish mud leaking into the brackish water. The town crouched back from the dock and within a wall, not of mannerly gray-white stone, but of felled logs prickling equally with their own sharpened tips and the iron noses of cannons. A forest loomed not far behind it, dark and threatening all the worst stories I'd heard of the colonies and the primitive men that lived here. Worry prickled along my skin. I didn't know how Elizabeth and I could have survived in London, but perhaps disappearing to the New World wasn't so clever an idea after all.

The rowboat judders to a stop at the dock. Two men peel off the small group waiting for us and help the sailors tie it down. Young, strapping men who look more like the sailors we just left than the gentleman-planters we've been told to expect when leaving London. Indentures, perhaps. Thankfully, Elizabeth only smiles politely at the one who offers her his hand out of the boat. I should trust her. She has been right about all the sailors staying with the *Waterlily*, and she knows when to show restraint. I put my worries aside and let the young, German-looking fellow help me ashore.

My first step onto dry land feels like a blessing from the Lord above. I nearly weep when the ground stays put under my feet instead of trying to tumble away.

Elizabeth curtsies deeply. "May I make the acquaintance of Sir Thomas Forrest, Esquire? I have a missive from the captain."

An older man, his shoulder-length curls shot through with gray, adjusts his slightly unfashionable but beautifully embroidered cloak and steps forward. "I am he."

Elizabeth turns slightly aside, then turns back with the scroll in her hand. Internally, I applaud her modesty. Sir Thomas plucks the scroll from her palm and breaks the seal with a crude knife, then studies the contents.

"Before us today," he reads, "stand Lady Sarah Wentworth, Lady Elizabeth Wentworth, Lady Felice Kennard, and Miss Winnifred Dunne, by charity of the fine men of Jamestown and grace of the Virginia Company for their safe passage. The maids will be quartered in my home and tended by my wife until such a time as one of the men who paid their passage sees fit to take them as a wife."

The crowd—overwhelmingly men, I realize with a small, unpleasant jolt—murmurs amongst themselves as they look us over. How do Sir Thomas or the Virginia Company expect to divide four women amongst three times as many men? I don't intend to be passed around between them.

Elizabeth naturally has none of my worries. She flutters her long, pale lashes like the governess Father fired after he found her with his valet and smiles a demure little grin. As always, the men take notice. What little attention is cast my way turns to her, as does the larger portion given to Lady Felice. She might only be the daughter of a baronet, but she has a lovely, fair face and red-gold hair under her cap. Miss Winnifred, who seemed sweet if self-contained on the voyage over, draws very few eyes without a title, regardless of how she might look.

Sir Thomas clears his throat and gestures behind him. "My wife, Mistress Margaret, will escort you to our house. Keep close. The streets turn to mud this time of year."

Mistress Margaret steps forward in an equally fine, and equally unfashionable cloak, then reaches her hand out to us.

"Ouch!" Elizabeth yelps and smacks some of the exposed skin of her neck.

I stare at her, wide-eyed, begging for any reason why she might behave so ridiculously.

"Something bit me." Her voice is pitiful and accusatory. She studies a reddish stain on the palm of her glove.

Sir Thomas sighs heavily. "Mosquitoes. You will become accustomed to them, in time."

The heavy, wooden gates of the fort swing open, beckoning us on that ill omen into whatever our future might hold.

2

MIDNIGHT

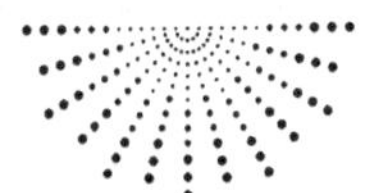

Sarah

Mistress Forrest leads the pack of us into the walls at her husband's instruction, and Jamestown unfolds before us. Fortunately, none of the men follow. The small welcoming party seems to be all the fanfare the colonial town can muster, and now even men in want of wives need to return to their work.

"This is our main street," she says with a vague gesture.

More of that gray mud churns underfoot in a narrow lane that would barely have dared to claim the title of road at home. Elizabeth takes one look at it and drapes her skirt over her arm, exposing inches of the kirtle underneath. My hands itch to correct her hold, hide a bit more of her, but the squelch of Mistress Forrest stepping onto the path encourages me to do the same instead. Mistress Forrest's cloak and dress, cut a bit shorter than propriety would have allowed in London, swish back and forth to reveal her shoes. Utilitarian clogs, with duly metal toes and blocks of wood that keep her tender feet up out of the muck. My leather shoes grow cold and pinching after only a few steps.

A whitewashed wooden church greets us, its culminating cross tilted at an odd angle. Two men hammer new thatch onto a hole in the roof, sweating in the midafternoon heat.

"Father Buck performs all our services," Mistress Forrest says. "Some of the men have not upkept their attendance as the Lord expects, and one of your duties as a wife will be ensuring they attend at least the Morning Prayer and Evensong on Sundays."

I nod, privately thinking that the men have failed to upkeep a great many things since moving to this wild place. The ones working on the roof have no hats to hide their hair, and one has doffed his jacket to expose not just his doublet but his sleeves as though the whole of Jamestown can't see him. The few people also on the street seem barely better dressed. A pair of women, likely indentures, wear their dresses draped higher over their arms than Elizabeth. I can see slivers of off-white linen, certainly the chemises that should've been hidden beneath their kirtles. Even Mistress Forrest's own shortened skirt would have drawn the eye in London. Though I do note that nearly everyone wears clogs much like hers, seemingly a universal concession to the bogginess of the land.

"The storehouse." Mistress Forrest indicates a long, low building. Stretches of daub connect the visible boards of the frame and peel up slightly at the corners. "In there, we keep all our communal supplies. It was that you could get a meal inside, but our fortunes have improved such that most meals are taken in family homes."

I've overheard a whispered conversation between Lady Felice and Miss Winnifred on the voyage over about the long, totalizing famine the colony suffered. That was almost a decade ago now, but clearly, it still marks the people here. Miss Winnifred is worried about another because barely a tenth of the colonists have survived, but Lady Felice is sure tobacco will keep us in fair wealth. I hope she is as right as she is confident.

"This is our home." Mistress Forrest strides past a low stone well and up to a single door in a row of houses so tightly clustered that I can't tell if they are built very near each other for space or share walls. She unlocks it with a single heavy key and allows us inside.

The Virginia Company representative in London had been quite clear that Sir Thomas is one of the wealthier men in the colony. He is a councilor in their nascent government and has survived from nearly the very first. Elizabeth has, on the long voyage over, often daydreamed to me about the luxurious house we'd surely stay in when our time in the swinging hammocks of the *Waterlily* was done. I'd thought her optimistic, but even I can't keep a tiny frown from puckering my brow as I take in our environs for the coming weeks.

Wood planks lay on the very dirt, barely cleaner than the mud we've left. An H-shaped chimney of clay and straw splits the two rooms. On one side, the roughest kitchen implements gather around the fireplace. Crockery the likes of which our scullery maids would've been embarrassed to use for their own meals hangs from the walls. On the other, a dining table lies empty except for a remarkably fine piece of lacework, half-finished, and a Bible. Something between a ladder and a set of stairs leads to an additional story.

"You'll all sleep in the garret," Mistress Forrest says. "The second story is for Thomas and I. You will help with the meals and the cleaning—and I would help well, as my word carries weight in this town. A successful housekeeper is more valuable than gold in the New World." Something in her face softens as she looks over us. "A living is a hard thing to claw out here, but all the more rewarding for its difficulty. And though the men may seem uncivilized, there are gentlemen below the surface yet. You will find your ways. I've knit a pair of stockings for each of you and left them on your pillows. Settle in, and I'll see you for dinner shortly."

With that, we are dismissed, expected to rustle ourselves up the steps on our own. While Elizabeth continues to stare around the small house in dismay, I take the lead. The second floor proves just as sparse as the first, and the garret even sparser, save four beds of straw and four sets of stockings on the lumpy pillows they bear. I set my portmanteau on one and look up at the thatched roof. A bit of sunshine peeks through in dusty shafts, too thin and weak to burn.

The more I see of Jamestown, the more I think I understand it. Here, there are none of the pretensions I often find so tiring in London. There is merely hard work, and those willing to do it. I will miss the days spent amusing myself in Father's library for the sheer pleasure of turning pages, but I know how to work. During our occasional lean periods, when Father was away at his business too long, I found myself in the kitchens or halls, scrubbing and cooking with the rest. Mistress Forrest is right—there is honor in difficulty. I can make a life here. And I intend to.

I don't fail to notice, however, that Lady Felice and Miss Winnifred take the beds as far from mine as they can and then shift them further still, leaving myself and Elizabeth alone on one side of the garret.

THAT NIGHT, I STIR FROM A RESTLESS AND UNCOMFORTABLE SLUMBER to the creak of wood. The third step down, which I noted on my ascent would give away any intruders. I blink my eyes open and peer through the unlit gloom as I couldn't have before my transformation.

Elizabeth's golden curls appear at the top of the stairs, the rest of Elizabeth close behind. She holds her shoes in one hand, obviously trying to soften her steps. I frown. What is she doing out of bed?

As she draws nearer, the answer becomes obvious in the crusted crimson around her lips. Blood—a feast of it, judging by how much she has spilled. And she hasn't even bothered to clean herself before returning to the home we sleep in. My pulse gallops.

"You must be more cautious," I hiss when she is near enough that I am certain not to wake the women on the other side of the garret.

"I was hungry," she says laconically, slowed with her meal like Father after a great feast. "Would you have preferred I eat something in here?"

"SOMEONE," I CORRECT. "AND YOU KNOW I WOULD NOT. BUT YOUR mouth—"

"Looks as if I've painted it." She flicks blood away with her tongue as she sheds the heavy kirtle she has alone covered her chemise with.

"These people have too many other concerns to trouble themselves with superstition."

People with a great many concerns are the most likely to be superstitious, I think, but all my clever arguments dissolve as her mouth turns the gore warm and delicious once more. Hunger gnaws at my guts. We have survived the voyage very carefully on rats, of which there are plenty, and the occasional fish. Enough to keep us alive, but certainly not enough to thrive. I have suspected that Elizabeth supplements her diet with Fergus and one of the cabin boys but have been unable to prove it. Now, with fresh human blood set in front of me for the first time since we fled London, a dark part of me wonders if she hasn't had the right of it.

No. I have learned to deny a great many hungers in my life, and this is simply another. I swallow the ravenous pit of myself down and marshal my thoughts.

I shouldn't like to give them reason to wonder if superstitions might be worth their time after all."

Elizabeth exchanges her chemise for a white linen nightgown with a delicate froth of embroidery around the neck and wrists. "The list of things you shouldn't like would rival the Bible for size."

I can't hide my shock at her blasphemy, and it only makes her laugh.

"I'll prove you worry too much," she says gaily, then raises her voice to slightly above the nonexistent whisper only our keen ears can pick out from the general nighttime hum. "Felice, Winnifred, you sleep next to a pair of vampires."

My heart crowds into my mouth, well on its way to escape. My skin turns to ice. Elizabeth has used that word, a few hours after she first woke up with this curse, and I told her never to do so again. We are demons. Monsters. Unliving things that ought to be in the cemetery yard rather than seeking husbands. But to name us so truly turns my stomach indescribably.

"You see?" She gestures at the still-sleeping forms of our companions. "They haven't leapt out of their beds with torches."

"It remains—"

"Perfectly all right," Elizabeth says with a note of finality. "We didn't travel all the way to the colonies to continue to hide like rats. I know how to handle these people, and I'll trust you not to interfere with my diet."

She lays down on her mattress, pulls her coverlet over her shoulders, and shuts her eyes. The conversation is over, but I continue to stare at the unfamiliar garret ceiling for many long minutes after Elizabeth's breaths have evened with sleep.

3

HUNGER

Sarah

"Here you are, Mistress Forrest," I say as I hand the lady of the house a bowl of cornmeal I have spent far longer than I expect grinding. My arms ache, but it is the sweet pain of hard work and knowing what I've done will become bread—or, if we're lucky, cake.

She takes the bowl delicately, as though even brushing my fingers would infect her with something. "Admirable work, Lady Sarah. You have your leisure for an hour."

I curtsy and leave the sweltering kitchen, dabbing at my forehead with a handkerchief as I go. Elizabeth shoots me a frustrated look from the open door to the back garden. She remains bent over a butter churn, flecks of pale cream dotting her skin. Mistress Forrest seems to have felt the same unnamable something that warned Lady Felice and Miss Winnifred away from us on the ship. It's only lunch on our second day in Jamestown, and already, we're assigned the tasks that keep us far from the rest of them for as long as possible. I return as comforting a smile as I can to Elizabeth, then leave through the front door of the house.

The dusky smell of mud and half-salt water that perfumes the air here greets me instantly. As does the sun, no longer hiding behind clouds. I tug on a pair of too-formal gloves to protect my hands and adjust my kerchief. Still, the nape of my neck and the slivers of skin between glove and sleeve sear as if I will burst into flames at any moment. I haven't, yet, but I don't intend to test it.

I wouldn't have tried my luck outside the house at all, except that my stomach is beginning to eat itself in its desperation. I can resist the allure of the forest no longer.

I traipse along the muddy street, my shoes growing quickly sodden once more. Perhaps on my return trip, I will see if the storehouse Mistress Forrest has indicated will give me any of those clogs. Neither my skirts nor my toes can endure this much longer.

Past another row of connected housing, this a bit less well-made than that we're staying in, I find the gate out toward the rest of the New World. The points of its logs jut into the sky, and two burly men wearing breastplates emblazoned with what Sir Thomas said at dinner last night was Governor Yeardley's crest stand before it. They eye me suspiciously. One of them puts a hand on the butt of the bronze pistol strapped to his hip.

"Pardon the intrusion." I curtsy. "I have business east of the town."

"What business?" the one on the left asks curtly.

Slaking an ungodly hunger. But I can't tell these upstanding men such a thing. Thinking quickly, I say, "Mistress Forrest gave me my leisure, and I would like to acquaint myself with my new home."

The one on the right snorts. "You're more likely to get yourself killed."

Sir Thomas warned us, at the dinner table last night, of the savages that control the woods beyond Jamestown. The Powhatans.

"Is that not my own business?" I ask. I wouldn't lie to these men, not truly, and that leaves me with few options other than trusting their charity.

They exchange a look. The deep lines on their cheeks speak to hard times they have endured, here or at home. They are the sorts of men who don't go about taking or indulging pointless risk.

"I didn't pay into this shipment." The leftmost one shrugs and grabs one end of the equally thick log that bars the gate shut. With a sigh, the rightmost one joins him, and the heavy logs swing apart.

I curtsy to them one last time and hurry out. Were I as fragile as I once was, I might worry more about their lackadaisical approach to a lady's safety. Now, though a small part of my mind wonders if Elizabeth engaged in a similar conversation last night, I think of little more than the welcome embrace of the trees ahead. The sun beats down on me, searing what little skin I have left exposed, and those mosquitos I have already grown to resent buzz in clouds over the exposed marshland. In the forest, everything will be cool and quiet.

In the forest, I will be able to hunt.

I set foot in the shade. My neck and wrists cease burning as if I've doused them in cool water. I exhale in relief. Hiding from the sun in London had been little trouble at all. In flat, uncrowded Jamestown, I will have to invest in longer gloves and heavier hats. For now, I shed my shoes to feel the earth between my toes and tuck them into my apron.

As I draw in my next breath, those so-called mortal concerns melt from my mind. The salt stink of Jamestown barely reaches out here. Instead, my nose fills with tempting scents like violets, fresh clover, leaves warmed in the sun. The trunks I stand between look nothing like those from home. Instead of the pale, pocked bark of a beech or the familiar darkness of a hawthorn, I find myself surrounded by giants that look like clusters of living veins or thick cords. Their tangled roots stretch and dominate the dirt in tripping knobs and clusters. A burst of frustration pulses through me. Were I in England, perhaps even in our country manor, I could hunt with perfect ease. I know every inch of those grounds.

But I have devoured so much of Father's library because I hunger for the world beyond the walls of our manor. Hard work might carry me through this new world, but so too will I need to rely on my curiosity. Every new discovery is a chance at new pleasures, not merely an obstacle between who I am and who I once was. I lay my hand against the strange trunk of this foreign tree and murmur, "Thank you."

I might not know its name yet, nor what makes it look the strange way it does, but it shields me as well as any familiar ash tree would have. I want to love this tree, as I had loved the ashes at home. With that curiosity closely guarded in my heart, I let my feet carry me deeper into the forest.

More strange plants pass me by. Tall, yellow flowers that twist their faces to pockets of sun, slumping sprigs of tiny white blossoms, ferns that spread their fronds like angel's wings to expose tall, brown stalks in the center. Each, I greet and thank for what they give me. Sweet smells, bursts of color, a laugh as they tickle my shins. Birds sing foreign songs in the branches, and I repeat their songs when I think I have the knack of them. The birds reply happily in kind, and I truly smile for the first time since I realized we would have to leave London. Of the two of us, Elizabeth has the better voice. In his kinder moods, Father would describe mine as "sweet," but I know that's merely a softer way to say "unpolished." Colonial birds don't mind, though, and I sing with them as I creep through the forest.

Once I have enough of my footing that I'm sure I can give chase without mistaking a root for steady ground, I turn my senses to the hunt. The birds overhead are too dear to eat, and they would barely make a mouthful. Smaller mammals scrabble by underfoot, reminding me of voles or martens. Too much trouble to capture for how little they, too, provide.

A stronger smell catches my nose. Hot, fresh blood pumped by a strong heart. Soft paw pads crunch over fallen leaves, another predator in pursuit of a meal. I turn and take up pursuit almost before I've finished discovering its existence. The dark hunger inside me swells, consuming all rational thought. I become one with the swampy, sodden earth, the strange, swaying ferns. Familiarizing myself with the terrain has done little. The curse has reshaped me into the perfect killer—I need nothing more than myself, a fact Elizabeth seems to understand far more instinctively than I do. The forest disappears under my feet as the smell takes on new dimensions.

Damp fur, not unlike the scent of a terrier I once had after his runs in the rain. My prey's prey, a deer just a few shades off from familiar. The plants both animals crush underfoot as they travel.

I pause behind one of those veined trees and peer ahead. A deer stands in a clearing, but my interest lies closer. Red fur bristles out of the greenery, and I realize I've been hunting a wolf. Britain has chased the scourge from our isle, but I still know the stories of the damage they cause. A single wolf can mean ruin for a whole village, if hungry enough. Can I truly face such a thing?

The hunger roars, and doubt dissolves. I'm cursed to kill; it's only right I kill killers. One breath, a bunching of my muscles under my skin, and I dive through the air.

My shoulder meets the wolf's, and we hit the underbrush together. The deer flees. The wolf swings wildly. I throw my hand up to block the blow instinctively. Claws shred the sleeve of my dress, but it feels only like being brushed with a cluster of twigs. Foreign instincts course through me. I know to pin the paws aside with one hand, to muzzle the snapping snout with another, though my fingers strain to encircle it. The wolf meets my gaze, its yellow-orange eyes startlingly aware. It's spent its life the stalker in the brush. It knows what being stalked means.

Something deep inside me aches. For a moment, I think it might be stronger than the hunger. But I bury my face in the wolf's throat, my needle-sharp fangs sliding neatly free of my gums, and pierce its flesh.

Blood gushes over my tongue. I can taste the deer the wolf must've eaten, the foreign herbs and grasses that came with the animal as well. A life in these woods, learning them as I had so briefly tried to. My one taste of human blood is lost to memory, but animals have always spread out before me like this, a tapestry of life in taste. I lower myself more comfortably onto the wolf's body as its struggles weaken. Soft fur cushions me. Strength pours into my limbs, invigorating me like no sleep or human meal ever will again. I drink this place, this creature, this life as deeply as I can and fold it inside myself.

I pull back when there's nothing more. The wolf lies limp beneath me, those knowing eyes empty. I swallow, and that ache in my chest redoubles. Tears dribble down my cheeks in burning trails. I shut its eyelids carefully, with two fingers, as I saw our vicar at home do when we lost Mother. Then, I open my mouth to say grace over my meal.

No words come to me, just as they didn't on the ship. I know half a dozen prayers of gratitude, but those holy words scorch my tongue now. And, in truth, I don't want God looking down on me anymore. I have left His domain, and any gratitude I have now is between myself and the creatures I kill.

I lay my hand on the wolf's chest, just as I did the strange tree, and muster all the ache into two simple words. "Thank you."

Some of the pain passes away from me, into the wolf or the world, I can't be sure. But I take comfort in the awareness in the wolf's gaze. It has killed a hundred times to survive. Perhaps, before the transformation, I was the deer. Now, the wolf and I are the same. I fix my dress, clean my mouth with some precious fresh water from my waterskin, put on my shoes, and make my way back toward Jamestown.

As I approach the edge of the forest, I spot another figure walking down the road to the gates. Alone here, I don't hesitate to indulge my improved sight. The figure resolves into a man with dark hair tied back away from his face and eyes as green as the grass underfoot. He has a strong chin, a thoughtful brow, and a neatly groomed mustache. The knowledge that he is the handsomest man I've seen since landfall shivers through me.

He pauses and turns toward the forest. I freeze. This is a mere flight of fancy—no man can hear me shiver from a hundred yards, much less see me amongst the trees–if he did. But this man looks for a moment as if he expects to be able to see something here. His gaze dances over the very patch of foliage I stand within and does not stop.

With something unnervingly like a shrug, he turns back toward Jamestown and continues on his way.

4

SUNDAY

Sarah

THE BRONZE CHURCH BELL SINGS OVER THE STREET, CROWDED FOR THE first time since our arrival in Jamestown a few days ago despite the spitting rain. Elizabeth and I walk arm-in-arm, behind the pairs of the other two tobacco wives and Mistress Forrest and Sir Thomas.

Elizabeth scowls up at the sky, her soft blue eyes still heavy with sleep. "I had thought the colonies would have more pleasant weather."

"Be grateful," I murmur, "that we need not endure the sun and holy ground."

"I can only hope this social gives us something to truly be grateful for," she replies.

While I would attend service and attempt to compel Elizabeth regardless, she has been easily won over by Mistress Forrest's announcement that we will meet the men who paid our passage, our prospective husbands, at a social held after Morning Prayer. For that, she donned her finest kirtle, pale green wool embroidered with twisting vines and minuscule rosebuds about to burst. The rain has, at least, warned her away from gowns too sumptuous to wear appropriately to church. She still shines like a jewel, as she always does. My own toilet takes second place—I can't hope to interest men with my looks beside her, and Lady Felice and Miss Winnifred want increasingly little to do with us. Elizabeth and I have to dress each other alone, listening to the other women giggle and chatter.

The shadow of the building swallows us, and my pulse speeds. Mistress Forrest and Sir Thomas enter the church. Lady Felice and Miss Winnifred enter the church. I take a deep breath. Elizabeth's grasp on me tightens.

We enter the church.

The aching, acidic burn that has plagued us both since waking up in this new life starts in the soles of my feet, as it always does. Knowledge fills me: I am not meant to be here. A thing like me is intended to stay away from this place and the safety it grants. Acid crawls up my legs as we follow the group into the Forrests' pew, only second back from the pulpit. Sir Thomas allows the rest of us first, then sits on the end. I take my seat on the hard, wooden bench. The burn dulls the impact of the gulfs that quickly form between the two halves of the household we've smuggled ourselves into. Lady Felice, Miss Winnifred, and Mistress Forrest press up against each other on the far end. Sir Thomas leans almost indecorously over the arm of the pew on the other side. Elizabeth and I sit alone, an island of pain. The acid reaches my knees, then my gut.

As the bells cease clanging, Father Buck, a cassocked man perhaps a decade younger than Sir Thomas but nonetheless weathered, takes the pulpit and begins the opening prayer. Words of confession and absolution fill the air. My ears burn just as my legs do, holy safety and promise torturing me for what I've become. Only the years of practice and repetition allow me to give the right answers at the right times. Only Elizabeth's white-knuckled grip on my hand keeps me from losing myself to the pain. Readings and prayers slip past me without a thought. The two spreading burns meet in the center of my chest, where my heart once beat, and consume me utterly.

"That we may evermore dwell in Him, and He in us, amen," I murmur along with the rest of the congregation.

At the altar, Father Buck finishes breaking the communion bread. The rest of our pew stands. I have to accept the body of Christ on my liar's tongue, and then I will be free of this agony. Elizabeth and I stagger to our feet with them and proceed down the aisle. Distantly, I notice the roughness of the pew-wood under my hand. Unfinished, like so much of this colony. Splinters bite into my palm without breaking my impossible skin.

Somehow, I find myself standing before Father Buck. I lower my eyes, hopeful it looks like a gesture of penitent respect, and offer my cupped hands.

"The body of Christ keep you in eternal life." He places the fragment of cornmeal bread in my palm.

"Amen." Devilish dexterity makes it easy to tuck the blessed morsel into my glove while seeming to place it on my tongue. Father Buck knows nothing of the eternal life I've already been granted, and he never could.

Needles of pain radiate up my legs with every step I take back to the pew, but they almost fail to hurt as much as the ache in the place where my soul once sat. Elizabeth returns to the pew after me, looking pale but markedly less troubled. Perhaps she simply has a defter handle on her own expressions.

Eventually, Father Buck gives the sign for the processional psalm, and he departs the small church with the same lack of fanfare as he arrived. Perhaps, if I could have heard him, I would've been able to evaluate his sermon and judge whether the colony is blessed by his ministry or merely making do. As it is, a dark part of my heart considers Father Buck a great enemy simply for how long the Morning Prayer persists.

Sir Thomas stands, and the six of us file out of the church with the rest of the congregation. I find myself grateful for the sucking mud of the road and chilling rain. Fire washes off me in their cleansing embrace.

"The social was intended to take place in the square," Sir Thomas says bitterly, "but it seems we must content ourselves with the storehouse."

"I will ensure the food is delivered correctly." Mistress Forrest departs in the direction of the row house, leaving us with only dour Sir Thomas. He stumps down the lane to the long, low storehouse, to which the doors already lie open. Inside, I can see a few rows of shelves, a counter, and a small square of open floor upon which we are presumably intended to have our social. Elizabeth smiles surreptitiously, the echoes of her pain already faded enough that she can grow excited about our potential future husbands once more. I envy her that.

Yet another sin I will confess to a reverend, if such an unburdening is still available to me.

Lady Felice and Miss Winnifred hurry ahead of Elizabeth and me, barely a pace behind Sir Thomas. Elizabeth tugs me faster and faster to keep up, until I am stumbling over the round toes of my shoes. What a lovely impression to make—that of a wet rat dragged along by a jewel of the kingdom. When we reach the storehouse, I keep my gaze low. I have no desire to see that same surprise or revulsion painted across the faces of a group that must contain my husband. Elizabeth releases me as Sir Thomas begins making introductions.

Names and professions flow past me like a muddy river. There are eight men, representing the fact that there were originally intended to be eight maidens on the ship, but half of our number has been delayed in London. We must each marry one of these men to fulfill our contracts with the Virginia Company. Most of them are planters and gentlemen–or simply gentlemen. One glassmaker stands out amongst their ranks, which explains the ashy glass-forge at the edge of the town. Another is a lawyer, like Sir Thomas. I watch rainwater drip off my dress onto a small puddle on the floor thinking I must be leaving a lasting impression.

"Clear the counter, if you please," Mistress Forrest says suddenly, her voice tight.

A clerk behind the counter scrambles to obey, and I look up to see her with two indentured men carrying in a steaming iron pot hanging from a log and a covered dish which she reveals to contain small, hard corn cakes.

"Allow me," one of the men says in a raspy baritone that instantly draws my eye.

The man helping the indentures heft the log high enough to lower the pot onto the counter is the one I saw on the road two days ago, the one who almost seemed to hear me. Every one of my senses springs to attention. Sir Thomas said his name, and the third place in the circle now stands empty while the other gentlemen watch my observer. The man who stopped on the road is Mr. Rafe Stone, a tobacco planter. Not a gentleman or aristocrat, which is perhaps why he claps the nearest indenture on the shoulder once they've set the pot down and ignores Mistress Forrest's worrying that he has broken the Sabbath.

He moves with surprising grace all the same. Watching him walk, one receives the undeniable sense that he knows every muscle in his body as well as Father Buck knows the creases in his worn *Common Book of Prayers*. No step or gesture is too large, too small, out of proportion with the rest of him. Mr. Stone is a study in masculine perfection, a man escaped from some master's brush and let loose in Virginia.

Sir Thomas clears his throat. "Eat, drink, be merry. The girls need to return to the house in an hour's time."

Mistress Forrest folds her hands in front of her peevishly after shooting Mr. Stone one last reproachful look, then she steps to the side with Sir Thomas, our chaperones for the event. Within moments, three men surround Elizabeth. Lady Felice draws two herself, and Miss Winnifred a respectable one. The final man, barrel-chested with chocolate curls, approaches me with the reluctant smile of a gentleman who finds every other lady's dance card full but still wishes to enjoy the song. I find a smile somewhere within myself regardless.

"It is a pleasure to meet you," I say with a curtsy. "Forgive me, I haven't a mind for names."

"I hope you've a mind for pantry goods." He laughs too loud, as if trying to draw the attention of the others. Then, he takes my hand and brushes a kiss so whiskery over the back I can feel it through my glove. "I am Mr. George Moore, and I own the Thistledawn Plantation."

I nod politely as if I know anything about the plantations around the fort. "How lovely."

"It most certainly is." He releases my hand and adjusts the lace falling band at his collar, obviously drawing attention to how fine it is. "Thistledawn now numbers just about a hundred and fifty acres, nearly all tobacco." He winks elaborately. "Nothing to worry about, I don't intend to smoke it all at once."

He bursts into another too-loud laugh, and I cover my mouth to laugh along with him. Mr. Moore is not a homely man, if a bit plainly made, and I recognize his name as belonging to a minor baronet from the north, but he has a spirit about him I can't abide for the rest of my days. It's a bit like Elizabeth at her worst: hungry for the eyes of those around him. He doesn't have a speck of malevolence about him, just a carelessness and self-focus I'm instantly sure Mistress Forrest hopes one of the tobacco wives will soothe out of him. I can't imagine him as a valuable contributor to the colony just yet.

.After another few overwritten attempts at humor, one of Lady Felice's men leaves her to pay a call to Elizabeth, and Mr. Moore happily cycles away from me. For a moment, I stand alone, listening to Mr. Moore's laugh bounce off the low ceilings of the storehouse. One of eight, decidedly not the sort of life partner I'm hoping for. If I'm to survive this transition, I need someone who approaches it with the work and curiosity I intend to.

"Lady Sarah?" Mr. Stone, the owner of that raspy baritone, sidles up to me with a bowl of Mistress Forrest's stew in one hand. "I noticed you had not eaten."

"Thank you." I take the bowl and spoon up a taste to be polite. Ever since my transformation, I can stomach only a few bites of mortal food before it sickens me. The meals in the colony hardly tempt my palate, either. Mistress Forrest's cooking bears the distinctive taste of a competent chef working with lackluster ingredients. "It is a pleasure."

"Do you like the troublesome weather here, then?" he asks with a glance at the rain outside.

Is he asking why he has seen me in the woods? "It doesn't trouble me any more than the moors around our home in the country."

"Then I suppose the sinking hasn't much irked you either." He nods.

The conversation between us dies away as if it had never started. I wait for the painful social awkwardness to fill its place, but it seems I will be waiting for the rest of my endless days. Mr. Stone has a strangely comforting presence about him, as if I've always known him somehow. He is also the first in Jamestown not to look discomfited merely by standing next to me.

"Mr. Stone!" Elizabeth flutes from her circle of suitors. "I must beg your expertise for a moment."

"Lady Sarah." He dips a brief bow to me then returns to my sister's side.

When the hour ends, Elizabeth slips her arm back through mine and leans her head close.

"Have you chosen your husband?" she murmurs. "If we collaborate, we can have our pick of the lot, regardless of what the other two decide."

I consider the men. The glassblower, Mr. Barnaby Whittaker, has a frankness I appreciate but carries a strong stench of liquor. A few of the other planters seem admirable, if unexciting. Mr. Stone's quiet comfort and—

"I have my sights set on Mr. Stone," Elizabeth gushes, forgetting she has even asked me a question. "Mr. Moore bragged so loudly about his near-one hundred fifty acres that I think those other two snakes failed to even hear Mr. Stone confess to his own one hundred seventy-five." She grins like a child who's been offered their favorite sweet. "And that's to say nothing of his looks. I am delighted to assist you in your search, but I shall become Mrs. Rafe Stone."

I turn my gaze to the mud once more.

5

BUILDING

Rafe

I stab my shovel into the dirt next to the knee-high hill I've just completed and dab my brow with one of my last fine handkerchiefs, embroidered by my sister, Esther. Her violet stitches have unraveled the slowest under the unrelenting Virginia weather. Mother used to crow over her embroidery. She swore Esther would have had a career in fine work, if she hadn't secured her husband so easily.

"Master Stone." Henrik, one of my newest indentured men, hurries up to me and bows. "Mr. Niklaus says—"

I hold up a hand to silence him then eye the young man. His pale hair clings to his brow, slick with the sweat that also darkens his linen shirt. He has been working himself far too long without a break—something I warned Klaus, my longest-held indenture and right hand, to watch him for. Upon first meeting Henrik, I recognized his type. Remarkably clever, efficient, driven to succeed, and cursed never to know his own limits.

"What did I tell you to call me?" I offer him my own handkerchief to clean himself.

"Rafe." He stares at the cloth for long heartbeats before taking it, uses it in a few brief scrubs when he does. Esther's embroidery unravels with the rough treatment, and I swallow the spike of pain.

Henrik needs to learn, as most of the men I pay for from the continent do, that the New World has accompanying new rules. The formalities of England and his native Germany must fall away if we are all to survive together.

"Try it again." I take my handkerchief back from him and tuck it away.

"Rafe," he grimaces with concentration, "Niklaus asked me to tell you that the hilling on Birch Log Field has been completed."

"Admirable." I nod to him in genuine surprise. Hilling my fields in advance of the upcoming tobacco planting is arduous work, I well know. I do not leave my men to do it alone, whenever I am able. To have hilled the entirety of Birch Log is such an impressive feat that, were it not Klaus giving me the news, I might be forced to doubt it. "Take your lunch. If Dinah has not yet finished preparing it, you are forbidden from helping her."

Henrik's young brow furrows. "Why? We are all strong enough to provide some assistance."

"*You* are forbidden," I repeat, meeting his gaze steadily. "If there are others whom Klaus designates able, they may assist as they see fit. You require rest, Henrik, or you will end your indenture bereft of the spirit that drove you here."

"Yes, sir," he replies with an almost sulky edge before bounding off toward Birch Log Field.

I lift my shovel and eye what work remains. Four hills yet before I reach the end of the row. On either side of me, soft grunts of labor and the occasional slap of a mosquito's death spiral up into the thickly humid morning air like smoke. Once again, I thank whoever might see fit to look after me that mosquitoes have no interest in my blood. The itching red welts look far too much like the pox for my comfort. I'll have to send someone to trade with the Powhatan for more of their repellent paste soon to keep my laborers in good health.

But for now, the next hill awaits my building it.

Perhaps three-quarters of an hour later, the unforgiving Virginia sun bright in the sky overhead, I pat the clay of my last hill into place.

"Finally caught up, have ye?" Fidelma asks with a wry smile.

"Finally." I shoulder my shovel, and we begin the long walk to the manor together.

She launches into a story about the three brothers she left behind and one of their many escapades that coaxes me into laughter even after half a day of hilling. Freckles dance across her ruddy cheeks like stars in the sky at night, and I think not for the first time about how unfortunate it will be to lose her when her indenture comes to a close next year. The men, at least, I can reasonably hope to hire as paid laborers. Fidelma, and the other rare women who come over, walk straight from my fields and into the church. I happen to know one of the Polish glassblowers has his eye on her already, though I will not give him permission to pursue her outright until I'm certain he will appreciate her as she deserves. She has an admirable work ethic and a sense of humor to match.

Until Sir Thomas approached me with the idea of funding these tobacco wives of his, I might have considered taking her as a wife. Station matters little, but a smile during the worst times cannot be overvalued. Twelve years in Jamestown have taught me over and over again that the worst times are never far off.

Perhaps the twenty years in England before that achieved much the same. In Jamestown, I have the scant comfort of them coming to everyone equally.

The sloped thatch of my roof rises over the swell of the last field, which has been strung already with the wooden supports required to grow the governor's grapes. The first year after Mr. Rolfe introduced his tobacco leaf to the colony, I planted this land with it and sent my grapes far afield. Both withered on the vine, and I learned the bitter lesson that the earth chooses its crop.

It is for those lessons, and for the thatch I find myself patching every sodden spring, that I paid into Sir Thomas's scheme. Fidelma might make a pleasant enough companion, but she does that just as well without the bonds of marriage between us. No, a wife matters very little to me. My chores are attended to by myself or one of my laborers, and as much as I might miss Esther's embroidery, I miss it more for the memory of her smile when I received it with awe than any great need for delicate flowers and vines on my belongings.

All I need—all I lack—is an heir to take what I've learned and build it into the sort of family home I left behind in England. Fidelma has no desire to settle into family life. She'll endure it, but being tied by her apron-strings to the home will grate on her spirit. And Sir Thomas was very clear: these girls from England come knowing that family life is what awaits them.

"Your kitchen, sir." Fidelma holds the knotty door open for me with a sweeping bow, her kirtle brushing the dirt.

I chuckle as heat and noise billow out at me. The hearth crackles, outlining Dinah, bent over her iron cauldron as she nearly always is, against its light. Half a dozen men, none of whom were hilling Birch Log with Klaus and Henrik, stand around the room and chatter like magpies between bites of fresh bread and dried meat. A block of hard, orange cheese sits on the butcher block with a workman's knife stuck in it, the bone handle swallowing the orange light.

I smile and step inside. Other gentlemen in town have expressed surprise, even disdain, that my workers eat with me in the manor when they have a serviceable kitchen in their quartering house. Those gentlemen seem to favor silence far more than I. Returning to a silent house seems a curse, more a coffin than a home. All my dearest memories from childhood are of Adam, Crispin, Esther, and me running around the house like wild animals, making such a racket that Father had to come out of his study to shush us, only to join in the racket himself. Yet another reason to seek out heirs before the season ends. Twelve years alone is quite enough.

"Rafe, tell these louts stew will weigh them down as heavy as stones," Dinah says. "Bread and cheese, that's what's good for the digestion at midday."

I pluck a warm corn roll off the tray, nearly burning my knuckles on the stone keeping them so, and look at the men. They all hide smiles like boys in trouble at school, a sure sign they are simply teasing my high-strung cook. Dinah has kept me alive many a winter, so I turn my gaze hard.

"Dinah's rules come from my own mouth," I say. She is correct in this, regardless of whether I've said it to her exactly. "Within these four walls, you will obey her as if she were me."

Just the same as those schoolboys, they cast their gazes at the floor and mumble apologies. Fidelma snickers as she gathers her lunch. I bow to Dinah, cementing that I will brook no disrespect against her, and leave the kitchen with my lunch in hand. More hilling remains, but I have another social with the women to dress for.

Sunlight pours in through my two glass front windows, illuminating the handmade seats of my parlor. A luxury, the glass, but more than worth it for the simple joy of opening my shutters without wondering what else I might let in. Between bites of dried pork sausage and sharp cheese, I hurry across the room to the stairs. Truly, I should not have stayed in the field as long as I did, but sitting at my desk and poring over papers I've read before seems a waste when there is work to be done, below my station or no.

Upstairs, in the square of my bedroom, I trade my work clothes for a clean suit. Green broadcloth, simple but fine. As I do, my thoughts drift to my potential brides.

Lady Felice and Miss Winnifred seem, by turns, pliable, trained, and well-suited to the home. But my mind seems unable to think on them for longer than a heartbeat. No, my attention returns over and over again to the sisters Wentworth, as a dog worrying a bone. Lady Elizabeth holds certain obvious charms. Her hair alone likely made half of London weep from envy, and she has the knack of giving just enough of herself away that a listener must stay to learn more. I am certain she was a favorite of the social circuit, which begs the question of their departure.

Baron Wentworth is a well-regarded man. Eccentric, but of an old line that begets a certain necessary respect. All I've heard of him is that he carries himself well and keeps above the fray of petty politics. His daughters did not enter society before I left England, but I knew he had two. For them to both have joined Jamestown is strange enough. For them to have come, not with adventuresome husbands, but in search of them, is stranger still.

Lady Sarah, hesitating in the feathered greenery at the edge of the forest, looms large in my thoughts. Her eyes, duller than the brilliant ice of her sister's, became luminous like deep pools in those shadows. A few cinnamon curls escaped her hat to cup her face as if they were soft hands. The sharp point of her chin contrasted the fullness of her cheeks, a shape that on any other face would have been merely uneven but on her, in that moment, became otherworldly.

She should never have been in the woods alone, much less a few scant days after her arrival in the colony. If she did wander out there, she should never have returned. Relations with the Powhatans have been worsening for some months now, ever since news of Pocahontas's death in England reached us, and her father passed soon after.

The mystery of the sisters Wentworth scratches at me, and it wears Lady Sarah's face.

6

JEALOUSY

Sarah

Days trickle by in Jamestown, an endless *DRIP... DRIP... DRIP* OF mosquitoes buzzing their sickening songs and earth turning from mud to dirt, then back again. By our first Wednesday, Miss Winnifred accidentally spilt a flagon of wine over one of the bedsheets she was intended to be washing, and Mistress Forrest saw no issue in allowing her to put it up across the middle of our garret. The red-spattered expanse of white now splits Miss Winnifred and Lady Felice from Elizabeth and I. Sometimes, when I hear Elizabeth slip out again in the night, I lay awake and look at that gory stain. A thousand ways Miss Winnifred could have gotten the separation she so desired...it only seems right that we should be marked for what we are, whether she knows how apt it is or not.

"Smile," Elizabeth says coaxingly, twisting one of her damp curls tightly around her finger while I pin the great mass of it back into a chignon. "Surely, I don't need to tell you that the gentlemen won't want a wife who is always frowning."

I can't find a smile within myself for someone I know has been out every third night since our arrival, but I manage to smooth my frown. "How long until we are to leave?"

She eyes the candle. "Half an hour, perhaps less. Shouldn't you dress?"

I open my mouth to inform her I've tried to dress three times, and each time, she has drawn me back with some help she needs, then close it once more. If she won't listen to me on matters of our very safety, she certainly won't on matters of her appearance.

"Which gown do you think?" I open my portmanteau and trail my hand over the four folded rectangles of fabric. We packed in a rush, but Elizabeth made certain we brought most of our finest things. Silks, velvet, and shining ribbons slide past my fingertips in a riot of colors I've so far found Jamestown lacking. All cloth made here is either drab or splotchy. Still, the drab and splotchy is quite sufficient for the labor that now marks my days. As much as I resent it, I've grown a bit grateful for the curse. It keeps me strong when I know I would otherwise lag.

"Not the crimson," Elizabeth says, smoothing the square neck of her carmine gown. "We would look too terribly like a matched set."

I run a reluctant thumb over it—Father always said red looked wonderful on me, and I've always thought it spoils Elizabeth's complexion somewhat—then turn to the rest. "What about the blue?"

"The sky or the cerulean?" She leans over the bucket of water we were allowed to clean with as part of our preparation, studying her own reflection. "No, there is no need to ask. The sky truly is a day dress. Cerulean would look lovely, even if the sky moves better in a dance."

"I'm not certain such details matter as they used to." I trace the embroidery on the sky-blue dress, a riot of silk and taffeta one of Mother's friends had made for me on my eighteenth birthday. The stitches have been let out once or twice, but the friend made certain to tell me that Mother had always dreamed of a dress in this color and never quite found the time to purchase one, so I will be letting them out and taking them in until the fabric cannot survive any longer.

Elizabeth lifts her head away from the water and looks at me seriously. "Sarah, you understand we must find husbands, yes? That this isn't merely another in a string of balls, where you might stumble into the arms of a man like Lord William and charm him with your alarm?"

My stomach knots over and around itself. Ice creeps through my veins. "I wouldn't like to talk about Lord William while pursuing other men."

"Lord William is my only proof that all hope is not lost in this endeavor." She takes my hands in both of hers. "He was a good, sweet man. The day he declared his intention to marry you, I wept tears of joy."

As did I. William spoke to Father first, arranged all the terms, and then arranged a private breakfast for the two of us. I rode over to his manor with my heart in my throat, knowing I wouldn't be able to eat a bite. William's attention had started exactly as Elizabeth described, a chance meeting, and I found myself unable to stop waiting for them to cease. If they were going to, he would have handled it exactly like that. He was an honorable man, too honorable to cease calling on me without so much as a word. Only the rustle of the sky-colored dress, chosen to bring spring into a dreary London October, allowed me to walk through his door with my head held high.

When I joined him in the solarium, I knew I was wrong, if not how. His sweet, rye-colored hair tumbled loose into his dark eyes and framed his soft jaw. His doublet hung open over his shirt, a nearly indecent gesture he had only allowed out of easy forgetfulness. When I came to call, he said, it was as if greeting someone he'd known all his life. Standing on formality seemed a waste of everyone's time. So I looked at William, my William, half-dressed in the morning sunshine, and knew something wonderful was coming.

He informed me quietly, my ungloved hand tucked tightly in his, and kissed me impulsively when I responded with equally indecorous excitement.

"Please." I turn away from Elizabeth, as if she can see the thoughts jabbing at me like a thousand pinpricks, and pull off my kirtle. "I shouldn't like to talk about Lord William."

She sighs. "I truly believe that to be a mistake. Lord William was a good man, but he has passed from this life. You do him no dishonor by seeking another husband, and studying how you nearly achieved a first might do you well."

The pinpricks sharpen, more like the rusting I found beside the well the day before last. "I believe that keeping my mind on the men here will be more beneficial. Might we talk of them instead?"

Elizabeth stands with a rustle, and the faint animal smell these cots never fail to give off, then comes behind me and begins unlacing my stays. For the cerulean, I will need a true underbust corset, boning I have not touched since I set foot on the *Waterlily*.

"Do you think Mr. Stone is much given to reds?" she asks. "I think they would look quite handsome on him, and it would be such a delight to arrive and discover we had dressed the same."

I cannot ask about the men here, or much in Jamestown, without Elizabeth mentioning Mr. Stone. What does she hope to do today? Attend to errands at the storehouse a bit after lunch, when Mr. Stone is often there. What did she think of the sermon? Mr. Stone seemed quite moved by the section about forgiveness. Is the grass green? She's not sure, but that would be a fascinating question to get the opinion of a planter like Mr. Stone on. It is as if she has forgotten every other name she's learned at times.

"I'm not sure red would suit his eyes," I say quietly. They are such a deep, true emerald that any color so opposite must dull their shimmer.

Elizabeth lifts the stays off over my head. "Now, that's not fair. Some would say red doesn't suit my coloring, but you need only look at me in it to understand those who would say so are incorrect."

Something hot and bitter pulses behind my breastbone, like I swallowed an ember from the hearth. She is wrong about herself, as she is wrong about Mr. Stone. A thousand colors would suit him. Visions of him in suits of arboreal greens, dove and charcoal grays alike, warm browns and tawnys, even deep, torrential blues that nearly match the richness of my cerulean brocade dance through my mind. In each, he looks handsomer than the last.

I dash the images away as if running my hand through my watery reflection. I ought to be imagining him alongside Elizabeth in red, even though I might prefer the look of myself with both. In both.

"Perhaps you are right," I murmur, lifting my hands for her to slide the corset over my chemise automatically. "Perhaps Mr. Stone is very like you."

"I believe he is," she says happily. Still, she yanks the laces roughly, tightening me in sharp jerks as she did when we first transformed and did not yet know our strength.

I endure my punishment silently. Envy is one of the mortal sins, and I won't indulge it. Certainly not when I am dooming myself to only ever envy. If Elizabeth wants Mr. Stone, she will have him. All of London knows she might've wed before me three times over. She only waited because she is the second sister, and her marriage would have dashed my prospects. Now that she intends to marry, there shall be no stopping her.

Fiddle music sings gaily out of the open doors of the storehouse, still the only building large enough to host these gatherings, and I do find a smile somewhere within myself. My fingers itch for my viol, at home in its case in London. Father said it was no instrument for a young lady, but string music has a liveliness others simply lack. Candles glow from every window, and bodies pack the muddy street almost as if it is time for service once more.

Tonight, Mistress Forrest has informed us, all of Jamestown has been invited. The men who paid our passage shall wear scarlet rosettes on their chests to mark them out from the crowd, a color which makes Elizabeth giggle. I won't deny it is auspicious, as if all the men are already marked for her. Lady Felice wears a lovely dress of lemon-colored silk that will move like the wings of a butterfly in the dances, and Miss Winnifred a finely made, dove-colored frock that repairs some of its plainness with slit sleeves revealing glimpses of green beneath. None of us will look much at home with the red ribbons at all.

The thought doesn't dull my growing excitement, especially as I recognize the opening strains of a galliard. An athletic, leaping dance is exactly what I need to shake off the lingering unpleasantness of dressing.

The six of us—the potential wives, Sir Thomas, and Mistress Forrest—enter the storehouse as one. Out of the strict organization of pews, the people of Jamestown seem far more plentiful. And, forgive me, more human. Figures I've only seen as shambling avatars of mud and linen shine in their best clothes, brightened by scrubbing and smiles. A few children dart through the group like a tiny school of fish, shrieking as they go. The shelves have been pushed against the walls to clear space, and exactly as I thought, a hopping galliard rolls across the makeshift dance floor.

"I have located Mr. Stone," Elizabeth hisses. "Please, talk to some of our benefactors. Select your favorite, and I will ensure he is yours."

She squeezes me, then swans away, circumnavigating the dancers with practiced ease. Foolishly, I trail her with my gaze for a moment. Mr. Stone stands to one wall, watching the dancers with those sharp green eyes of his. With a stab of satisfaction, I note his richly green suit. The only hint of red on him is the rosette at his breast.

"Lady Sarah." The glassblower, Mr. Barnaby, bows with a swaying looseness that would have given him away, had the now-acrid stench of wine not. "I was h-hoping to speak to you this evening."

The appeal of his frankness melts like an ice chip left in the sun as I meet his reddened eyes. "Is that so?"

"I thought we got on quite well," he says.

"I certainly enjoyed speaking with you on Sunday." For the scant minutes I did. I glance across the storehouse at Elizabeth and Mr. Stone once more.

That swallowed ember sears with bitter delight. Though Elizabeth is using every trick I have seen her use, Mr. Stone leans slightly away from her, his gaze still on the dance.

"Well then." Mr. Barnaby rocks as if aboard a ship, forcing me to catch his arm or let him topple into me bodily. Only the ungodly strength in my limbs keeps him upright, and the lascivious smile I earn for my efforts is hardly a reward. "What more is there?"

The music changes. Even brighter than a galliard, this could only be suited to what my friends in London called country dancing, a swinging delight of rounds and switched partners.

"There is dancing." I bob a rushed curtsy and hurry to the floor. If Mr. Barnaby takes that as an invitation, I will be free of him before long. If not...I sincerely doubt he has enough of his wits about him to hold the slight against me.

I enter the flow of the dance like slipping into the current of a river. Mr. Barnaby catches my arm a heartbeat late, and I cannot find it in myself to mind. Though this particular pattern is not familiar to me, country dances all have a comforting familiarity about them. It is simple to release oneself into the pressure of a partner's hand on one's arm, pushing left or right. To see the next step in the great, weaving knot of it all. Were this viewed from above, would it be more beautiful to step in or out? Whichever it is, I do, and I am always right. The bouncing fiddle plucks something inside me, leaves it quivering like a string. I hardly notice when I pass away from Mr. Barnaby. My partners are little more than stepping stones across this river; it is the music making my feet light enough to walk over the very water itself.

Or so I think, until I spin into the arms of a man in a green broadcloth suit that very nearly matches his eyes.

"Lady Sarah," Mr. Stone says seriously, as if we were walking into church instead of spinning with arms linked.

I giggle, then cover my mouth. Giggling always makes me sound nervous. But perhaps all the handsomest men I shall ever meet are charmed by nervousness because the corner of his mouth curls.

"Mr. Stone," I finally manage. "You are a fine dancer."

His smile grows. "You may be the first living soul to ever say that to me."

I furrow my brow. Mr. Stone has the rhythm well in hand, like a dog brought to heel. His posture is neat, and he hasn't trod on my feet even once. He is almost the very model of a dancing instruction pamphlet. "I find that difficult to believe," I admit.

"I rarely dance." He twirls me. The next rotation—the next switching of partners—is almost upon us.

"Perhaps you should." I smile up at him. "You've got a grace many men in London would envy."

Something ripples across his face, and he tenses. My fingers ache as he squeezes them too tight against each other. With a small grimace, he relaxes once more. "My apologies," he murmurs. "I often crush fingers when I get a bit distracted."

His green eyes glow with honesty, and he spins me off to my next partner. Dreadfully, that turns out to be Mr. Barnaby once more. A fine dancer, Mr. Barnaby is not. At least my newfound strength softens the blow of squashed toes.

Something cold takes root in my stomach, and I look over my shoulder at Mr. Stone. It should soften the blow. Yet somehow, that gentleman planter crushed my fingers to bruising.

How very strange.

7

RECOMMENDATION

Rafe

THE MORNING AFTER THE DANCE COMES EARLY, GOLDEN FINGERS OF sunshine reaching in through the slats in my shutters and jostling me awake even before Dinah takes up her breakfast clattering in the kitchen below. My eyes open, and the quiet rhythm of routine drags me from my mattress. Yet another matter to consider, in this search for a wife. I will no longer be able to simply roll off whichever side of the bed most pleases me and over to my chest of drawers with the thundering steps of a giant. Protected as I am from waking my workers in their quartering house, I've grown quite hoggish. Surely, any of those tender women from England would expect a husband rather than a bear. Perhaps I ought to wait until the next ship comes in and attempt to regain some shred of gentlemanly manners in the meantime.

Yesterday's undershirt needs laundering, as any I wear to hill do, so I free the next loose, linen garment from the drawer. Simple breeches, cut at the knee, and my good boots to keep my legs from the constant churn of mud inside the fort follow. Though I'll surely end up in the fields by this afternoon, as I always do in the far too short stretch of time between planting the tobacco seeds in their initial beds and moving them to their final fields, errands compel me into town first. The storehouse occasionally stocks that pest-repellent paste, and Dinah informed me that, should she be asked to make do with what cornmeal we have once more, we will all be eating bread thin enough to see through. So I don a simple, brown doublet and a wide-brimmed hat, stop downstairs for the earliest serving of the porridge Dinah nearly always makes for breakfast while she hides yawns behind her ladle, and step out into the early morning.

Birds sing from the trees still near my manor. Other, more mercenary men have told me I ought to clear-cut a circle round my house and build out from there. Perhaps they are right, but I've never felt quite steady without some wood nearby. Leveling the land merely to the east has been more than profitable enough for me to wish to lose that song, my only companion in those early days before I had so many living beside me.

I set off down the thin lane leading toward the fort, and my thoughts drift to last evening's dance. It was pleasanter than I expected. Usually, such affairs broadly consist of council members politicking while an indentured man saws away on a fiddle as if his very life is caught in the strings. But Sir Thomas saw fit to add a few other pieces to the band, and the furor of excitement over the women distracted near everyone from the day-to-day maneuvering.

It certainly distracted me. I can't quite explain how I found myself amidst the dancers. I have a distant memory of Lady Elizabeth asking me if I might like to dance and beginning to refuse when I saw Lady Sarah on that drunkard Barnaby's arm. Somehow, the word *yes* seems to have tripped off my lips instead. It's been more than a decade since I've danced, and yet I agreed simply to lay my hand on Lady Sarah's arm and watch her turn that pointed little chin up to me. If I were a romantic, I might have told her that her dress turned her eyes to stars caught in ocean waves.

I thank a god I know has long since ceased listening to me that I was not born a romantic.

"Mr. Cole," I say to the soldiers outside the gates as I approach. "Mr. Spraggins."

"Mr. Stone!" Cuthbert Spraggins, one of the youngest of the cohort Governor Yeardley brought with him from overseas, tips his helmet back to get a better look at me. "How is the old plantation?"

I hear the question he is not asking behind his words. Cuthbert Spraggins is ill-suited for military work and hopes I might have a job for him. One which pays well enough that he can justify to his merchant of a father back in England why he left the traditional role of the third son.

"Bluebonnet is well," I reply. "Though hilling takes its toll."

Cuthbert grins. "If you find yourself needing an extra pair of hands—"

"Open the gates, Spraggins," Roland Cole growls tiredly. Cuthbert hops to it, and I am admitted to the fort mere moments later, sparing Roland a grateful nod as I depart.

I shall write to Governor Yeardley when I return home. Roland is a veteran of the Nine Years' War, and he ought be afforded a more comfortable position than standing in the worst spit of land in all Virginia for his service.

The palisaded walls surround me and the relative bustle of Jamestown in the morning. I tip my hat to the few women I pass, mostly indentures carrying baskets and jugs from one building to the next. Barnaby stands outside the glass forge, his decisions last night painted in dark swaths under his eyes and in sickly green on his cheeks. Truly, all of Jamestown's glasswork will be better if he can find himself some saint of a wife who will keep him from the bottle.

"Mr. Stone." Sir Thomas steps out of the storehouse doors ahead of me and offers a short bow. Perhaps the reason last night was so free of politicking is his involvement in the matter of the wives; the lawyer has spent as long in Jamestown as I have, but his elevated position of council member upon our arrival means that he is far more the man he was in England than I am. The bobbing turkey feather in his hat alone belies how many of the old customs he still holds dear. "I trust you had a pleasant evening."

"Give my compliments to Mistress Forrest." I bow perfunctorily in return. "It was one of her most splendid events."

"A compliment from such a difficult gentleman to please as yourself will surely pink her cheeks." He steps slightly aside, allowing Mr. Ballard, a smaller planter, to pass between us.

Sir Thomas is settling in for a longer conversation. I hide a sigh in my own shift. Only the likes of Sir Thomas, who has nothing waiting for him at home but the occasional letter to write, would believe others wish to linger and talk while the sky is still orange with sunrise.

"Have any of the women caught your eye?" he asks.

Curiosity throbs. "The sisters Wentworth are particularly interesting specimens. What can you tell me about them?"

"Ah, Lady Sarah and Lady Elizabeth." He leans forward, a gleam in his eye, far more excited than I expect. Almost hungry—or desperate. "I'm certain you've heard of Baron Wentworth. Your family held a certain station, did they not?"

"My father had a knighthood." My voice is tight, unyielding. Sir Thomas knows there are many in Jamestown who prefer never to speak of the lives they left behind, and he well knows I am one of them. "Though I never had the pleasure of making Baron Wentworth's acquaintance."

"He is a serious sort, occasionally eccentric, but I've never met a gentleman more willing to put all on the line for his fellow man. He has raised his daughters in their mother's image—though, of course, you wouldn't know that, if you have never met the baron." He glances side to side surreptitiously. "Their sainted mother was lost to illness, but Baron Wentworth made certain the girls were trained properly all the same."

This is little help in unraveling the strangeness of the sisters. I step toward the storehouse doors. "Very impressive. If you shouldn't mind, I ought—"

"Have you read their letters of recommendation?" Sir Thomas lurches forward, all but grabbing my arm to keep me in place. Rarely have I seen the council member so out of sorts.

"I…suppose I haven't." They arrived, with those of the other two women, in a packet still sitting on my desk at home. Glowing praises certainly bought and paid for hold little interest for me when I can look at my potential wife in the flesh and judge her abilities for myself.

"You ought." He nods, that turkey feather bobbing like another head. "They come highly recommended. Even Viscountess Hargraves, a notoriously difficult to please woman, had lovely things to say about them."

"Perhaps when the planting is finished." I move to leave once more.

"They each know how to make lace. Arrived with yards of it, and Mistress Forrest tells me Lady Elizabeth's is particularly fine. She also plays harpsichord, Lady Elizabeth, and it would be quite simple to send away for one when the next shipment arrives."

I clench my jaw and exhale slowly through my nose, soothing the annoyance rippling too close to the surface of my skin. Sir Thomas is an honorable man, if not the company I would ever choose to keep and a block between myself and the days' work.

"I care not for lace," I tell him. "And I lack the desire to give up space in a home I built for a harpsichord. Every soul living on Blue-bonnet Plantation works, myself included, and I require a wife both willing and able to do the same."

Sir Thomas stiffens back into formal posture, finally out of my way. "Of course. I should have known a gentleman like yourself would possess more… prosaic concerns. I shall see whom Mistress Forrest believes the most competent housekeeper."

The sting of his accusation does not even puncture my doublet. Sir Thomas and others may believe I've given up civility and turned myself common. What I have turned myself is wealthy and industrious. I would not trade my workaday life for theirs unless held at the mouth of a cannon to do so.

"Thank you. Good day." With another, much shorter bow, I step finally inside the storehouse.

Thankfully, my business is simple. Griffith, behind the counter, knows better than to try holding my attention with chatter. In truth, I think he enjoys the respite himself. Keeping the colony's stores means most believe he knows nearly every scrap of news there is to be known, and the man isn't a gossip by nature. Within minutes, I reenter the tepid April sunshine with a pot of salve under one arm and a twenty-pound sack of dried corn clenched in the other fist. I might have brought a pair of men and a cart with me, but the corn is a pleasant stretch to the muscles after a night's sleep, and holding it tightly alchemizes some of my irritation with Sir Thomas to simple effort. My steps are light and my head high as I turn back toward home and the joy of plain, hard work.

To avoid Mr. Moore's cart, extravagantly horse-drawn despite how little ground he must travel within the walls, and whatever endless conversation he might see fit to trap me with, I cross the street. Row houses march by in near-orderly lines. I remember when the studs for many of these were still trees in the encroaching forest, remember the *thud-splat* sound of hammering them into the swampish ground. Now, they are some of the stateliest and longest-lived within the fort.

Outside Sir Thomas's house, a woman in a bonnet bends over a garden patch. She's too slight for Mistress Forrest, but I cannot be sure which of the potential brides it is at this distance. I prepare a respectable smile and hope, deep in my breast, not to be confronted with Lady Elizabeth. Last night made it more than clear that she likes conversation nearly as much as Mr. Moore.

A quieter *thud-splat* splits the morning air. I frown. That is a labor sound, a wood-driving sound, the sort one isn't accustomed to hearing in the presence of the sorts of young ladies staying with the Forrests. I quicken my steps, curiosity throbbing in time with my own heartbeat like a living thing.

The woman shifts. Her tawny skirts swing aside to reveal both that she has cleverly accepted the local custom of clogs to avoid the worst of Virginia's mud and that she is erecting triangular bean supports in the Forrests' front garden. Vegetables she will certainly leave their home before being able to taste. She does not reveal her face, and I am nearly at the edge of the garden.

Mr. Moore cracks his whip, and his horse treads on. The sun is high enough in the sky that my men will be wondering where I've gotten off to. I ought to cross the street once more.

The woman looks up, and my decision is made.

"Good morrow, Mr. Stone," Lady Sarah says with a shy smile. Merely shy, though. There is no hint of embarrassment at being caught doing such work, cheeks not even red with effort.

"Good morrow." I bow and continue on, knowing Lady Sarah doesn't wish to be delayed in conversation any more than I. After all, we both have work to attend to.

I exit Jamestown with a faint smile on my lips.

8

SETTING DOWN ROOTS

Sarah

On the second Friday after our arrival in Jamestown, I huddle in the shadow of the house away from the sun as I churn butter. My hands sting, rubbed raw from hours wrapped around the handle and scorched red already. Elizabeth loathes the task, and her glances behind Mistress Forrest's back were becoming downright mutinous, so I offered to endure it in her stead. I did not then realize just how little churning butter accepts all the minor sun protections I have come to rely on during my days here. My gloves lay abandoned at my side, and I have had to knock my bonnet back enough to see inside the churn often enough that my cheeks and nose scald nearly as much as my hands. By the end of this, I shall be as red as the cooked crabs Sir Thomas has all but banned from his table.

Worst of all, I am once again alone. The longer we stay, the more the reaction to us seems to spread. Now, people I have not yet met scurry out of my path when I walk the street. Mistress Forrest certainly does not find herself in possession of a quiet tongue, but I believe Lady Felice is responsible for the lion's share. She has become

51

extremely popular, Miss Winnifred always at her side, and I sense they may be telling stories, swaying any who may not have noticed our unnaturalness away before we have even the chance to convince them otherwise.

The solitude grates on me. I'm not much given to always talking, as Elizabeth is, but that doesn't mean I don't prefer the quiet comfort of another's breath or footfall in a space with me. The militant curiosity I have turned on Virginia is scant comfort when I have no one to share my discoveries with—and my discoveries are plentiful enough that Elizabeth warned me off sharing them with her some days ago. She says she cares not to learn this place any further than will keep her alive, and she is powerful enough that she needs learn hardly anything.

Bitterness seems to have taken up residence in my chest near permanently, a smoldering coal that confession and reflection has yet failed to douse. Sometimes, I am certain Elizabeth was not so very… herself before we left England's familiar shores.

The back door squeals like a stuck pig as it opens, and I turn to see Mistress Forrest grimace briefly at it, then pluck something else off the counter I know stands just to her left inside.

"Lady Sarah," she calls from the step, "how comes the butter?"

I plunge the stick in my cramping hands a few times, listening for the distinctive *splash* of the separated layer of buttermilk. "Nearly, Mistress Forrest."

Her face tightens into something resembling a dried fruit, an expression she seems to reserve for broken items in the house, and Elizabeth and I. "Hm. You would be going faster on a proper stool, instead of crouched against the wall like a beast."

"Apologies." I bob my head in a mock curtsy. "Is there anything further?"

"When the butter is complete, I need someone to travel into the forest and trade with one of the people there. As you are the only one of the young ladies under my roof who has seen fit to leave the fort under her own power, I thought the task might suit you." She extends a single delicate hand, holding a small canvas pouch and a many-times-folded parchment. "They favor these glass beads. The paper is a map and a list."

I can't release my hands from around the churn and convince them to return to it, so I simply smile gratefully and ask if she might leave them inside for me. That earns another dried-fruit face, but she quits the yard without another word.

Perhaps Elizabeth is right and I should choose a man to pursue. Remaining under the Forrests' roof grows more unpleasant every day.

Such thoughts fade from view as I step out of the gates, bonnet and gloves neatly back in place and beads tucked into a pocket in my kirtle. The air out here tastes even cleaner than that inside the fort, though both improve over London by orders of magnitude. Of the many things I miss, the close feeling of a hundred thousand bodies packed within walls that haven't been expanded in nearly three centuries is not one. Freedom is freer when one can see it all around them.

"Hello, vein-trunk." I pat the strange tree that greeted me when I first stepped into this forest. "Hello, golden blossom. Hello, angel fern and nodding-bishops."

Having something to call the plants makes them all feel as if they were friends, rather than new acquaintances. Had I anyone to discuss my discoveries with, I may have learned the true names of these plants by now. Instead, I am left to my own imagination. I unfold the map, scrawled in Mistress Forrest's precise hand and study it. A few landmarks pock the page; particularly notable trees, the curve of a river. Though I've scolded Elizabeth for her outings, I must admit I have ventured into this forest far more often than proper. So many of the landmarks are recognizable at a glance. I set off deeper into the forest than I have ever ventured before.

Talk of the savages in the forest is hard to avoid. I've heard a few men whisper the name Powhatan, but I do not know whether that belongs to a person or a people. Perhaps it is simply their war cry before they attack. The fear that creeps through me on many crawling legs is not nearly so strong as it might have been before my curse, but I shouldn't like to find out the legends about demons like myself have skipped out some important way I might be killed. It is only the fact that the place on the map where my list sits has been scraped many times, other lists achieved and expunged from the vellum, that keeps my feet moving along the predetermined path. Mistress Forrest believes they will trade because they have before.

I will not be forced to taste human blood today.

The map leads me to a towering vein-trunk, taller than any other I've yet seen. Its bark is scarred with a shape I half-recognize from the village nearest Father's country manor: a simple symbol for unlettered people in England to recognize shops.

"Hello?" I call tremulously.

A cluster of angel ferns rustle. My heart dances a nervous galliard. Leaves part, and a woman becomes visible between them.

She pauses, searching me up and down with her gaze. I know it is impolite to stare, but I can't quite help myself. A thick braid, black as a crow's wing, drapes over her shoulder and brushes the bottom of her rib cage. In place of a gown, she wears a swath of tanned leather slung over one shoulder, leaving half her chest bare. Her sharp features seem to turn even sharper as she studies me.

"You are strange to me," she says, her tongue slow as if used to words of other shapes.

"I come on behalf of Mistress Forrest," I reply carefully. Though I came in search of trade, some part of me didn't expect her to speak English.

She raises her chin, then steps from the angel ferns. That swath of leather reveals itself to be a skirt which ceases well above the knee, thankfully ungirded with a belt of weapons. In that leather, I recognize something of myself. A lovely, twisting pattern of abalone and feather lines every hem, just as I embroider my own most beloved skirts. I see hours of labor and a familiar desire to be near beautiful things.

"My name is Lady Sarah Wentworth."

"I am called Matatishe." She cocks her head to the side, still studying me with unafraid frankness. After my long days alone, I welcome even open suspicion. It is far more soothing than the furtive sort. "What do you want, Lady?"

She says my title as if it's a name, and I realize my mistake.

"Apologies." I curtsy on instinct, and her mouth curls into a smile. "I am called Sarah. All the other words are mere accessories."

"Accessories," she repeats slowly, as if tasting the word. "Second names. I understand."

I blink. How on Earth do the people in Jamestown believe Matatishe to be savage? This is more civilized conversation than I've carried on since departing the *Waterlily*.

"I am here to trade." I look at the list on the parchment, two scant items. Climbing-bean seeds and, seemingly hastily added, bear oil.

"What else?" Matatishe's gaze wanders, as if I've immediately become dull to her.

The rejection throbs like a bruise smacked. I cannot lose this woman as well, not when I just began spinning visions of having this chore always assigned to me and stealing a few minutes' peace and conversation each day.

I put my hand on the towering vein-trunk. "A selfish question, if you'll allow it. Do you know this tree's name?"

She turns back to me, interest alight in her dark eyes. "Your name or mine?"

"Both." I take a step forward, trying to express my sincere interest.

"Your name is cypress," she says. "My name is a third name, and you cannot have it."

"Cypress." I stare up into the budding branches. "I've been calling them vein-trunks."

That curling smile once again. "It may like a second name."

I grin back at her. I've never been the best at telling such things, but it seems to me as if I've just made my first friend in Jamestown.

THAT EVENING, I PINCH THE *BOOK OF COMMON PRAYER* ELIZABETH AND I are sharing delicately between two burning fingers. Though Sir

Thomas organized this prayer meeting, followed by dinner, with all the men he considered serious prospects in his home rather than at the church, the word of God still sears. Elizabeth's eyes filled with tears mere moments after the meeting began, so I have been holding the book for the two of us and counting down until my release. There is no timepiece in the Forrests' parlor as Father had, so I have been counting the logs as they burn through in the fire roaring to stave off the last of a winter chill I can no longer feel. Mr. Stone sits with his back to the blaze, and I steal occasional glimpses at his face.

His green eyes, glowing with flame, remain steadily on his own book. His jaw looks rougher-hewn like this, as though he is less a forgotten masterpiece and more an unfinished one, waiting for a kindly artist to smooth out the jagged edges. He reads with his lips moving, graceful and quick. Certainly, he is a man of enough breeding to have been taught better, so I allow myself to imagine he likes the taste of the words.

"Amen," Sir Thomas intones.

Everyone lifts their heads from their texts, and my unnatural reflexes finally fail me. Mr. Stone catches my gaze. My face prickles as if I would blush, but I haven't eaten in long enough to have the blood for it.

Elizabeth giggles and plucks the book from my hands. Mr. Stone looks away from me–at her. A breath escapes my chest like a spring flood, relief and fear blending as mud and water do. He has such a terrible habit of discovering me.

"If you would all join us at the table," Mistress Forrest says.

Mr. Stone stands and strides off. The other three serious bachelors, Mr. Moore, Mr. Ingram, the lawyer, and Sir Ellis, a gentleman, follow suit. Elizabeth drops the *Book of Common Prayer* on one of the vacated seats and eyes me accusingly. She wants to know why I held onto it as long as I did. My fingers are now scorched redder than they were by the churn or the sun, as if I stuck them into the fire.

Or perhaps she wishes to know why I was looking at Mr. Stone.

Having no answer for her in either regard, I hurry to the kitchen to assist in setting the table.

"Mistress Forrest—oh." I stop short a step into the kitchen when I discover Mr. Stone standing in front of the dressed platters.

He bows. "I thought a hand might assist with the heavier dishes."

"Certainly." My words tangle around each other like the uncareful lace bobbins I am always fixing for Elizabeth.

"Now that I have you, however." He steps away from the dishes, toward me. "I have a proposition for you."

The prickling worry of his unexpected strength, his impossible attentiveness, wars with the strange ease I always seem to feel in his presence. I know, somewhere in the remains of my soul, that he does not need me to say a word and welcomes any I have.

"How do you feel about labor?" he asks. "True, hard labor, the sort you must scrub out from under your nails when the day ends."

"I like it better than idleness," I admit honestly. "It does not scare me, nor do I resent it. But I am not sure I could ever live a life without a scrap of leisure."

"I don't believe the human animal can." He takes another step closer. It's almost as if he's growing, filling more and more of the kitchen. "And what of children?"

Sour guilt churns my stomach. I will not lie. "I have always wanted children and many of them."

He nods resolutely. "You are in want of a husband. I find myself equally in want of a wife with the qualifications you've just described. What say we dispense with the distraction of these events and wed each other? I will provide you with occasional leisure if you provide the required work and heirs to the fortune I've built."

My mind turns to nothing but the roaring of a strong wind through treetops. Somewhere under those trees is William, his easy smile and tousled hair. Above them is nothing but noise upon noise.

The kitchen door opens behind me, and I recognize my sister by the quick step of her feet alone.

"Mistress Forrest said you had offered to manage the dishes, but I could not let you do such a task alone," she declares to Mr. Stone. I may as well not have been standing in the room, even though she passed me so nearly that her skirts brushed my hand. "Tell me, what is delaying you?"

"I have asked Lady Sarah to wed me," Mr. Stone replies frankly. "And I was hoping I might have an answer to the question before sitting down to dinner."

Elizabeth turns to me slowly, frostbite in her blue gaze. "Is that so?"

I look between the two of them, a rabbit caught in an inescapable snare. "I…you must understand that I need time to consider your offer, Mr. Stone."

The word *consider* turns Elizabeth's face into a snarl and Mr. Stone's to a grimace. Having gnawed myself from the trap, leaving blood and pieces behind, I turn and flee the cramped kitchen.

9

THAT MAN

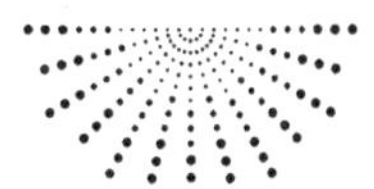

Sarah

OVER DINNER, ELIZABETH DOLES OUT VENOMOUS LOOKS AS IF THEY were second servings of the rich, rabbit stew. Her eyes rime the air between her and her target in the rare moments between Sir Thomas's and Mistress Forrest's watchful gazes. Most of her looks, distilled from Father's worst and most scathing, land on Mr. Stone's plate. Every droplet of warmth she has kept reserved for him over these past two weeks has dried up as if it were a puddle in the sun. I stare at my bowl, uneven earthwork showing grayish clay through the glaze, and try to avoid the few pointed in my direction. Elizabeth knows—she *must* know—that I have not pursued Mr. Stone intentionally. I don't even believe I have pursued him unintentionally. In truth, I have no idea how I found myself in that kitchen, listening to him lay out the details of a marriage proposal as if it were a trade deal.

Briefly, I glance up from my bowl and discover Mr. Stone looking at me. His green eyes shine, nearly glow, in the firelight, and once again, I am struck by the tingling feeling of ancient recognition.

59

Something in me has always known something in him. Were I to accept his offer, to stand by his side, I would fit there as if the space was made for me. My mind fills with images of the two of us, arm in arm on the main road or sharing a pew in the church. Perhaps even the acid of the blessed ground wouldn't agonize me so if I had his arm to lean upon for support.

Between Elizabeth's palpable rage and my own errant imaginings, dinner whips past. Sir Thomas is ending the meal with a second grace what feels like a heartbeat after the first. The suitors are escorted to the door with a flurry of goodbyes, and the four of us are dismissed.

Elizabeth somehow manages to hold her tongue until we climb the stairs to the garret, and Lady Felice draws the curtain between the two halves of the room. The moment it slides into place, however, she whirls on me.

"You shall not marry that man."

I knew she would say such a thing, but that somehow fails to make hearing it any less painful. I realize I would, in fact, rather like to marry Mr. Rafe Stone. To hide my expression, I step behind her and begin releasing her from her gown.

"He is quite clearly a serpent in the grass," she continues, nearly snarling. "How dare he lead so many of us on then ask the hand of the only woman he barely spoke with?"

Elizabeth's anger is often like a summer storm. It arrives suddenly and with great furor, but it frequently peters out on its own before long. With this in mind, I pull at the closure of her gown and hold my tongue. It will do neither of us any good to note that Mr. Stone paid neither Lady Felice nor Miss Winnifred any mind.

"That man does not deserve a single woman who survived the voyage," she spits. "Neither the four of us nor whoever else arrives, you have my word. I would not be surprised if he were a drunk, or a philanderer, or... or... a bore!"

I cannot imagine myself minding a husband who was a bore. That seems almost relaxing, but of course, it would drive Elizabeth wild. I tap her upper arm, and she raises them both so I might free her from her gown.

"Mr. Ingram strikes me as a particularly interesting fellow," I say carefully as I fold the silken top and lay it in her trunk. Perhaps, if I can turn Elizabeth's attention elsewhere, she won't mind if I choose to accept Mr. Stone's offer. It is certain in my mind that he will never turn his to her, so this is the kindest thing I can give her. "He tells the most wonderful stories about his practice."

She snorts, disgusted. "Mr. Ingram is a lawyer, and his father was a mere cobbler. Whatever money that family has is as fragile as a sheet of muslin. One unlucky break would upturn their fortunes entirely. No, he may have nice hands and a decent story or two, but I value my life too highly to waste it with him."

"Of course." The ties on her skirt are so tight that I must focus my attention on them for a moment. My own knots ring with earlier frustration. "What of Sir Ellis? His family is reasonably moneyed, and he is certainly devout enough that you needn't worry about philandering."

Elizabeth shudders from tip to toe. "I have never seen a man with wetter lips than Sir Ellis. If I had to lay with him, I would be sick."

Sir Ellis is a perfectly nice man, if a bit overburdened with saliva, but she cannot hear that now. Perhaps I am wasting my efforts. Perhaps I ought to set my sights elsewhere and allow Mr. Stone to select his wife from the next group.

"And of course, a devout man would be always in church." She lowers her voice, a rare concession to my desire to hide our secrets from the other women. "To enter that place every day might well kill either of us."

That, I cannot argue with. But it conjures up a tiny detail from the back of my mind, a ray of sunshine in the darkness.

"Mr. Moore lives far enough from the fort that he has built his own private chapel, and I have heard he failed to consecrate the land properly."

Elizabeth pauses in her various elaborate displays of disgust, and her fair brow furrows in consideration. "Mr. Moore has the look of Father's chestnut mare."

That gains a snort from me. Basil, Father's childhood horse, does have coloring shockingly close to Mr. Moore's. And something of his way of drawing all attention to himself, if not also his barrel chest. For a moment, Elizabeth and I are reunited again, simply sisters gossiping like young ladies oughtn't after another ball. Mr. Stone and the curse both fall away. I free her from her skirt and begin combing her hair without even a flicker from that bitter ember behind my breastbone.

"He is only the second-most landed planter in the colony," Elizabeth says hesitantly.

"But he comes from wealth, and his father has extensive connections in the east." I slide my fingers through her golden curls, untangling them gently. "He told me that Lord Moore is one of the most sought-after jewel traders in England. Raw stones, so we would not have any cause to truck with him."

Her mouth pinches in further thought. The more I speak, the more clearly I see that Mr. Moore is the obvious choice for Elizabeth. He may not have the look she so favored in many of her suitors—even Fergus, the lascivious sailor on the *Waterlily*, outdoes him in that regard—but he meets her every other requirement. And Mr. Moore strikes me not as the sort overburdened with the kind of curiosity that might lead him to discover Elizabeth for what she is. But on his arm, she would be always at the center of attention, a rich man's beautiful wife, and she has never wanted more than that.

She twists and meets my gaze, the ice in her eyes thoroughly thawed. "I shall consider Mr. Moore, as it seems *that man* is not a suitable husband for myself or anyone else."

Her feelings toward Mr. Stone and myself may not have softened yet, but I shall not give up hope. That night, I dream of a life next to a green-eyed planter.

THE NEXT DAY, ELIZABETH AND I WALK ALONG THE MAIN ROAD TO THE storehouse on an errand for Mistress Forrest. I duck my head low, as always, praying my bonnet will protect enough of my face that I needn't mind the sliver of burning on the back of my neck. Though Elizabeth has finally consented to a proper bonnet, rather than the kerchief she prefers, she walks with her head held high.

"Good morrow, Mr. Warren," she flutes gaily.

"Good morrow, ladies Wentworth," the older widower I have seen only at service thus far replies with a short bow. "I am surprised Sir Thomas is not keeping all his young ladies inside today."

Worry prickles over my skin like a stinging nettle. "Why is that?"

"A deer was found at the gates this sunrise." Mr. Warren glances around nervously. "Those woods-folk, they don't like it when we touch the deer, and this one was utterly drained of blood."

I turn my body to stone so I do not look at Elizabeth. Last night, I slept far too heavily to have caught her on another excursion, but there is no explanation for this other than her carelessness.

"Oh, how horrible." Her voice is all breath, pure feminine concern. "Why do people believe such a thing could have happened?"

How can she be asking that? How can she be standing here, the mortal sun searing her skin, and play-act humanity?

"Some say it was a threat." Mr. Warren frowns. "I'm not so certain. There are creatures in those woods, beasts no kindly God put there. But I won't worry your fine young ears with that."

After a brief goodbye, he hurries on his way. Slowly, I melt and allow myself a single glance at my sister. Amusement dances on her face, as if we have just learned of a ball or seen the result of some practical joke.

"What were you thinking?" I hiss.

She does not waste breath denying it. "Everything is so dull here. I just wanted to rile everyone a bit."

"Mr. Warren suspects." Just saying the words strikes ice into my heart. The moment I begin to settle into a life here, consider that I might be happy in addition to merely alive, our existence is threatened once more.

"He is an old eccentric. I would not be surprised if he suspects a banshee or ghost." She giggles, high and delighted. "Oh, I hope he begins telling people he does."

"You must be more careful." Every place I look, I see pairs of people in conversation. They all huddle close, brows drawn. News of the deer seems to have permeated the colony, and it is on everyone's lips.

"Don't worry yourself too much, Lady Sarah, or even Mr. Stone will give up his perverse fixation on you." She pats my hand and strides down the street, her chin even higher than before.

10

AGREEMENT

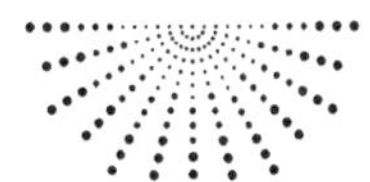

Sarah

Sunday dawns with the first true heat since our arrival in Jamestown. I wake with the coverlet stuck to my chest, wondering vaguely how a creature like me still sweats. The few itching mosquito bites I have collected beg the same question. I feel so pitifully human and weak on Sunday mornings, as if the Lord Himself is reminding me that I was once one of his children.

Or perhaps it is merely that I know this will be the first time I am forced to face Mr. Stone since his proposal. There have been no formal events since that fateful dinner, but a public social awaits me. I dress with shaking hands, barely listening to Elizabeth's chatter, and endure the pain of service with a distant mind. Mr. Stone sits in his family's pew alone. His gaze does not drift from Father Buck or his posture falter. Once again, I am visited by visions of balm at his side.

I blink, and I am one of a crowd around the primary well, watching the other three women flit like butterflies from man to man. Potential husbands preen under their attention. I cup my hands around an earthenware mug of chilled beer and wish that I could

65

exchange my heavy bonnet and cloak for the lightweight kerchief and capelet Lady Felice swans around the perimeter in.

Other citizens of Jamestown watch us with quiet interest, talking amongst themselves. More than once, amidst the names and petty gossip none of these God-fearing people ought to be engaging in on the Sabbath, I hear whispers about the deer. No attack has followed from the Powhatans, and suspicions are turning from them to more inauspicious explanations. Mr. Warren's theories are picking up speed in ways that make my skin crawl, though the fondest explanation is currently ghosts of those lost during the Starving Time. Reverend Buck adamantly denies any otherworldly potential, and I find my heart softening toward the weather-worn preacher more than I would have thought.

"Now, you must be joking, Mr. Moore," Elizabeth giggles. "Surely you couldn't give me a necklace of all freshwater pearls in less than a season."

While this is the first formal event, Elizabeth has found more than enough ways to seek out Mr. Moore since I pointed out his eligibility. Every errand somehow coincides with one of his, leaving me stranded out in the sun for burning minute after burning minute as she drapes herself over the side of his carriage like so much fabric and giggles.

"Less than a month, I would say," Mr. Moore crows.

I must admit the two of them make a well-matched pair. He is dark where she is light, and her slimness complements his breadth more than I would have thought. More than that, they both shine with the implication of finery smothered out of respect for service—respect I have had to remind Elizabeth of more than once. Embroidery gleams at Mr. Moore's wrists and pockets. Fine buckles that look so much like gold I almost wonder if he didn't ignore conventional brass fasten his shoes. The falling band at his neck is so intricately detailed I am surprised he wore it in this weather. He makes perfect sense alongside Elizabeth's fragile crepe gown which I had to sew a wristband onto that she might not drag it in the ever-present mud.

Your sister is a turkey, Matatishe says in my memory. *Always flashing tail feathers.*

My hidden smile turns to a hidden snort. The only errands on which I have not been delayed by conversation with Mr. Moore are my increasingly frequent trips into the forest. Elizabeth disdains the place for anything, but as the deer showed quite clearly, hunting. She says she doesn't like to risk her clothes. I've explained to her about the aprons I wear, how simple it is to step lightly once you begin to know the plants, but she refuses. In truth, I do not much mind having Matatishe to myself. Mistress Forrest has begun to complain about the length of my trips for how long we spend talking to each other. She is brilliant, a fascinating woman, and the only one other than Elizabeth in the whole colony who will speak to me a moment longer than required by etiquette.

She is also the only soul who knows my unkindest thoughts about Elizabeth. I trust Matatishe not to repeat my words. She has been very clear that most of what she calls Chawnzmit's people, those of us in Jamestown whom she has apparently named for John Smith, are not the sort she would ever talk to intentionally. She knows the rest of the colony thinks of her as little more than an animal. The idea incenses me, and if I believed my saying so would make a bit of difference, I would stand up in church and declare its wrongness. As it is, though, it means I have one friend to whom I can trust my every secret without fear of revelation to any but the rest of her people.

Well, not my every secret. I have told her all my thoughts about Elizabeth, save those about her nightly outings and the deer. Matatishe believes Elizabeth to be vain—perhaps even vainglorious— but not swayed by the irresistible hunger that now lives in both our breasts.

"Pearls and rubies?" Elizabeth presses a falsely shocked hand to her chest, drawing every eye to the square neck of her gown and just how tightly she had me lace her stays in the brief moment of primping between church and the social. Mr. Moore's eyes seem particularly happy to linger on the pale, exposed flesh. "Oh, you are too kind. I merely asked out of curiosity, but if you insist on giving me such a present...."

"That and more, my sweet." He pats her other hand, immodestly tucked into the crook of his arm. "If you give me the time, I will pull the moon down from the sky and have it fashioned into a comb to suit your glorious hair."

She ducks her head coyly and catches my gaze. A brief, sly smile flickers across her lips. She is more than happy with the suitor I have chosen for her. That sly pleasure turns my stomach in a way I find myself not quite able to explain, and I turn away from the pair of them. Mr. Moore has no real idea the sort of woman he is promising the world to or how dearly she will hold him to that promise. I remember all too well the scandal when Elizabeth broke off with a count whose attention she had garnered simply because it was discovered that he was from a lesser branch of his own family tree. It mattered not that he had already inherited the land and title; that there might someday be a more legitimate heir that questioned her claim was enough to dispose of the man entirely. The next week, she had another charming suitor on her arm as if the count had never existed.

Turning brings my attention to the other side of the well, where Mr. Stone stands between Miss Winnifred and Lady Felice. He is wearing a dark brown suit I have seen him in before, a handsome piece which makes him look as warm as a fire on a winter's evening but shows signs of inexpert patching in the knees and elbows. My heart sings at the image of him bent over his own breeches, a needle clutched in one hand, graceful even in his inexperience.

Elizabeth's laughter rings through the gathering. Heads turn in her direction from all over, and I know all of Jamestown has gotten her message. The attention she has been lavishing on Mr. Stone now belongs to Mr. Moore. That is why Lady Felice and Miss Winnifred have taken the risk of approaching Mr. Stone for the first time since the very first meeting. Though everyone avoids me, they treat Elizabeth as if she is one of the aggressive, striking snakes that Mistress Forrest warned us will begin lurking in seemingly innocent piles of leaves as the weather warms. I know not whether news of Mr. Stone's offer to me has become public knowledge, but the other two women do not fear me as they fear her. Lady Felice tosses a curl of red-gold hair, and for the first time in my life, that bitter ember in my chest burns for someone other than Elizabeth.

I lift my kirtle delicately and stride across the half-dry mud toward Mr. Stone and his admirers. Elizabeth's reaction, the fact that she has still not spoken Mr. Stone's name since he made his offer to me, melts from my mind like the last of the snow clinging to roofs and shutters. For reasons I may never understand, he is interested in me. And, no matter the disrespect I fear it does William's memory, I am interested in him. My presence may be a curse upon his life, denying him the heirs he stated so clearly were his only desire, but I have no hope in this New World if I do not lay that curse upon someone. I should like to make a selfish decision and enjoy, just once, the immorality my curse offers me first and foremost.

Lady Felice eyes me steadily as I approach but offers only the barest curtsy. "Lady Sarah."

Miss Winnifred at least has the faculties to respect what remains of my superior position and curtsies a hair deeper, though she does not address me. Sourly, I feel sorry for her. She will end up on the arm of someone like Mr. Whittaker, and hers will be an unhappy life. But I shall not abandon my chance at happiness here in favor of hers.

"I should like to speak with Mr. Stone." I bob my own curtsy, solely to him, then finally lift my gaze to his face, my skin a welter of worry over what I may find within. Mr. Stone is an efficient, businesslike man. He may resent the days I have made him wait.

What greets me is simply the glowing, all-consuming green of his eyes. Sometimes, it is as if he is devouring me with his gaze. Not in the lecherous way of so many men I have long avoided, but as if he wishes to reach under the surface layers of etiquette, social utterances, my very skin and see the soul which hides beneath. His eyes beg understanding, something deep and wanting which I have perhaps never seen before but which I would happily give myself up to. Had I met Mr. Stone before this curse befell me, I might have even turned over William for him. Now, I approach him with want tempered by slick, sour guilt.

"Apologies, Lady Sarah," Lady Felice says acidly, "but Mr. Stone, Miss Winnifred, and I were—"

"Just concluding our business," he says over whatever the end of her sentence might have been.

Lady Felice makes a small, shocked noise. My cheeks flame. He is pushing them aside for me, and with no care for the fact that I may simply be here to turn him down. His interest in me is as all-consuming as his gaze.

"Then… I suppose we shall go." She takes Miss Winnifred by the arm, and the two of them flounce away with their noses in the air, clearly put off by the interaction.

"Well?" Mr. Stone says, a note of impatience I haven't yet heard in his voice.

My tongue knots. The ember which powered my journey here seems well and truly burnt out, with Lady Felice put so neatly in her place. I had no true intention of what I might say to Mr. Stone when faced with him once more.

"The weather is stifling," I find myself mumbling. "Might I expect this the rest of the summer?"

"This and worse, though my home has some cooling abilities." He takes a step closer, indecorously near me. I can pick out slim knots of gray tweed in the wool of his doublet. "I would like your answer now."

"Yes." The word bursts from my tongue, escaped from a pin I didn't know I was holding it within. "I shall marry you."

His answering nod is sharp, businesslike. I flatter myself that I see a hint of a curve in his lips, as if he might be pleased with my answer, but it disappears so quickly that I fear it may have been simple vanity.

"Sir Thomas," Mr. Stone calls.

The lawyer joins us quickly, glancing from one to the next. "What may I do for you?"

"Discharge Lady Sarah's responsibility to the Virginia Company and draw up a marriage license. We shall be married on the next

Sunday." Mr. Stone's voice is crisp enough that I could find myself cut by the words if I wanted to. However, I find his demeanor comforting. The world that exists between husband and wife is blessed by the Lord, but it grows and thrives in the home and has no heavenly business with such matters as the Virginia Company. Completing the formalities is nothing more than this—a brief conversation between two men at the well, relief on Sir Thomas's face, and satisfaction of a deal complete on Mr. Stone's.

What shall come next will be what determines whether I have made the correct choice.

11

WEDDING BELLS

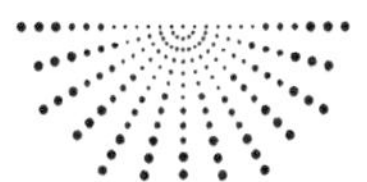

Sarah

"I suppose the red does suit you reasonably well," Elizabeth says as she pins another section of my hair back.

I offer her a tentative smile. On Wednesday, Mr. Moore asked Sir Thomas for her hand, and she has been far more gracious about my acceptance of Mr. Stone since then. She even offered to organize all the details of my toilet, other than the dress itself. On that, I was firm. I have not worn the red gown since arriving in Jamestown, and today, I should like to look as beautiful as I believe as possible. If I cannot give Mr. Stone everything he hopes for, I shall give him everything I can.

Thinking about what I cannot do, however, sends another wave of tension prickling over my skin like so many little shocks from touching a door on a winter morning. Mr. Stone was quite clear that we would be wedding in Jamestown's church, with Father Buck performing the service. No amount of Elizabeth's careful finicking with my hair or gown can allay the burning I know will leak up from my feet and into the rest of my body until I can hardly hold the bouquet of wildflowers Matatishe helped me select yesterday. And after the service is done, my life with Mr. Stone will truly begin. I will discover whether he is everything I believe him to be, whether I am truly able to keep this dark secret of mine when I am sharing everything, even bedclothes, with another soul.

I shall also be parted from Elizabeth for the first time since her birth. A sudden throb of sisterly feeling has me grabbing at her wrist and stopping her attention for a moment.

"I love you," I say, desperate for her to hear the words. "I believe I am going to miss you terribly."

She smiles indulgently and kisses both of my cheeks. "In only a few days' time, we shall both be wives. The walk isn't so long that we cannot make it between our two homes, and we'll no longer need each other as much as we did."

My sleep will be soothed by not waking every time she shifts, awaiting another nighttime hunt, but I do not believe I shall ever need her less than I need her right now. Still, I know she is right. Our bond will carry us to the end of time, even if our shared curse means we reach that end with only each other. Perhaps it is a blessing that, according to a text I discovered in Father's study, Elizabeth and I shall never bear children. Burying them would be too painful to imagine.

The bells begin clanging. Elizabeth's grin widens. "It is time."

"Am I ready?" I stand, straighten my skirts, and present myself for her approval. She looks me over with a critical eye then nods.

We hurry downstairs to join the rest of the household and walk to the church together.

Stepping inside eats through the soles of my boots and up into me in a single heartbeat, but I keep what I hope is a sweet smile fixed upon my lips. As agreed, the first pew has been ceded to Mr. Stone and I. He stands at the end of it, and I fancy his eyes glow even brighter as he takes me in. Regardless, he sets a warm hand against the small of my back and guides me into the seat next to him like I am already his, and the feeling of it thrills.

Father Buck launches into the usual prayers. Mr. Stone sits stiffly next to me, a few inches away, and all warmth dies. Noticing any detail is difficult through the haze of pain calling smarting tears to my eyes, but it is almost as if he is leaning away from me. I have never seen his posture so ramrod straight, almost militant, and every muscle in his jaw bulges beneath his skin as if he is clenching it just as tight as a human jaw may be clenched. My worry returns, a rime of ice over the spot where he touched me. Mr. Stone does not wish to marry me, and he's realized only now that is the case. When Father Buck calls us to the altar, he shall revoke his claim. The marrow of my bones riots at the idea, but I know it. I am certain.

"Would the couple take their places?" Father Buck says.

I rise unevenly. After a heartbeat, Mr. Stone follows. Though he takes my arm, our every step lands like that of an executioner taking the stage. Only doom awaits.

"Dearly beloved," Father Buck intones in a thin, worn voice. "We are gathered together here in the sight of God, and in the face of this congregation, to join together this man and this woman in holy matrimony."

Mr. Stone's mouth twists. Each heartbeat draws us closer to the moment in which he will rebuke me. I would not be surprised if Mistress Forrest then set me on the next ship to England, a failure who needn't remain in the colony any longer. Distantly, I hope I may have a moment to bid Matatishe farewell.

"I require and charge you, as you will answer at the dreadful day of judgment, when the secrets of all hearts shall be disclosed, that if either of you do know any impediment, why you may not be lawfully joined together in matrimony, that you confess it." Father Buck looks at us both severely and mournfully, as if he, too, knows the doomed moment we approach. It seems as if my day of judgment is upon me now.

"I do not," Mr. Stone replies, steady and full-throated.

Shock washes every word from my mind. Does he know what he is doing?

"Lady Sarah?" Father Buck prompts.

"I…I do not," I say.

The reverend nods and continues with the service, blessing our union and the prosperity it will bring to the colony. My hesitation fades from the air between Mr. Stone and I. When I look at him now, he seems far less cold, merely stiff. Perhaps he likes the eyes of all upon him as little as I do.

Agreeing to serve him as my wedded husband is much simpler, the fear melted from my bones when he accepts me as his wedded wife with the same ease. We exchange simple rings of gold, forged at the blacksmith, and a chaste kiss that surprises me with its suddenness. I have never seen a kiss within a church before, and I suppose I haven't seen one yet. The brush of Mr. Stone's beard against my cheeks is rough but appealing, a sensation I find myself craving when he retreats.

For the rest of the service, we kneel at Father Buck's feet. He places the blessed, now sickening bread upon our very tongues, and I am obliged to swallow the poison that should be the sweetest morsel I have ever tasted. But at long last, the concluding hymn echoes off the walls of the church, and Mr. Stone and I lead the procession outside just behind Father Buck.

A small celebration awaits us. Elizabeth—who, I am certain, happily volunteered to leave the service a few moments early—stands beneath a striped tent and beside a table bearing the iced groom's cake and the fruit-studded bride's cake which Mr. Stone and I will bring home with us, to eat in a year's time. Her face glows with a smile, and she sweeps me up in a hug the moment the procession softens. I hug her back, heedless of how it may crush my gown. I am a wife—I am Mrs. Stone.

"I suppose I should call you brother now," Elizabeth says impishly over my shoulder.

I release her and turn to see Mr. Stone mere inches behind me, as if the invisible tether of marriage tugged him along.

"Whatever you prefer." He rests his hand on the small of my back once more, and I marvel at his warmth, so intense as to be palpable through so many layers of clothes.

Elizabeth giggles. "I shall, if you also call me sister. We are family now."

Mr. Stone inclines his head. "That we are."

"Oh, we shall have to have a dinner once you and Mr. Moore are wed," I say, barely recognizing my own breathy voice. I am free of the church, and something delirious fills me like sloshing wine.

Elizabeth is quickly caught up in my own excitement, but Mr. Stone only mumbles something noncommittal. As other colonists join us, we find ourselves quickly at the head of a receiving line. To my greatest surprise, many of those in line offer us small gifts. Mistress Forrest provides a pair of much more comfortable clogs, shaped by her own hand. Lady Felice and Miss Winnifred offer a handkerchief each from their own stores, a gift I know costs the latter far more than the former. Privately, I decide to make Miss Winnifred another for her own wedding, so she does not find herself wanting. Reverend Buck gives us a few words of wisdom, which burn only slightly, and an offer of counseling should we need it.

What awes me most are the gifts from strangers or mere acquaintances I have barely nodded at on the street. Quickly, it becomes clear that Mr. Stone is not only well-respected but loved by this community. One of its pillars, with his quiet, easy way. When the celebration ends, not long after the receiving line peters out, I nearly weep with gratitude as he produces a handcart from beside the storehouse. I was imagining staggering down the road under the weight of so much pottery, glasswork, and other gifts.

He begins loading the cart silently, our first moment of privacy since exchanging our vows. I take up a place next to him, sorting through the goods for how best to stack them, and hand him a wooden firkin of French wine, a rare gift from Mr. Moore himself. Mr. Stone takes everything I hand them and fits them together with practiced ease. Were I not here, he would load the cart just as quickly, but if the uncareful patches in last Sunday's suit are anything to judge by, not quite as well. Perhaps that is what I can offer to this marriage.

"I would appreciate you calling me Rafe," he says after a few minutes of quiet work.

"Rafe." The name flips off my tongue, sharp enough to suit the man in front of me. "Then you ought to call me Sarah."

"Everyone on Bluebonnet is called by their baptismal name." He slides a jug in tightly, safely. "Working folk and myself. I won't be changing that for you."

I nod. Visions of running a house as tightly as a warship, everyone saying, "Yes, Mistress Stone," fade from my mind, but I won't miss them too sadly. I have never had the sort of spirit that inspires obedience.

He slides the last platter into place and lifts the handles of the cart himself. The muscles in his shoulders, only visible due to the clinging of his linen undershirt and slightly gapping doublet, tense and strain. With promises of service and forsaking others ringing in my ears, I hurry forward and pull one of the handles into my own grasp. Only otherworldly strength keeps me from dropping it. Mr. Stone—Rafe is very strong indeed.

This time, I am certain I do not imagine the small smile on his lips. He drapes the hem of my dress over his free arm, and together, we set off for the home we now share. The road is far from short, and dark hunger tears at my innards. It has been too long since I ate of the forest, especially if I am to be straining myself like this. But there is something satisfying in the long-forgotten ache of strain in my arms, the same something echoed in Rafe's quiet, steady footfalls beside me.

We reach his plantation, Bluebonnet, just as the sun is beginning to streak the sky with its most vibrant hues. I wish to spin up and join it, my crimson dress blending with its richest reds. Even Rafe seems to take it in with a pleasanter eye. For the first time, I wonder if he might be a valuable source of the knowledge I have been seeking about Virginia.

"Dinah?" he calls as we trundle up to a side door rather than the front.

"Lads, they have arrived!" a brassy, middle-aged woman's voice yells back.

A moment later, the wooden door swings open, and a rosy-cheeked woman I assume is Dinah grins at me from the mouth of a kitchen. Yellowish corn flour streaks her cheek, and she dries her hands on her kirtle.

"You must be Sarah," she says.

In a heartbeat, I understand why Rafe has done away with titles entirely. Those visions of my militant kitchen become little more than a child's fantasy, replaced with the much sweeter image of myself beside Dinah and whoever else may emerge from this house, working and talking as equals. Only when the pitter-pat of feet racing to join us intrudes do I dismiss the thought and greet the woman in front of me properly.

"Dinah is my cook," Rafe says. "Though you will be responsible for the house from this day forth."

"I can give you all you need on the morrow," Dinah says brightly. "Tonight, the two of you ought to enjoy yourselves."

My gut wrenches. Rafe cares so little for social convention that I hope he will not mind that I allowed William to sway my convictions and spent an evening or two in bed within him before our marriage. I should like to hope he will not notice, but if there is one thing I have learned of the planter at my side, it is that nothing escapes his notice.

The "lads" quickly make themselves known. Indentured men, charging in from deeper in the house, from the squat quartering house not far off, a few even from the fields despite the Sabbath. Rafe sets the cart down and tucks my hand into the crook of his arm, a gesture of silent support and protection that steadies me more than I would have thought. As they arrive, he introduces them. Names fly past me like birds on the wing, far too fast to catch in the net of my mind. I do notice not all of the lads, are in fact, lads. Of the nearly forty indentures that arrive, perhaps a fifth their number are women. Stocky, sunburnt women who seem used to a day's labor and unused to patching a gentleman's trousers. To my surprise, not a one of them stirs that ember in my breast.

"And this is Klaus." Rafe claps a smiling, off-blond man on the shoulder. "My right hand in all business about the fields."

"It is lovely to meet you all." I curtsy. "I hope to meet you more sincerely over the coming days, and I hope we might all become friends."

My pronouncement is met with somewhat limited excitement. Especially at the outside of the gathering, which has been drifting apart almost as quickly as it forms, leaving behind a dozen or so laborers, looks all too similar to those I received inside Jamestown begin to wing my way. They, too, can tell what I am. Soon, Rafe must. And Matatishe—and then I shall be alone.

"Obey her as you would me within these walls," he says.

Then, he leads me inside. Though his space is rustic compared to any I saw in London, it is markedly larger than that of Sir Thomas. Rafe shows me a sunken cellar beneath the kitchen, as well as a separated sitting and dining room. His brick chimney radiates warmth into the open, sparsely decorated space. Though he speaks little, the quiet comfort of his presence is enough. Upstairs, his office and the bedroom flank the entrance to the garret. The office, I am pleased to note, is well-organized and shows no sign of having been lived in more than it ought.

At the door to the bedroom, Rafe pauses. Something prickles through the air between us, incipient like a storm. When he opens that door, it will become our first night as husband and wife. I know my duties, and looking into his eyes, I find it difficult to resent them.

"When I asked of labor, I did not exaggerate," he says, his hand on the knob.

"The house alone is large enough to keep my hands busy," I admit. "But do you mean there is more?"

"I often assist in the fields. I expect the same of you." A muscle in his jaw flickers as if he is waiting for me to refuse.

"I have tended garden beds alone, so I may require some guidance." I smile up at him. "When I set my future on living here, I knew what sort of labor would be required, and I have decided to enjoy it."

"An admirable quality." He opens the door.

My heart flutters, even though I am looking only at an unmade bed and a simple chest of drawers. This is to be my bedroom for the rest of my days, my mattress which I share with my husband.

"Make yourself comfortable," he says. "I shall be sleeping in the garret, if you find yourself in need of me."

Rafe turns and departs before I can reply, leaving me very much alone.

12

UNIQUE

Sarah

ON THE FOLLOWING THURSDAY, I SLIP MOTHER-OF-PEARL BUTTONS THE size of apple seeds through loops of silk along the back of the new gown Mr. Moore commissioned for Elizabeth's bridal wear.

"Is it not the finest gown you have ever seen in all your life?" She admires the sheathes of fine, pale blue material around her arms leading up into dramatically slit sleeves.

"I cannot believe Mr. Moore had it made in time," I say honestly. It looks like the sort of gown that would take the best seamstresses in London a month or more.

"He said he started work on it when he first put in for a wife," she says proudly. "He knew he would only marry a woman who suited it, and the moment he saw me, he sensed I was that woman."

Mr. Moore might do better as a poet than a planter, but that is another thought to tuck away and giggle over with Matatishe later. For now, I am happy for Elizabeth.

"Of course, certain changes had to be made," she continues. "The skirt was terribly out of style, and I favor different flowers than those previously featured in the embroidery. But he was quite happy to make the changes for me, you know. He insisted we spare no expense."

"And it is lovely you can wed him in his private chapel." I finish her buttons and smooth the back down. For all I disbelieve much of Mr. Moore's braggadocio, he certainly has managed to give Elizabeth a dress which fits her as if it were made on her very body.

"If only Father Buck were as obliging," she grumbles. "He says, if we forego the prayers, the wedding will not be legitimate in the eyes of the Lord. And I could not tell him that the Lord has no truck with me any longer, at least until I have properly wedded Mr. Moore."

"Elizabeth!" I gasp.

"Surely, you cannot still worry over blasphemy when we cannot set foot in service without burning." She shakes her head at me. "Our eternal resting place, should we ever be sent there, is chosen."

"There is no risk in attempting to keep what commandments we can." I position the lace-edged kerchief over her hair and pin it in place.

"There is no amusement in it either." She purses her lips. "I shall see if Mr. Moore even requests attendance in the chapel of me. I have the sense he isn't much more devout than I, and the chapel may be his own excuse."

A pang of worry for her immortal soul, regardless of what I knew about our curse, strikes me quite hard. Another deer was found, though this time at the edge of the woods, and Mr. Warren's conviction is only growing. Governor Yeardley is believed to be visiting Jamestown soon, and I am worried Mr. Warren will capture his ear. Any news in the governor's hands is liable to reach London before too long, and then all our efforts will have been for nought.

"Have you new shoes for the occasion as well?" I ask to deflect Elizabeth before we find ourselves in a fight mere minutes from her marital vows.

Her glowing smile tells me I know my sister just as well as I think I do.

"I, Lady Elizabeth Wentworth, take the Mr. George Moore to my wedded husband, to have and to hold, from this day forward. For better, for worse, for richer, for poorer, in sickness, and in health. To love, cherish, and to obey, till death us depart, according to God's holy ordinance, and thereto I give my troth," she repeats, her mouth pinching sour around the blessed words.

Mr. Moore seems unable to notice. He has not ceased grinning so wide I am certain I could count each of his teeth since Elizabeth entered the chapel, and I do not expect him to do so soon. It is a blessing, to have something so outlandish to pin my attention on amidst the far slighter discomfort of the service in his chapel. And a marvelous chapel it is, nearly as finely made as that within the fort and still half as large. Though Mr. Moore does not rival Rafe for sheer quantity of land, he certainly seems happy to make the most of that which he does have. My gaze strays to the stained-glass window in one wall. It is simple, especially compared to those rumored in the far-off reaches of the Papal States, but to see glass windows alone in the colony is a miracle. The rainbow of colors sparkles over the simple wooden floor and the train of Elizabeth's gown like jewels.

"Thereto I give my troth!" Mr. Moore declares.

They exchange gold rings, yet another element Elizabeth's new husband has apparently been preparing since the moment he purchased his wife. His overbearing confidence, his certainty that his perfect wife would arrive, suits everything else I know about Mr. Moore and makes me more and more pleased that I have Rafe. I am not sure I could live in a world where my husband was sure how everything would come out and told me so.

With a few more prayers—though the list is truncated from what I endured, I cannot help but notice—the ceremony draws to a close. Elizabeth clings to Mr. Moore as if she were moss while the two of them parade out of the chapel together. Rafe takes my arm before we join the procession. It has become a small habit of his whenever we walk together. He still shows no interest in sharing our bed with me, touches me no more than this or the occasional chaste kiss on the forehead, but I no longer travel unescorted. That is, other than into the forest for my occasional hunts. His touch on my arm is a small symbol that he is not unhappy, that he feels a little of the same peace I do with him, though I am increasingly worried about the distance he places in our marriage bed.

From the chapel, Mr. Moore and Elizabeth lead us and the others who watched the ceremony—Sir Thomas and Mistress Forrest, a few of Mr. Moore's friends—down a soft hill and toward a tent that makes the one Rafe and I celebrated under look like something a child dashed together in an afternoon. It blankets most of a field, tilled but not yet planted and covered with a sheet of canvas. The groom's cake is brilliantly white and two layers high like a stepped pyramid. The more modest bride's cake is nowhere to be seen. A fiddler and two other musicians already play, and other colonists who were not invited to the service flow in from the main road. As if they knew what sort of event Elizabeth and Mr. Moore would put on innately, everyone wears their finest.

Rafe sighs as we approach then turns to me. "I will stay two hours at the most. Then, I shall tell everyone that I have planting that must be completed before sundown."

Relief washes through me, and I nod. "If, at an hour and a half, you have concerns about completing your planting in time, I would not fuss."

We enter the tent together. Just as at our own wedding, Elizabeth and Mr. Moore head an elaborate reception line. Rafe and I decide we need not enter it; I gave Elizabeth her favorite of my necklaces as a gift already, and we have intentions to sup with them before next Sunday. Instead, he takes up residence at one of the many long tables and sits me beside him. Despite the noise, the finery, the glimmering groom's cake, I nearly feel comfortable.

Sir Ellis saunters up to us and sits. After a few pleasantries, he says, "I don't believe I have seen a wedding celebration this elaborate in England."

A woman I only faintly recognizes pauses in her path past us and nods. "I heard Mr. Moore borrowed some of this finery from Governor Yeardley directly."

Rafe's eyebrows tick up a notch, but he does not speak. I waver. Elizabeth is my sister, and I ought to defend her. However, with a few more jewels, this may have put a royal wedding to shame.

"You know, I had my sights set on her." Sir Ellis licks his remarkably wet lips. "Cannot say I am displeased to have lost out, imagining this expenditure. She is a singular woman."

At that, I nod. "There has never been a soul to walk this Earth quite like Elizabeth."

Every other person who comes to speak with Rafe and stumbles into conversation with myself comments on the same. I fall to the same response each time. Elizabeth is singular. It is perhaps the truest compliment I have ever paid her. She is a great many things, but she alone is all of them.

As these visitors come and go around us, I realize Rafe is saying very little. That seems his way with most people. However, I also cannot fail to notice that he seems more relaxed, more prone to the occasional rejoinder or slim smile, the more people who gather round. He has spoken little about his family, or anything he may have left behind in England, but I am left with the unshakeable sense that he is used to being surrounded.

At the two-hour mark on the nose, as I see on the timepiece in his pocket, Rafe stands, stretches, and says, "As much as I loathe to say it, my tobacco will not plant itself."

Objections fill the air. Why does he purchase indentures, if not for the very thing? Surely, he doesn't intend to plant himself? I stand with him, the picture of the dutiful wife, to hide my own smile. I have seen him in the fields, as he has promised, but these people needn't know we are merely sneaking away. The secret fizzes between us, precious and delightful, as we make our apologies and escape.

"Mr. Moore." Rafe bows to the other planter as we pass. "Mrs. Moore."

Elizabeth shivers with overwrought delight. "I don't believe I shall ever get used to hearing that, brother. Say it again for me?"

Rafe's mouth tightens. "Mrs. Moore."

She repeats the gesture all over again, and Mr. Moore guffaws.

"This little wife of mine," he says, then bows to me. "I hear we are to address each other as brother and sister now."

"If it pleases you." I squeeze Rafe's arm, silently pleading with him to make our escape once more. He has the way of these people as I do not, and while I believe George will make Elizabeth as happy as she can be made, I shouldn't like to stand here and pretend I enjoy his company.

"Apologies, the planting awaits." Rafe bows and begins to step aside. I follow him gratefully.

"I understand." George belches another laugh, and Elizabeth looks up at him with eyes so adoring I can almost forget my certainty that she loathes that sound. "Foremen never crack the whip as well as those with real money on the line, eh?"

Rafe offers him a tight nod and hurries away as my stomach knots. I have seen many corners of Bluebonnet, but only a fool would believe they had seen every one after a mere week. Though there has yet been no sign of a whip, I do not like to picture one in Rafe's hands, nor even Klaus's.

"Do you whip your men?" I murmur when I am certain the music of the ongoing celebration will swallow the noise.

Living rage consumes Rafe's expression for a single heartbeat before he covers it once more. "George Moore is a fool. Take nothing he says to heart, and any practice he describes, you may safely assume I subscribe to its opposite."

The knot unravels on a single breath. If I were clever, that rage might alarm me, but I feel I understand. Rafe cares for his laborers as if they were family. The idea of cracking a whip over their heads must be as awful as the idea of doing the same to Elizabeth would be to me. The deep place inside of me which has always recognized Rafe hums. He would not lie about this. No one on Bluebonnet will ever be punished like that.

We return home quietly. Rafe undresses first, changing into simple work clothes, then allows me the bedroom so I might do the same.

My belongings remain in my portmanteau until the carpenter he contracted completes my chest, but I have found myself reaching for the same two sturdy dresses over the past week. I love to see my fine gowns, but I don't truly wish for any more occasions to wear them. Sloughing them off with the help of Dinah's expert fingers, replacing my half-corset with looser stays, and settling into a routine of work is already far superior to nightly balls and worrying over which man might have me.

Rafe is already gone to the fields by the time I reach the kitchen, and my old worries resurface, nevertheless. I take a deep breath and face them. If my husband does not wish to bed me, I have not failed in my wifely duties. I may yearn to discover what lies beneath the many layers of his clothes, but that is not for me to demand. The life I share with him feels like a long, slow exhale after many years of holding my breath. I could certainly be unhappier. And if he never wishes to bed me, he may never discover that I cannot provide him with what he wants most. I turn my hands to the work in front of me, a bit of knitting I wish to complete before summer is truly at its height, and I should rather lose my fingers than set them to wool, and listen to Dinah sing to herself in the kitchen.

THAT NIGHT, I TOSS IN MY EMPTY BED AS IF IT WERE A HAMMOCK ON the *Waterlily*. Vivid dreams, too intense to remain asleep through and too brief to remember, plague me. My thoughts dance in macabre and inhuman patterns. Before my transformation, nights like these made me wonder if I had been possessed or hexed. Now, I merely wonder if I am slowly becoming the creature of the night all the stories promise. When I fell asleep, the first midnight after I awoke something new, it frightened me so badly I thought I had died. I suppose if this restlessness is a sign of some more permanent change, then the Puritans have the right of it, and I was always doomed to become this creature. I have simply never understood what comfort they glean from such a cold destiny.

A howl splits the silent night. My heart lurches. Rafe is by far a planter, but we have a few head of cattle, a pair of pigs, and a chicken coop I thought to myself just yesterday might use some reinforcement. I fly out of bed and to the window, my nightgown flapping around my legs. If the wolf is stalking the coop, I have no choice. I shall simply have to end it and boil my nightgown clean before the rest of the plantation wakes. Though I know Rafe is more than comfortable, I cannot allow a war to start against a simple, hungry wolf. Nor would I prefer to lose my occasional egg at breakfast.

My stomach gnaws at itself, gnashing through every reasonable line of logic. I understand Elizabeth a shred. Despite the risk, I may hunt the hunter regardless of what it wants.

I throw open the shutters, an iced evening breeze whipping through the thin linen, and peer outside. My eyes pick out movement in the close-drawn forest with a predator's ease. The wolf is taller than even the last I saw, nearly as high as my breasts at the shoulder, and dark as pitch. Were it not for the unnatural power of my eyes, I would be forced to assume I imagined the howl. Hunger claws at me. I lick my lips, then think briefly of Sir Ellis.

The wolf throws back its head and howls once more at the sliver of a moon. Its eyes catch the light—a luminous, haunting green. I suck in a breath. I have never seen that color in a natural animal in all my days.

As if it heard me, the wolf cuts off its howl abruptly. It turns and pelts deeper into the forest, saving itself and our fragile coop. I stare after it for a few long moments, then close the shutters with a shudder. I shall eat tomorrow...and avoid wheresoever I believe that monstrous wolf may have gone.

13

CAUGHT IN THE ACT

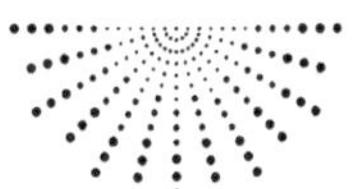

Rafe

THE FIRST RAIN OF MAY IN JAMESTOWN HAS SOOTHED ME, SINCE I discovered the bounty of growing tobacco. Virginia's hard weather softens the clay and gives the fields the last preparations they need before the delicate, dangerous dance of transferring sprouts from seedbed to final field. Of late, I have taken to allowing myself a run in my other form on the night the rain falls. Last night, I could taste it in the air, heavy as over-mulled wine, and I took the risk. In all truthfulness, I should have realized that was a mistake.

Klaus claps me on the shoulder hard enough to jar me from my thoughts. "Trying to drag your heels slowly enough that your strapping young men will work your day for you, *Master Stone?*"

I scowl at the title and pick up the pace. Distraction in the form of Sarah's eyes, turned almost indigo in the night, has haunted me since I woke in the garret. She did not say a word as we partook of a quiet breakfast together, but neither did she flinch when I left my now-customary kiss on her brow. All reason dictates she merely thought

91

the experience a dream or particularly odd fact of colonial life. However, I cannot escape the sense of an arrow through my breast when I met her gaze for the first time through lupine eyes.

"Forgive me for taking care with the crop." I heft the handles of the wheelbarrow scratching at my palms, and the fragile fronds of sprouting tobacco within rustle. "I should like to plant some of these."

"Now, you know I'll cosset the little bastards like they were my own children just as soon as they touch clay." My second-in-command grabs his own barrow with two hands once more, and his seedling shift back into position. "I only thought I might cosset you a spot first."

Klaus reminds me most of my eldest brother, Crispin, and not least in how often I am forced to grimace at his turns of phrase. Crispin was a rebel, ill-suited to inherit Father's position and resentful when made to try. I was raised knowing he would abdicate whatever came to him the moment he was allowed. He was raised knowing Father wished he would choose otherwise, but that he would always have a home in Stone Manor. Somehow, we both grew up laughing.

When I first met Klaus, on the then half-built dock jutting into James River, I thought him the usual sort of stolid German. Well-built, even-keeled, and perfectly dull. In truth, I sometimes wonder if Bluebonnet wouldn't have benefited more from a man of the description I expected. Instead, she and I both received the sort of indenture who, upon meeting me, had promptly chosen to mock me for what he termed my "court accent" while I stood knee-deep in mud.

Perhaps Bluebonnet might've taken to the stolid German of my imagination, but I firmly believe I benefitted far more from Klaus.

We trundle up to Birch Log Field, the largest of my discrete holdings, and set our wheelbarrows down at the edge. A small army of laborers—my indentures combined with as many hands as I could hire on the day half the colony is transplanting—scuttle over it like particularly efficient ants already. Watching them work, I can very nearly forget the impact of Sarah's gaze.

I lift pots of seedlings from the wheelbarrow delicately. They wave up at me, green with the promise of months of growth to come. We shall not transplant everything; only a fool leaves himself with no ability to replant if some of his stalks fail the transition. However, the smaller beds nearer to the house are nearly empty in a frenzy of work. Only today will the ground be soft as a pillow for the insubstantial roots that are the plantation's lifeblood. Anything that remains will have to wait until the next rain.

Klaus and I join the bustle. A row to my south, Fidelma takes up a working song. Klaus picks up the next line, full-throated though he could not carry a tune if someone offered him a basket. Laughter ripples across the exposed clay, and others join in easily. I let the rhythm steer the pace of my hands but keep my voice to myself. Singing and dancing are far too bound up with bygone days for me to partake of them easily.

My muscles groan and stretch as I work. After a night as my truest self in the forest, returning to a man's form always requires some adjustment. Certainly, throwing myself into planting is not the cleverest course of action. However, if I were a truly clever man, I would not always run the night before planting in the first place. There is simply something animalistic that pulls me creeping from my bed in the night to taste the morning dew under the pads of my paws. Father called it our inheritance. Crispin called it moonsong, even though only he had it bound up with the moon's rays in the least. I only call it sleepless nights and exhaustion I so rarely feel in my limbs.

Had I been for a run more recently, I would not ache so. But I have been on behavior so good that it would awe the string of nannies who passed through Stone Manor in England, attempting to put my new wife at ease. She is strange, though of course I knew that before making my offer. Her very strangeness was what made it so impossible to stop thinking about her. And she is markedly more skittish than her sister, so I believed allowing her to adjust in privacy might comfort her. Some of my aches, perhaps, originate from the lumpy mattress I dragged to the garret in advance of her arrival. It is still superior to Klaus's winking offer that he hurry the process along by allowing me to share his bed until I have, in his words, earned my own, at least.

Yet, Sarah seems no more comfortable with me than she did on the day we wed. I could have misunderstood, rocking with the pain of the holy ground underfoot, but I believed for a moment that she looked as though she would rather be hung from the neck until dead than marry me. The dress she wore was red as an English rose and made her quiet beauty sing like a plucked harp string, but her face was drawn up as if anticipating a dash of cold water. That expression had cleared, or I might not have gone forward with the ceremony, but I still discover it on her face sometimes. She never deflects my caresses, but neither does she seem to seek them out.

And then there are these fleeting moments, like the one in which I admitted to her my plan to flee her sister's celebration. She smiled like the dawning sun, as if I was the thing she had been waiting for all her life. She tucked herself alongside me and did not wander an inch. It is very nearly the most confusing thing about her.

The most confusing is her unexplained penchant for the forest. I know she trades with the Powhatan emissary, Matatishe, for household essentials now and then, but Dinah reports she has disappeared into the trees every three days, as if she sets her watch by it. Bluebonnet is a growing plantation, but even we do not require trade every three days.

"Forgive Rafe," Klaus trumpets, abruptly informing me the work song ended while my attention wandered. "He has a fatal affliction… husband!"

Laughter rocks the field. I smile tightly.

"How is the lady wife?" Fidelma calls teasingly. "Everything you paid for?"

More raucous amusement. I have been avoiding requesting Sarah's assistance in the fields for this very reason. If my presence discomfits Sarah, I cannot imagine what this brash cadre might make her feel.

"I would thank you to treasure her name as you do my own," I say stiffly.

Fidelma cackles. "Prudish, then?"

"Or perhaps he likes her a bit too well." Klaus grins at me, wide and careless. "Our generous master has found the one thing he will not share."

The very idea of loaning Sarah out, as if she were some piece of equipment, explodes through me as hot and bright as a muzzle flash. She is not to be touched by another. It is part of the contract we agreed to before a God I doubt has any truck with me, but it means something to the rest of these people, and I intend to enforce it. She is mine.

I open my mouth to say just that, and Klaus's easy grin becomes Crispin's in my mind's eye. He never wanted anything more than when I told him he could not have it. I do not fear my right-hand man or his designs on Sarah. I merely know I will be hectored until the end of my days if he decides this is a lever he can pull to rile me.

"Your generous master has simply entered into another business arrangement." I place a tobacco plant into a pre-dug hole brusquely. "Sarah is an honorable woman, and I will not dishonor her by speaking about her with you, but that is all."

"Not even how lovely she is?" Fidelma laughs.

I watch another of my younger indentures, a Scot called Allistor, nod in appreciation.

"I like a dark-haired lass," yet another offers. "The lighter-haired sort always seem a bit too insubstantial."

"And she's got a sweet little face." Klaus strokes his own chin, evoking the point of Sarah's.

That sharp something takes a clear form in my breast: they have not understood her correctly. The charms which led me to Sarah Wentworth as a wife, despite the strangeness of her circumstances and behavior, have so little to do with her looks that I almost do not recognize her in their descriptions. They speak not at all of her tireless and unflinching work, the way she has not even commented upon the calluses that now mark her soft palms, and the ease with which she shares my quiet.

"Are we gossiping spinsters or laborers on the most productive plantation in Virginia?" I bark. "Work, or take your leisure, but do not combine the two."

I smell my chatter-ridden doom in the slight lift of Klaus's brows, but the teasing dies off into another song at least.

14

THISTLEDAWN

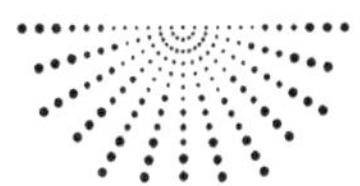

Sarah

I'VE NEARLY GROWN USED TO THE BEATING OF THE LATE-SPRING SUN upon my neck and the swirling dust of the dry path by the time I reach Elizabeth's new house. For all we talked of visiting, nearly a week has already passed, and Elizabeth has not taken herself to me even once. I have seen her in town, but it seems I must travel to her if I wish to see her longer than a few moments at a time. Perhaps that is not a surprising state of affairs, but I will admit myself somewhat surprised it has come about so quickly. My nerves have been rattled by sleeping alone as I have.

That is, of course, the only explanation for that strange beast I saw in the forest. I may have been dreaming or have simply heard an earthly wolf and imagined the monster at the tree line. After all, there are no such thing as werewolves, or I would have seen some proof of them by now.

I take in the spread of George's land as I approach. It is easier to see without the hubbub of a marriage afoot. Fields grope in every direction, shoving the forest back with almost indecent force. There

97

are no sheltering trees clustered close around the house—the nearest leaves are those of the mulberry trees Governor Yeardley mandated every planter must grow to bolster the colony. Even the other buildings, the quarters and barns required to produce everything George makes it very clear he does, are several minutes' walk away. Set apart as it is, Thistledawn Manor looks a bit like an aging maid without a dance partner; still lovely, but unmistakably lonely.

The final stretch of path winds between two initial fields. No work songs color the air as they do at Bluebonnet—at what I am surprisingly swiftly beginning to consider home. And amidst the familiar sun-pinked fair skin of European indentures, a few dark-skinned Africans pluck weeds from tobacco hills. My eyebrows raise. I have seen them before, at the sides of Father's wealthiest friends, but I believed they had not yet been transferred to the colonies.

One straightens, wipes sweat from his brow with the hem of his thin, linen shirt. The simple, human gesture reminds me abruptly of Matatishe, and my stomach twists. So many in Jamestown call her and her people savages, just as those at home spoke of the Africans. But Matatishe is no more savage than any other woman I have met, and I cannot believe these Africans are so different simply because they come from another spit of land we have not previously set European foot upon.

The front door opens, jarring me from my thoughts, and I turn to see Elizabeth standing in the opening.

"Sarah!" she exclaims. "I thought I heard tender foot upon the path."

Homesickness seizes me, and I sweep the final few feet into her arms. "It has been far too long."

"Do you truly need me so dearly that half a week is too long?" she teases.

I merely embrace her tightly. The bones of her corset jut into my arms, far more formal than anything I would don for a day about the house, especially if I did not expect company.

Crack!

I whirl out of her arms toward the noise of a whip slicing through the air. The man I was watching crumples under its tail, the other end clasped by a tall Englishman I do not know. Blood fills the afternoon with its metal stench.

A cry bursts from my lips, and I take a step forward to run to him. My thoughts chase each other in senseless circles. Did the Englishman miss his intended target, some livestock I cannot see? I cling to the notion, the hope, that such a blow was not intended for a man who merely wiped his brow.

Elizabeth grabs my arm, her fingers iron and her gaze ravenous. "What is wrong?"

"He needs assistance." The man stands, ruby painting the back of his shirt. Unearthly hunger growls through me, but I shove it down. "He cannot continue to work."

She laughs, desire unfading. "He is a blackamoor, sister. They do not hurt as we do. George has that man's body bought and paid for across time, so if Foreman Burns believes he can continue working, I assure you he will." As carelessly as waving a handkerchief, Elizabeth lifts a hand to the tall Englishman. He waves with equal ease, and my hunger turns to true, mundane sickness as the African winces back to his weeding. "You shall understand when I have shown you the house. These slaves are far more economical than indentures. George believes we'll turn the whole plantation over to them before long."

Without a backward glance, Elizabeth turns and begins pulling me through the open front door. I wish to go back. My grasp of medicine beyond tending simple scrapes and colds is limited, but I might be able to offer some palliative treatment. If I did not believe Elizabeth would pull me bodily from the field and reveal our unnatural strength in the process, I would. Perhaps I can induce Rafe to purchase the man, or all of the men, from George. There must be some method for converting slavery to indenture. No human deserves perpetuity in bondage.

"I truly was concerned when I saw his such-called *manor* from the road," Elizabeth says as if she has already forgotten the man outside. Perhaps she has. "But it is lovely, for a house on the edge of civilization."

I hum a vague affirmative. As usual, that is all she needs to continue.

"This settee comes from France." She runs her hand over the wooden back. Plush, pink upholstery embroidered with a dancing pattern makes up the body of the piece, easily the most luxurious item of furniture I have seen since setting foot on the *Waterlily*. "A present from a dear friend of George's, or so he says. I placed it in front of the door as it is. There is no finer way to welcome guests into a home than to offer them somewhere to set down their troubles." She grimaces. "I only wish it weren't uglier than the mortal sins combined."

With half my mind behind me, I am unable to stop my mouth from falling open. "If you dislike it so much, why set it here?"

She looks at me as if I have grown another head. "Are you not impressed? I assumed you would be able to identify how fine a piece it is, even if much of the colony could only guess."

I take in the settee again, searching for any clue to unravel the knot of my sister's logic. Its legs are finely turned, the embroidery the sort that would make most seamstresses weep…an impressive piece, certainly, but it looks as though it would repulse any behind set upon it.

Elizabeth shakes her head in disbelief. "I shall take this as confirmation of my suspicions about how my new brother saw fit to decorate his own home. Have you anything not crafted within the walls of Jamestown?"

"I…." In truth, I haven't asked. The furniture in Bluebonnet is serviceable stuff, adept at its purposes but otherwise not noteworthy. "I'm not sure."

Elizabeth tosses her hair over one shoulder. "Well then I am even gladder you've come. You deserve what droplets of indulgence can be found here."

She leads me on a grand tour of the rest of the house, which is all very like the front room. Pieces of furniture that would not look out of place in the most stylish sitting rooms of London hobnob with common colonial goods, pine and mahogany jostling each other uncomfortably. Those exceptional pieces always sit near the fronts of the rooms, as if Elizabeth is cordoning off the rare concessions to her circumstances from public view. I am forced to admit that the Thistledawn Manor casts in stark relief how little art or decoration lines the halls of my own home. Though I do not begrudge Elizabeth her French settee, I might like a hanging, a vase of flowers, perhaps even a painting or two.

I also cannot help but notice that this house is larger. It sports a sitting room, a separate dairy, and a room which Elizabeth simply calls "hers," currently draped with pieces of various gowns and a few incomplete fiber projects. A half-darned sock lies tucked beneath the corner of her trunk, forgotten. Strangely, though, I discover nary a glass-paned window, and the chimney is ill-positioned to heat the whole house, as if it were built and then expanded recklessly.

Breathless, Elizabeth returns me to the sitting room and plunks me on the French settee. As I expected, it offers all the comfort of a bed of nails. I attempt to recline while Elizabeth settles on a plush armchair. Mere heartbeats after, an indentured woman pushes out of the kitchen, deposits a platter of bread, cheese, and fruit for a late midday meal on a table beside Elizabeth's chair, curtsies, and disappears. Were we at Bluebonnet, Dinah would have remained at least long enough for an introduction. Unease creeps across my skin.

"I see George is treating you well," I venture.

Elizabeth sighs, weariness crossing her expression. "He is quite wealthy and quite willing to expend that wealth."

I leave the settee to gather a few morsels from the platter. It would not do to have this woman, whatever her name might be, wondering why the elder Lady Wentworth does not eat. "Does he not make you happy?"

"Happy?" Her laugh is bitter as horseradish. "I suspect the Lord could not have designed a man more perfectly to make me unhappy."

The blasphemy stings, but I let it slide in the face of her upset. Guilt stirs my gut. Have I led her astray by suggesting George as a suitor? Perhaps even into danger?

"What has he done?" I ask breathlessly.

"Name one thing he has not, and you may drag the damnable settee home with you." She shakes her head. "You know how particular I am about quiet in the night?"

I nod, stomach sinking.

"He insists on chattering until I am forced to falsify snores!" She drops her head back against the chair. "And when we eat together, he endeavors to keep my hand in some inescapable clasp. Perhaps I needn't eat as I used to, but he does not know that. He would starve me!"

"He may have noticed how you eat," I say carefully. My thoughts rest on the elaborate decoration of the seat beneath me, the blood of the man outside. Elizabeth is under stress, I know. As well as I know that she has a tendency to take refuge in frivolity when life becomes difficult. The first morning I woke in this state, the taste of blood on my lips, she told me she thought I ought to start coloring them because it lifted my complexion so. She is not nearly so shallow as she pretends to be. In moments like this, however, I struggle to remember the long years of heartfelt talks in the night, that she is my beloved sister to whom I would entrust my life. She pretends at shallowness too well.

"Then how would you explain the way he talks as if he is always shouting to a far-off participant, though I have explained my sensitive ears?" She narrows her icy eyes at me. "Or how he is always huffing and puffing through the house as if he desires merely to interrupt me at whatever work I am intended to do, then demands to know why I have not completed what I've set my hands to?"

"His…breathing?" I furrow my brow. "Are you distressed by his very breathing?"

"I was not when we wed." The anger at me softens, as if a greater frustration has sapped it from her. "And then we came upon our wedding night, and I discovered how he truly sounds."

My cheeks burn hot enough that I glance left and right for rays of sun that might be searing me. Elizabeth has always been too flippant with what happens between a man and a woman.

"You would think a man as large as him would have an equally large—"

"Where is George just now?" I ask before she can complete her sentence and burn the ears off my head.

She levies a glare at me for interrupting her then seems to take in the expression on my face. A sly smile pulls at her lips. "Skittish, sister?"

"I—" Sometimes, I imagine being pinned by Elizabeth's smile much as a field mouse might be pinned by the talons of a hawk. There is no clever way out of this for me. Either I shall have to hear stories of George, or I shall have to bear mockery for my own lack thereof. Only silence holds a splinter's hope of freeing me, the field mouse playing dead in the hopes the hawk selects fresher prey.

"I'm sure that man is a devil in bed." She shakes her head playfully. "I would not be surprised if you've chosen a gown with this matronly of a neck because he has purpled you all over with his touch."

I squirm on the settee as though there might be a more comfortable position just out of reach. The idea of Rafe looking at me like that, touching me like that, sparks a fire deep in my gut. The idea of Elizabeth knowing such a thing stamps it out a heartbeat later.

"Men like him often are devil's in bed," I murmur.

"Sarah," she says seriously. "Look at me and stop wriggling."

I meet her gaze. A fatal error, I recognize the moment her smile grows.

"Has he touched you yet?" she asks.

My heart thumps like a panicked rabbit. I open and close my mouth. Before, I was not pinned. Now, I am well and truly so.

Elizabeth sets one pitying hand on mine. "Oh, dear. I've told you—worry less, smile more. Men don't like women lined all over with hardship before they've even born their first child."

I flinch at her choice of words. There shall be no first child for either of us, and no growing lined with anything other than hardship, if I can even become so.

"You may also wish to tempt him." She traces a finger along the high, square neck of my simple gown. "Dress as I would. For all of

George's innumerable flaws, bloodlessness is not one of them. I am surprised to find it in that man. You may wish to see if he is not getting what he desires else—"

"Another one?" George says, loud enough that even though I am certain he is outside of the house, I can hear him perfectly clearly. "That's the second goddamned pig this week."

Elizabeth catches my gaze, saying without words that she warned me about her husband.

"I've already put up a notice in the storehouse to hire a few guards," a man whose voice I do not recognize replies as some door I cannot see swings open with the barest hiss of hinges. "Are you certain we cannot simply arm a few of the laborers?"

"Arm?" George scoffs. "I would sooner arm the pigs themselves."

How terribly charming. I stuff a few bites of the bread and cheese into my mouth and chew furiously while Elizabeth adjusts her skirts and posture. The door leading from the kitchen swings open a few heartbeats before I can swallow, and George enters with the foreman, Burns, at his side.

"My little wife." George sweeps her into a kiss which I know from a distance Elizabeth is only enduring. I find myself forced to admit that his full, whiskery beard would put me off as well.

"And my darling sister!" he declares when he pulls back.

I should have known better than to think such cruel things. George crosses the sitting room toward me, arms out, and I am made to submit to the whiskery press of his cheek on mine that I so feared. Finding a smile is difficult, but I manage it when I consider the potential terror of being banned from my sister's home.

"Apologies for intruding," he tells me. "Elizabeth, have you finished my sock yet?"

She clenches her jaw. "Nearly. Lady Sarah was here to help me with the very thing, just as soon as we complete our lunch."

"Of course." George bows to me and rejoins his foreman. "We are only passing through. Business awaits, as it always does on a plantation of this size."

Burns bows as well, and the two of them exit into George's office.

Despite the closed door, we remain able to hear them as clear as a bell. Elizabeth meets my gaze tiredly, as if to say, *"You see?"*

"Was this one like the other?" George demands.

"Bloodless?" Burns asks. "Yes."

Gooseflesh crawls up my arms like a living thing. I hold Elizabeth's gaze in mine, hoping to see confusion within.

"Drained, like that damnable deer." We hear a thump, as if George has slammed his hand down upon the desk. "I must know if whoever did that has turned their attention to me in particular."

Recognition shines in Elizabeth's eyes. I hope my sour mood is causing me to miss the attendant guilt, but I cannot find any.

"If you like, I can ask around," Burns offers.

"No, the last thing I need is rumors." George huffs.

I shoot to my feet. "Will you show me the sock?"

Elizabeth sighs and whispers too softly for mortal ears, "I know you already saw it. Just admit you wish to scold me in private."

"I wish to scold you in private," I say as evenly as I can with the gooseflesh now threatening to throttle me. Her very own livestock, from her very own barns! The deer was reckless enough.

With another sigh, Elizabeth stands and escorts me back to her room. "I already know all you can think of to say. Sarah, these people are too foolish to consider what we are. Perhaps the reason your husband has no interest in you is because you are always looking behind you for a stake on the other side of the ocean."

I squeeze my hands into fists tight enough that all my frustration can rattle through them. It is not enough. "Trees here can be sharpened just as well. You might have led them to your front door."

"If the colonists are fools, George is their jester." She flips a hand at the sock, expecting me to retrieve it. "Alerting him does little more than alerting the pigs themselves."

I obey only so I do not begin tearing at my own skin. The wool is fine on my palm, the stitches of Elizabeth's attempt sloppy and rough. I yank them out in jerks. "You know what Father said."

"The hungers you feed grow hungrier," Elizabeth repeats so rhythmically that I can picture her at the slate our tutor left behind for

Father to teach us upon. "I suppose you eat every fortnight and only half-dead vermin."

Every three days, or my stomach gnaws me to shreds, but I shall not give her that confession now. Father's mantra taunts at least my waking thoughts enough that I dare not feed more often than that.

"I am leaving after the sock is complete." I lay the kinked yarn she attempted to use on a small table and select a different, better matched skein. "I should like you to visit Bluebonnet next time."

"As long as I am greeted with the same warm hospitality." Elizabeth smiles. "And something to eat."

15

ROUTINE

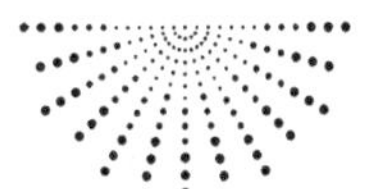

Rafe

SUNSET DRENCHES MY FIELDS IN ORANGES AND REDS, BRIGHTER HUES than I believe I ever saw in England. This time of day was the first I grew to love in Virginia. Many hungry afternoons were made far less unpleasant by the fiery skies I knew awaited, even if only barely. I whistle a faint tune to myself as I walk back to the house, a day's work caked upon my clothes. Of late, I have taken to lingering in the fields a quarter hour or more after the rest have quit it for supper. The slight delay allows the kitchen to clear of its first rush before I return. Though I still enjoy the sounds of a full house, there is a different enjoyment in sitting down across from Sarah to eat quietly. This way, I can eat with her and hear others about.

"Sarah set a plate aside for you," Dinah calls over her shoulder as I step into the kitchen.

Ah. I forgot she was visiting Thistledawn and her sister today.

I acknowledge Dinah with a nod, accept the dish my wife ensured for me, and step into the dining room. In addition to the hearty stew Dinah has bubbling in the hearth, my plate sports a rare delicacy: a tender biscuit smeared with persimmon jelly. I forgot I'd squirreled a few pots away in the cellar. I smile as I take my seat at the empty table. Sarah is as hard a worker as she promised, but she retains her taste for the finer things in life. Small indulgences like this have become more commonplace, and they remind me each time how much pleasanter life can be. I have perhaps three years of persimmon jelly lurking in the crevices of my cellar, and I might never have opened them. Denying myself for no true reason other than the memory of being denied. The Starving Times carved gouges from my body, even despite my special constitution. I will be happy never to endure that hunger again. Still, enduring a state of perpetual parsimony is no better.

I lift my head from my plate to inform Sarah as much and find only a candle for company. If I needed company, I could join the laborers in the kitchen. Their chatter and laughter leaks out through the cracks in the door I made the sorry mistake of milling myself. But their presence, the teasing with which they would greet such a simple revelation, holds no savor to me.

I shall not be the sort of man undone by the absence of his wife, and certainly not after a scant fortnight. My stew beckons.

THE DOOR SWINGS OPEN A FEW MOMENTS AFTER I COMPLETE THE LAST morsel of biscuit, just as I am considering rising from the table and taking up the book Father Buck leant me. Sarah steps inside, her hair tousled by the wind from its tight bun into a cinnamon corona. Her bonnet hangs heedlessly loose around her neck, as if she ran out of her sister's house without taking a moment to right it. I frown at her in concern.

"Apologies." She pulls the stiffened fabric into place over the riot of hair I have already seen. "It loosened on the walk."

"Are you all right?" I stand but do not cross the room to her. False-hoods have no particular character I have yet noticed on her lips, but

I do know she often rejects my advances when I catch her unawares and begin asking questions.

"Of course." She offers me a faint smile. "Truly, there was nothing to it but the wind."

I rap my knuckles on the table lightly. "Have you eaten? I am certain Dinah would prepare you something."

"Elizabeth fed me well." Her tone turns wry. "Did you enjoy your biscuit?"

There it is, another of those tender gestures I do not yet understand. "Very much. I am pleased you opened the jelly."

"I hoped it might be a reasonable substitute for my absence." She doffs her gloves and cloak, then steps deeper into the house.

I follow her into the sitting room as a sheep follows the one ahead of it. "Due to your sweetness?"

There is a heartbeat of silence in which I am certain I've overstepped. Then, Sarah looses a laugh. It is not her sister's high, feminine giggle; Sarah's laugh has as much roughness as a bolt of tweed, a thousand places to hide warmth away in and seek comfort from. I tuck it into a pocket of memories I intend to treasure with a small smile.

Conversation dies a natural death. We do not need to speak as we putter through the sitting room, piecing together our evening. I retrieve the book, a treatise on the human soul, from my study; Sarah produces a stocking she is knitting. I take the leftmost armchair by the fire; Sarah takes the rightmost. In a few moments, Dinah will exit the kitchen and offer us warmed wine or chilled ale. Sarah shall take the former, and I the latter. For now, the quiet clack of needles and rustle of turned pages fills the room.

Until this moment, I did not realize how many small pieces of our life have already fallen into place. Her absence from the supper table jarred me more than I thought it might. We work steadily side by side through Dinah's offer and the delivery of the drinks.

"Mr. Howe indicates your chest will be complete by the next Sabbath," I say.

She looks up at me, surprise at the broken silence painting her face. "I am pleased to hear it."

"As am I."

When quiet falls once more, it is surprisingly unpleasant, like an overzealous application of leeches. In England, I did not need to rely on others to create noise. And though I treasure the quiet between us, Sarah holds her sister very dear, which indicates she may not savor it as much.

"Your father is Baron Wentworth," I find myself saying, graceful as a deer taking its first steps on blood-slicked legs.

"Yes," she replies without lifting her gaze.

I slot a bookmark into my treatise and stare into the fire dancing in the grate, watching her from the corner of my eye. The firelight casts her as a spirit from some ancient fresco. Her eyes are alive with it, blue and gold in an impossible combination. Her hair dances with it, alive and curling as a fern in the wind. She wears only a simple, brown kirtle, but I envision her in the red of our wedding day, and she is utterly transformed. I have never before met a woman so given to becoming unearthly under the influence of mere light and shadow. A whole life lies behind the careful precision of her fingers, weaving yarn into fabric, and I wish to know it as I have so rarely wished to know another. Sarah will not open herself to me gladly, that much is clear. I must press.

"Elizabeth is your only sibling?" I venture.

She nods. "Mother never quite recovered from Elizabeth's birth. She was too ill to bear children until we finally lost her."

Grief aches like an old wound before rain. Sarah knows the shape of loss, though I have yet to meet one who knows its breadth as I do.

"Then were you much alone?" I ask. "I imagine a country manor would be quiet with but two children to fill it."

"We spent a good deal of time in London." She frowns slightly at her work. "Why are you asking me all this now?"

The rejoinder pulls me up short. Curiosity aches, too large to speak. "Merely making conversation."

She hums a gentle affirmative and says nothing further.

"Were Elizabeth and Mr. Moore well?" I sip my ale, enjoying the bite of Virginia hops. These questions seem so desperately prosaic in the face of her fiery metamorphosis.

Her lips pinch. "I saw George very little."

The exclusion of Elizabeth is painfully purposeful. Something happened between them, and it has set her on edge. I ought to leave it be; quarrels between sisters never benefit from the interference of outsiders. But the notion of taking my attention away from Sarah still pains me.

"And Elizabeth?" I press.

"As she always is," Sarah says tightly. "Though that does remind me, are you aware that George has purchased Africans to work his plantation?"

All the glow and warmth of the fire dies away, becomes the threat of violence. I sit back and choose my words very carefully. "Mr. Moore, Governor Yeardley, and a handful of others have chosen to pursue the route of slavery. I understand it may increase their yields. However, it is not an avenue I will ever be willing to consider for Bluebonnet or any other land I own. If this is a disappointment to you, I suggest you speak to those men and women and ask how they enjoy their condition, then to my own."

Sarah releases a breath I am surprised to find colored with relief. "I was terrified you were going to say you felt the opposite. No, the only ownership I wished to suggest was the potential of purchasing George's men out from under him and giving them their freedom."

My own reliefs laps at my mind like gentle waves upon a shore. I should have known the woman who discovers a store of jelly and only smears one biscuit with it would have no interest in the tentacle-like grabbing of power and surplus that is enslaving Africans.

"I shall speak to him." I smile gently. "Is that what distressed you, or did something occur between you and Elizabeth?"

A door slams shut between us. All tension released from Sarah's posture snaps back onto it like armor. "As I said, Elizabeth is as well as she ever is."

More time. She merely needs more time. I have pressured her

enough for one evening. I drain my ale, set my treatise on the table between us, and stand.

"Sleep beckons. I hope it comes for you shortly." I move to kiss her on the brow.

Sarah huffs, frustration blotting out her careful control. I draw back. That is an emotion I have never seen on her before.

"What is it?"

"Nothing to trouble yourself over." She keeps her face stubbornly turned toward her stocking, hiding any glimpse of truth I might glean from within.

I return to my seat. "How can a husband honor his wife if she will not confess her troubles to him?"

"By obeying her request for peace," she answers quickly.

I frown. She has told me what she wants. I ought to leave. But I can only think of Mother and Father, joined at the hip when they were not at their own business. Every evening, they sat with their hands intertwined. Mother was obliged to take up crochet merely to indulge Father's desire to be near her. When I purchased a wife through Sir Thomas, I assumed she would be very like Dinah to me: a woman, perhaps even a dear one, who helped me to maintain this household. When I look at Sarah, I understand why Father obliged Mother to take up crochet and never complained about the holes that left in his stockings.

"A wife might obey her husband's requests as well," I say with a hint more heat. She could be that woman to me, and I sense I could be that man to her, if she only allowed me to be.

Sarah grimaces. "I assure you, I stay my tongue for our own best interests."

"If my interests are involved, I deserve the chance to make that determination for myself," I reply. "And I am satisfied to sit here until dawn if that is how long it takes to wear you down." I pluck my book off the table and open it once more, though I cannot focus my gaze on a single word.

She huffs once more, then says, "How am I to give you an heir if we never so much as share a bed?"

I look up at Sarah slowly. She no longer hides her face in her work, and the fire that animated her before now takes her up as one of its own. She is a living flame, flickering from head to toe. For the first time, I feel as though I may be seeing something of the true woman beneath the manners and quiet. It very nearly shocks me more than the fact that she thought to desire my presence in bed beside her.

"*Never* was not my intention," I say slowly. "I thought some time to adjust might bring you comfort before we began."

Fire dances off her very teeth as she declares, "You cannot treat me as a tree in the fields or the kitchen, but a delicate flower in our bedroom. I am no flower."

I burn with her. I launch to my feet, haul her out of her chair, and throw my wife over my shoulder as the animal passion I have been denying for two long weeks breaks loose.

16

DELICATE

Sarah

RAFE'S SHOULDER, HARD AND UNYIELDING, BOUNCES AGAINST MY GUT. I
open my mouth to yelp in surprise, and a sound far lower and
hungrier escapes my lips. When I challenged Rafe, I had no true idea
what I was expecting. Perhaps proof of Elizabeth's accusation that he
was satisfying himself elsewhere. Perhaps a dull refutation that would
leave me as cold and lonely in bed as I have been since we wed.
Perhaps even anger, the storm of fury that sometimes left my unlucky
friends caked in powder at balls to disguise the explosions of their
husbands, brothers, or fathers.

I did not expect the shift in his gaze, the green instantly deepening
to something far richer than grass or even emeralds. His eyes became
living forests in themselves, reaching and devouring wilderness
snatching what society has taken from them. A consuming possession
—or repossession. I did not expect his iron grasp around my hips, his
heavy feet on the stairs, moving faster than I have ever heard him
climb them before. It reminds me of the crush of his hand on mine
when we danced in the storehouse. My husband is stronger than any

man I have ever known, calling into question my own unearthly power. Perhaps I have only been elevated to the highest extent of women, and he will always overpower me still. I clutch the front of his doublet at the idea.

I have survived the ravages of Jamestown thus far, when even I thought I could not. I want to know whether I can outlast my husband just as well.

Rafe shoulders open the bedroom door, storms inside, and kicks it closed once more. Moonlight streams in through the open shutters, carried on a faintly salty breeze. I brace for the moment he sets me down, the long and careful minutes of undressing which must follow. He laces his breeches differently than William, and I shall have to—

He throws me onto the bed as if I weigh no more than a sack of corn. The tight-strung ropes supporting the mattress groan in objection, and I gasp. Rafe stares down at me through the darkness, his eyes shining with that same devouring want. All fear is banished from my mind in a heartbeat. He was offering no persimmon-sweet lies about waiting for my comfort. Rafe has wanted me, perhaps since before our marriage, and that want lays bare in his glowing gaze. I shiver with it, feeling almost ungodly. Nothing I have ever been taught about what happens between a husband and wife includes such naked desire.

He pounces. His body covers mine entirely, warmer than my thickest quilt, a furnace in human skin. But he will not allow me a moment of stillness, not now that I have told him I am strong enough. His mouth greets mine like a long-lost friend, that clash of bodies in an overzealous embrace. Skin splits, and a droplet of my own blood spills between us. I taste jelly on his tongue. The two blend into a heady concoction, my hunger for him and my hunger I dare not name sated in a single moment. He slides covetous fingers through my hair, frees the last few pins and lets it fall.

On the two occasions I lay with William, I found the experience pleasant enough to endure a lifetime of. A bit of diversion, perhaps as exciting as the occasional picnic or trip to visit the country. I laid back and allowed him to take what he wanted from me, as I had been taught.

With Rafe, I cannot imagine doing such a thing. My hands claim his body as ravenously as he does my mouth. I trace the embroidery on his doublet, graze the muscular flesh beneath his breeches, twirl raven locks between my fingers like spinning wool. My sprouting calluses catch on hems and threads, and neither of us pay them any mind. It is only right that I touch a man like him with hands like these. A delicate flower has never been a particularly accurate description of me; Elizabeth lay claim to it early enough that I dare not encroach. I have never felt less like one than as I map my husband's body through touch alone.

I bow into him, offer myself up to be claimed by the forest of his eyes, and he does not refuse me. He snarls against my mouth. One of his hands surges out of my hair and down to the top of my gown. *Now*, I think, *he must slow*. My stays are tightly laced to support me through the journey to Thistledawn, and he knows the value of money too well to try something as foolish as destroying them.

He scrapes the neck of my gown down to the top of my corset, exposing the pale skin of my breasts without a moment's pause. The moonlight and his body shadow me just enough to hide from my own meekness. I know I haven't the figure most men dream of, too narrow to mimic a corset's shape without its boning or suggest I am likely to survive childbirth. Even Father commented on it when he thought I could not hear. But Rafe does not hesitate, does not even seem to notice. He drags his searing lips from mouth to neck to tender skin as inexorably as a river drives toward the sea. By his low, throaty hum I am forced to believe he is satisfied with what he finds. Soon, I am too lost in his touch to think of anything but it. His fingers dance, always more graceful than I ever believe a man of his size might be. His tongue traces shapes, letters in a language I do not speak but would dearly love to learn. Though perhaps it is the one we have been trading silently back and forth in our nearest moments, a few of the figures already familiar in his slivers of smiles and gentle touches.

There is no gentleness in his touch now. There is no gentleness in mine, and I do not wonder if there ought to be.

Rafe draws back from my skin, meets my gaze. His eyes are glowing with moonlight, anointed with it. I nearly wish I could drink it down as water from a pool, but I am too consumed with squirming beneath him. He has infected me with his own desire, and I cannot cease moving with it. He watches every twitch with those devouring eyes.

"I do not believe without proof." He slides off my body and lays on his back beside me. "If you are no flower, prove yourself so."

Chill night air whisks over my exposed skin. He is offering me the reins, but the look in his eyes remains. This is no abdication, no tepid acceptance of the wife and life he has been handed. It is a challenge—to see if I will claim my place in his bed as he has claimed his place in the New World. Nerves jangle through me like clanging bells. This goes against all I have been taught.

As does my very existence, and my willful continuance thereof. As does the idea that I might be in this place with Rafe at all. I reach for him slowly.

The unnatural instincts lurking beneath my skin seize control, and my hands shoot out. Want flares. For once, I feel as though the evil inside me may better know my desires than I do. Godly men and women do not touch each other like this. It is as if a stranger is unlacing Rafe's doublet to reveal the fine haze of dark hair on his chest, the planes of his muscles. A stranger laughs when he smirks up at her. A stranger pulls his linen undershirt aside to reach the points fastening his breeches.

No. If the woman doing these things is a stranger, then I am the flower I declared myself not to be. I have survived nearly two months in Jamestown, and I do not shrink from newness any longer.

I free my husband's cock from the prison of his pants and make a hungry sound when he grabs my nearest wrist with bruising force. I let him guide me to touch him, curve my fingers around his length and press. I find myself all movement again, too full of want to contain it in frozen limbs. Rafe watches me with those devouring eyes, tracking every shift as though he is the hunter, and I the prey. He shall learn he is sorely mistaken. I resist his grasp and shift the rhythm to something that would keep pacing with the rolling country dance we once shared. His groan rumbles through the bedroom. I roll with it, a ship upon the waves of his desire, steering in whichever direction I so choose. His hair comes loose of its ribbon and falls wild around his shoulders. He is undone in the moonlight simply by my touch.

"Are we…making an heir," he hisses through gritted teeth, "or are we not?"

A contrary impulse to deny him flashes through me. I should like to see the look on his face, what he might do in return. And it would delay the moment at which he discovers I can never give him the heir he so desires. But I cannot resist the pull of his eyes. The deep forest, swearing to swallow me whole and never return me. I wish to be swallowed.

I lift my skirts, silently thankful I had no space in my portmanteau for a cage to full them, and straddle my husband's legs. Rafe grabs my hips, quickly purpling fingerprints into the skin just as Elizabeth predicted he might. There is one sweet, gentle brush before his cock finds what it wants most.

My moan pours out of my throat, despite my efforts to claw it back. Rafe snarls and thrusts. I ache with the stretch, out of practice and unused to a man of his size at all, but I savor the ache as much as the tingling rush of euphoria. His face contorts, somewhere between passion and violence. I kiss the slash of his mouth, the ropes of muscle standing out in his neck. Then, I attempt to roll my hips in time with his.

I have long chastised Elizabeth for her blasphemy, so I am ashamed to admit that, in this moment, I believe I have discovered a forgotten miracle. An unwritten one, perhaps, left to the New World and its disorder. I did not feel this with William, not ever before in my life. Rafe and I move as one at a pace fast enough that I envision vine and ferns and trees sprouting from our very bedroom to rejoin their brethren outside, kindled simply by the desire between us and the green of his eyes. Noises I have never before heard tumble from my lips. Rafe takes the Lord's name in vain with the casual ease of a lifelong sinner.

We reach something beyond life as I have known it together. Euphoric, brilliant light cascades through my body. A thousand sunsets, crammed into a few interminable heartbeats. I feel more, better than I have felt since the first moment I woke into this new life. Rafe stiffens below me, my name on his lips.

His ecstasy fades before my own, so when I finally descend from the heavenly heights, I find his gaze upon me. His eyes shine, not with that furious hunger, but with something far softer. The luminous sunrise to the blazing sunset, a promise of a new morning and what hopes that might bring. If I want to make a fool of myself, dizzy and glowing in the wake of my first true pleasure, I may even call it love.

"Have I proven myself?" I ask, as if my greatest desire in life is to dash my own chances at success.

He only smiles, broad and full, and runs his thumb over my hip.

17

NEW NORMAL

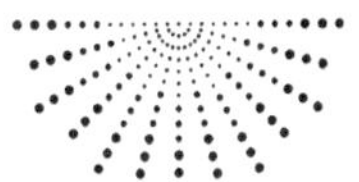

Sarah

I WAKE A FEW PRECIOUS MINUTES AFTER SUNRISE, JULY SUN RAYS pouring in through the window and bathing me in the warmth lost from Rafe's early departure. As always, he has beaten the sun itself into the fields. Since the advent of this month, he has been always at the tobacco, priming and topping the now nearly knee-high plants. Well, nearly always. Ever since the dam broke between us, in a May that feels so long ago, he has been quite adept at making time for me in the evenings. The apex of my legs aches sweetly, a reminder of how late we occupied ourselves into the night. I've grown quite accustomed to feeling my way around his body long after the candle burns out. My fingers alone could map every inch of taut skin and muscle.

But the clattering from below means Dinah, as well, is already long at her work. The weekend approaches, which means we have much cooking to do so that we needn't work on the Sabbath. I am not entirely certain why, but Rafe is as likely as myself to spend the day abed, once we have escaped service, and both of us count it only fair that the workers should be able to rest as we do. There are a few

121

Jewish men among the indentures who rest on Saturday, as their book dictates, but otherwise the plantation is still. Such a difference might have bothered me before, but I found it as painful to cross the threshold of the makeshift temple they set up beside their beds, so I care not.

I roll from the bed, strip off my nightgown, and deposit it in the basket of linens for boiling on Saturday. Habit induces a prayer of gratitude to my lips, but I catch it before the pain. Acid pouring down one's throat is a quick enough teacher. Humming a song I heard Fidelma singing the other day, I dress. After I finish around the house, a few errands await me in the fort, so I withdraw a maroon kirtle with singing birds embroidered on the pockets. Thankfully, one of the many formalities which has fallen away in the colony is the requirement to cover every inch of skin with quite so many layers of cloth, so I am able to don it over merely a simple chemise. Less thankfully, the Virginia sun has grown no more merciful, so I am forced to pocket a pair of gloves and carry my bonnet downstairs as concessions to its rays. Would that I could go about in a mere kerchief! I would save hours of work in boiling sweat-soaked linens. But the bite of summer rays is even sharper than those of spring, so I dare not discover whether the old legends of burning in the sun hold more truth than Father claimed.

Thus arrayed, I march downstairs to begin my day as the lady of Bluebonnet Plantation. Dinah and I bake bread. I tend the rows of grape vines tangling through wooden supports. I clean Rafe's study simply because I have the time and I enjoy how it makes him smile. Then, I check my list one last time and set off down the sweltering path toward Jamestown proper. Thankfully, we live far enough from town that I can travel at least the first mile scurrying tree to tree like some kind of frightened prey animal. The method, though truly ridiculous-looking, allows me a few extra minutes of attempting to make pleasant conversation with the guards at the gate before I must rush inside and to whatever destination I may have.

Mr. Cole and Mr. Spraggins respect Rafe enough that they at least put forth an effort to indulge my chatter. Not so for the rest of

Jamestown. When there are errands that require visits to Matatishe, I leap for them. Trips to the town itself only serve as a reminder that my husband is a respected member of the community, not myself. Lady Felicity, now married to Sir Ellis, has tarnished Elizabeth's and my reputation with citizens I have yet to even meet. No, a trip into Jamestown is a day by my lonesome, watching others cross the street to avoid my path and the few remaining rules of courtesy potentially inducing them to talk to me.

Dark thoughts slow my steps until I am near enough the fort that I must stride down the center of the path, at which point the searing sunlight distracts me from any personal considerations. My attempt to arrange my hair to protect the back of my neck is an utter failure. As well, though I may be imagining the effects, my chemise is so thin that the sunlight crawls underneath it to scratch at my skin, more threat than true burn. Every morsel of thought in my head devotes itself to keeping my feet on the path and my expression placid. Summer in Virginia grows more agonizing with each passing day. I long for autumn. Matatishe says the leaves turn brilliant colors, even brighter than those in England, and though I am not sure how she knows that, I would like to see it.

The pain distracts me so completely that I nearly stumble into the crowd at the gates. Sharp, angry voices pop like overheated kernels of corn, a blend of English and Powhatan that catches my ear just in time. I stop a few feet from the largest cluster of Powhatan people I have ever seen, perhaps as many as a dozen, blocking the path into the fort. All of them wear skins like Matatishe's, though in different arrangements. The men favor skirts or aprons, in addition to the occasional necklace of woven turkey feathers so long and broad it looks nearly like a chest plate. All have the same thick, dark hair I have come to envy on Matatishe, braided and decorated. A few bear half-faces of brilliant red paint or ink.

"Mistress Stone!" Mr. Spraggins calls, a note of desperation in his voice. "Please, come here, and we shall keep you safe."

I circle toward him slowly. Certainly, a few knives and knapped axes jut from belts, but every Powhatan I've seen has traveled with similar weaponry. Mr. Spraggins' concern seems much the same as warning me to fear at a ball where gentlemen all wear bejeweled rapiers, or on the deck of a ship where sailors carry rope-cutting blades. So as I move, I try to understand what has brought so many of Matatishe's countrymen out of the forest.

Sir Thomas comes into view, standing between the closed gates and the Powhatans with his hands up. "I am very sorry," he says, "but I have no idea how this could have happened to you."

"Manteo is dead," a man I do not know growls. "Drained. We have lost dogs, discovered our agreed-upon deer and bears destroyed in the same way. You have done this."

Gooseflesh pimples my skin despite the heat. I have not touched fang to human skin since the first morning I awoke in this form. There is only one creature unnatural enough to do such a thing in the New World.

"Our animals have often suffered the same fate." The usually composed Sir Thomas is red in the face, sweat beaded all along his oiled hairline. I do not know whether the Powhatans or the heat makes him look so, but jaded Mr. Cole has not taken his hand off the butt of his flintlock pistol or his eyes from the man who just spoke in a way that portends violence. "I intended to write to Governor Yeardley and see what help he can offer."

"Ha!" The laughter, though acrid with pain, is familiar to my ear. Matatishe! I seek her out in the crowd and find her nearly at the center. Garish crimson streaks her hands, and I know it could be only one substance: blood. "What justice from your leader? A young boy is dead. Will you give us one of yours?"

Sir Thomas opens his mouth, face twisted in refutation very much like Mistress Forrest's prune mouth. Despite my slow steps, I am now near enough to Mr. Spraggins that he reaches out to grab me and pull me to his chosen safety. If I wish to try to assist in any way, I must do so now.

"Matatishe," I say quietly, hoping the clamor of her companions will ensure my words reach her ears alone.

She does turn, and her dark gaze meets my own. The whites of her eyes are nearly as red as her hands, as if she has been crying. She squares her shoulders and strides up to me.

"What would you have now?" she spits. "Trade?"

"I wish to know if you are all right." I frown.

That merely earns me another bitter laugh. "At sunrise, I discovered my youngest brother dry of all his blood but a puddle around his head. Would you smile and talk peace?"

My heart aches for her. I reach out a hand of comfort, even though that exposes more of my tender wrist, and she recoils.

"Opechancanough is right. You did this." She shakes her head, and cold fear spears me to the dirt. Does she know the truth of what I am? "You and all of Chawnzmit's people. You drag your evils to our shores. I will not repent your crimes."

Relief and despair war in my breast. She is correct; I brought this evil to her shore. Had I not been so careless, Elizabeth and I would never have had to flee London. And yet, I am relieved to know she does not think me the unnatural monster that I am.

I fold my hands behind my back and incline my head respectfully. Matatishe is my only friend, and I will not lose her. "I offer sincerest condolences for your loss. If there are any funeral preparations in which I might assist, my hands are yours. If I have anything which might help you, my things are yours. I have not lost a brother, but I have lost a mother." *And a father*, I add in my mind. "There is no deeper grief. I will grieve with you, whether I can help any further or not, and I will do so from a distance upon your word."

The rictus of pain and fury on her face softens slightly as the clamor grows around her. "You will be informed."

It is all I can hope for in this moment. Had another illness offered its hand in the wake of Mother's passing, I would have slapped it aside.

The man who spoke to Sir Thomas spits something in rapid Powhatan, and Matatishe twists her head toward him. Murmurs in the same throaty tongue ripple through the cluster. Her face stiffens once more.

"We leave," she says. "Though there remains debt to pay."

She and the other Powhatans proceed back up the path. Mr. Spraggins finally succeeds in seizing my arm and pulling me toward him.

"Mistress Stone!" he says breathlessly. "Were you accosted?"

I shake my head, Matatishe's warning ringing in my ears. It has the tone of a bone-chilling prophecy, and one only I may halt.

"Good." He shakes his head. "I am sorry you were forced to interact with those savages. Mr. Stone would be furious if he knew. Shall we open the gate for you?"

Rafe would be barely alarmed, but arguing will earn me nothing. Especially as Mr. Cuthbert is already waiting to release Sir Thomas back to his row house.

"No," I say quickly. Our supplies can wait; violence hangs over Jamestown like a swollen storm cloud, and I cannot endure mundanities while that is true. With a brief curtsy, I turn down a different path, leaving a startled Mr. Spraggins in my wake.

The road to Thistledawn is far longer after I have already been walking for some time, but emotion powers me through any wink of pain. The ember in my chest smolders, threatens to burst into true flame. Elizabeth has been reckless for a long while now. I have seen colonists wandering around with a daze in their eyes and an unseasonable scarf about their neck. She has been drinking from humans nearly as often as she slaughters her husband's livestock—though I believe that particular practice tapered off as soon as she discovered how it damaged their profits. But to kill? To take a living soul and turn it to dust? That was a sin I hoped would only ever be mine to bear.

I reach the front of the house and discover Elizabeth, sitting in the shade with a parasol over her head while she flips idly through a book. She looks the picture of pastoral ease, her cheeks pink with youthful color and her curls round as stacks of coins. The ember rages in my breast.

"Sarah," she says casually, "I was not aware we had scheduled a visit or I might have dressed."

I do not need to look at her clothes to know they will already be more exquisite than what I am wearing. "What were you—"

The door opens, and George pokes his bearish head out. "Ah, little wife. Where have you put my clean falling band?"

I sink my teeth into my tongue so intently that my fangs slide from their sheaths and puncture it. My own sour blood fills my mouth as Elizabeth sighs disdainfully.

"As I told you, George, one of the indentures is doing the washing." She looks at me as if for support. "A lady like myself cannot be seen hanging laundry."

George notes my presence with furrowed-brow irritation. His face, like Sir Thomas's, begins to go red. "I am certain our sister would inform you to the contrary."

Elizabeth raises her eyebrows at me. If I release my tongue, I will fly at her over the life she has taken, and all will be ruined anyway. I remain silent, swallowing sickly sweet iron as if my life depended on it. In many ways, it does. Far more of the legends around demons like myself are true than false.

"Even she will not enter our marital discussions." George throws his hands up. "I did not come to fight, little wife. Can you at least tell me whom you assigned the washing?"

"Dark hair, scrunched face." She shrugs. "One of the Italians, perhaps?"

"We don't have any—" George cuts off the end of his own sentence by storming back inside and slamming the door hard enough to shake some thatch from the roof. I watch it fall slowly, looking for all the world like the last straw on the camel's back.

"He has been irritable ever since I informed him of my latest bleeding." Elizabeth settles comfortably back into her seat, all frustration of the fight melting from her posture as if it never occurred. "He says I could lounge this much if I were pregnant—which, of course, he uses as a justification to continue trying each night." She shudders.

Slowly, I pry my fangs from my own flesh. A final gout of blood paints my tongue. I take a long breath in through my nose. Elizabeth hates almost nothing worse than feeling scolded, so if I can restrain myself enough to approach the problem from another angle, I may make more progress.

"It has only been two months," I say, hoping she does not see the spatter of my own gore on my lips.

"Two and a half, as he's fond of reminding me." She shakes her head in plain disgust. "Though it's not as if time will solve the issue. Disappointment awaits him, so perhaps it is better I discover what sort of man he is now. If he isn't to my liking, perhaps I shall—"

"Slaughter him?" I ask before I can catch the words.

Her face becomes carefully neutral, nothingness sharpened to a cutting point. It is an expression I know all too well, that of Elizabeth caught, and the very one I hoped to avoid. But as soon as the words touch open air, they catch flame alongside the ember in my breast.

"There was a crowd at the gates." I take a step forward, still nowhere near the shadows which protect her, but I barely feel I need them anymore. The pain is a wick, and I am the candle. "A mob, Elizabeth, of grieving people. His loved ones. His name was Manteo, did you know that?"

"Sarah—"

"No." My voice snaps out of my throat, punishing and hard. "For once, you shall listen to me rather than mock or dismiss. You committed a mortal sin. Your choices threaten not only our continued safety here, safety you swore to when we boarded the *Waterlily*, but also the two communities that preexist us here. This reckless disregard ceases in this moment, or I swear before the Lord my God and the acid he pours on my tongue that I will ensure it ceases by my very hand."

Elizabeth stares at me. She blinks, long lashes sweeping her cheeks in perfect arcs. She opens her mouth—and laughs. "Oh, you should see yourself. Like a mouse learning to squeak. Perhaps you can, with what awe-inspiring views you must enjoy from the back of a horse that high. You speak to me of mortal sins, Sarah? Whose sin chased us aboard the ship?"

Guilt takes root in my gut, threatens to boil me alive. My sins are lost in the fugue of transformation; I have only the evidence upon my wakening and the sour sense that I am everything Father warned us of as proof of my actions. They are proof enough for me, and Elizabeth is right. But that ember sears at me, urging me that there is a difference between us.

A whip cracks in the nearest field. Torn in a thousand directions by my heart, I cannot still my feet. Impossible speed sends me racing toward the sound. I skid to a stop and throw my hands up to catch the blow. Pain scours a line across both my palms.

"What in God's name?" the foreman, Mr. Burns, mutters.

The African man behind me stares at me with wide eyes. Over his shoulder, Elizabeth smiles delightedly, assured in her victory. I am no more careful than she, by her estimation.

I lower my voice and say to the man, "If you swear I was standing near enough to justify my interference, I will guarantee your freedom."

He nods, relief bright in his eyes. As I expected, he is just as human as Matatishe or myself.

"Mr. Burns, you have struck me!" I cry.

"You stood in front of—that is, how did you—" the foreman splutters.

"I was walking a survey of the fields." I blink innocently to cover the lie on my tongue. "Was I not,…?"

"John," he answers, despite how uncomfortable the English syllables sound on his tongue. "I saw her, foreman."

Mr. Burns looks between the two of us, confusion and fear battling across his face. I stare up at him, praying fear wins out. If he decides to accept our explanation simply because the alternative terrifies him, that shall be enough for me.

Elizabeth flounces up beside him. "My sister is absolutely right."

How does the lie make me so sick when she reinforces it? I am obliged to nod along or perish and let John die with me. Mr. Burns shakes his head but agrees.

"I think it is time for this visit to come to a close," Elizabeth says tightly once he wanders off.

"I hope you shall visit me again soon." Alone, she will only fall deeper into her worst nature. I have some hope of bringing her back if we stay close.

She snorts. "Of course."

I look at John one last time, memorizing his features so I might describe them to Rafe, and depart.

18

GAPS IN THE STORY

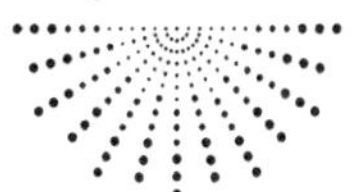

Rafe

LUNCH OFFERS A BLESSED RESPITE FROM THE HARD WORK OF TENDING the tobacco plants. They are growing in strong this year, but twitching off the clusters of compact leaves at the top and the suckers that grow in their place is never especially pleasant. I lean against the wall outside the kitchen to escape some of the hearth's heat and watch the path. Sarah has gone into town on a few errands, and I am hoping to see her before I finish my meal and work summons me once more.

The stir of caked dust on the road makes me smile. She still has not quite mastered the way ladies here hold their skirts so as not to cause such a cloud. However, that smile fades as I realize just how quickly Sarah is walking. Her footsteps approach a run, something I have never seen from her before. I scarf the last of my lunch and circle around to the front.

She storms down the path, her face lowered as it always seems to be but still at an angle where I can see the frown pulling it out of its normal beauty. No, not merely a frown; I believe my wife is scowling, a look I have truly never before discovered upon her before. She clutches her hand to her chest, and I can smell something like old blood in the air.

"Sarah," I say, holding my arms out, though I am not certain whether I intend to hold her or merely stop her.

She looks up without a hint of surprise, her scowl flickering like a dying flame unable to truly disappear. "I thought you would be in the fields."

"What happened?" I reach for her hand.

Instead of offering it to me for inspection, she pulls it tighter to her bodice defensively. After all these months, surely she is not still afraid of me. Something has gone terribly wrong for her to react so.

"Did someone accost you?" I ask, hearing the note of violence in my voice. None may touch my wife without facing the consequences.

She begins to shake her head, begins to nod, opens and closes her mouth as though she is a fish recently pulled from the water. A thousand answers dance through her eyes, and I realize sourly that Sarah is deciding whether to lie to me. Beneath all of that, though, lies a fear twisted taut as a fiddle string that keeps the burgeoning blaze of my anger from burning toward her. She is shaken, terrified. I can only hope she will trust me enough to allow me to destroy whosoever did this to her. I hide my fists in my pockets so I do not scare her any further.

Sarah takes a step toward me, her face turning up like a sunflower reaching for the sky. The shadows of the roof turn her eyes into luminous, depthless pools. She places a single, delicate hand on my arm. "Would you take me to bed?"

She is ill. I brace one arm around her back and thread the other behind her skirts, lifting her off her feet the moment after I understand what she is saying. But when I bring her closer to my face, she cups my cheek and claims my mouth. Every flutter of conflicted emotion I watched play across her expressive face pours between us with the speed and violence of a summer storm.

A very different sort of bed, then.

I open the front door and hasten upstairs before one of the many hands enjoying their lunch can spot us. That they tease me is permissible, if occasionally irritating. Sarah cannot endure such a thing, especially now. And, perhaps, the flame of my rage has burned into a hunger far more concentrated but no less consumptive. Keeping my lips from my wife's is an act of will for which I ought to be commemorated.

Finally, we reach our bedroom. I try to lay Sarah gently on the mattress and tend to her as I have so often of late, but she sits up the moment I set her down. Her fingers go quickly to the hem of her kirtle, and she pulls it up over her head, doffing her bonnet in the process.

"My stays," she says breathlessly, turning her back to me.

I fall upon the crisscrossed laces, my hands dancing through the patterns she has taught me to understand these past two months. She tugs off her gloves as though she cannot wait to touch me. Thankfully, practice has made me adept; I have no use for my eyes, so I bury my face in the crook of her neck to inhale the scent of her. She smells of rosemary, a pleasant side effect of the cloth baths she takes nearly every evening, and the animal musk of want that stirs something primal within me. Perhaps she will not tell me what occurred, but she has come to me for comfort, and I intend to provide it to her. Still, though, the rusted reek of old blood taints her skin as well as the air.

Her stays loosen, and I tug them over her head. Sarah gasps with the freedom and turns back to me, skin now only hidden by a loose chemise. I push it up and run my bare hands over her softness. She crushes her mouth to mine, all my hunger reflected in her. That initial promise that I needn't treat her as a flower has proven more than true, but this is the first time I have not had to tempt her into taking as much from me as I want from her. The animal inside me howls for more. I grab hungrily, fingers scraping over flesh, as I trace the path from ankle to that most intimate part of her. Sarah hooks one leg around my clothed hip, dragging me ever closer. I find myself stumbling to obey, unexpected and nearly irresistible strength in the simple movement. Her usual poise is gone, shredded away by whatever occurred before she returned and leaving behind something far more similar to my wolf than I would have expected from the woman I have slept beside for so long now.

I sink my teeth into the swell of her lower lip, barely soft enough not to break the skin. Sarah mewls and tears at my clothes. Laces clatter against the floor, and my doublet becomes the mere suggestion of a shirt, allowing her to run her hands over my skin as well.

The wet heat of her greets me like an old friend. In merely two months, I have become well acquainted. She squeals with the strum of my fingers, and want becomes a living animal in my breast, as real as my very own wolf. I haul her off the bed, one handed, and lift her back to my chest. Her chemise rucks up such that she is bare nearly to the collarbone, miles of porcelain skin mine to enjoy, and she holds her own weight with legs around my waist. Her warmth radiates through my thin summer breeches.

Her conflict remains palpable. Fingers flicker from one place to another, gentle one moment and searing the next. She scrapes her nails along my skin then kisses as sweetly as the morning dew. I can only hold her to my chest as her breathing races and attempt to coax enough joy from her body to overcome whatever else troubles her. By the way her hips roll like crashing waves, we are swiftly approaching that moment.

I twist my hand between us to loosen my pants and release the near-painful hardness of my cock. Her body welcomes me, already perfectly positioned. She moans as I slide home, and we move together in the dance of creating our heir. I clutch at her hips, her thighs. She tugs on my hair and fights to keep her hold until she shudders apart with my name on her lips. In her boneless relaxation, I am obliged to hold her weight exclusively, everything she is relying simply on my strength.

My heights of pleasure subsume me utterly with that moment of trust. If she would allow me, I would carry her and anything else she wished to lay down until the end of time. My pace slows, drawing out the sublime moment as long as possible, until Sarah squirms for her freedom. This time, she allows me to lay her upon the bed without popping back up. I strip off what remains of my clothes until only my bottommost shirt remains, then join her. A peaceful haze fills her eyes, and she smiles up at me softly.

"Now may I see your hand?" I ask.

That softness crumples like it was only thin fabric. Complex emotions dance through her gaze once more. She does turn her palm up to me, however, displaying a thin, scabbed scrape on its surface. It looks no more dangerous than what a child might get upon catching themselves from a fall, but the shape is strange for such an injury, even if she were wearing her gloves at the time. More than that, the smell of old blood strengthens the moment she offers the wound to me, as if it has already been long healing.

"I shall be fine," she says.

Nothing further. I take her hand in mine, study it. "And if I were to ask how you received this?"

"On the road." Her lips snap together at the end of the final word as if trapping any additional details on her tongue.

She came to me for comfort when frightened, I remind myself. If I force her now, I will only prove that such a choice was a mistake, and that is the very last thing I want.

"Did anything further happen?" I roll onto my side and stare down at her, hoping to read the truth in her face.

"There was a commotion in town," she answers slowly, as if choosing her words carefully. "The Powhatans discovered one of their own dead."

I grimace. When Governor Yeardley took office from Governor Dale, many things improved in Jamestown. Dale's laws bordered on dictatorial, and he was a dark cloud whenever he entered a room. However, Yeardley has declared a number of policies against the Powhatan which have, coupled with the movement of their own leadership from Pocahontas's diplomatic father to her militant uncle, led to more than a few skirmishes along the coast stretching up to the governor's manor. Nothing severe enough that I thought to warn Sarah, but I have endured this often enough to smell violence on the horizon. The long years of war that preceded Pocahontas's marriage are only barely not the least favorable time in Jamestown in my memory.

"A warrior?" I ask.

She shakes her head. "A youth. And they seem quite certain we colonists are to blame."

There is something in her gaze as she says that. A very slight sliding away, or a blush of unspoken emotion. If forced, I would name it guilt.

Warmth stirs within me. Was my tenderhearted wife so troubled by the advent of bloodshed, so guilt-ridden by her own potential association with it, that it put her in this mood?

I stroke her cheek softly. "If things become more dangerous, I will ensure we are safe."

"And who is ensuring the Powhatans are safe?" she exclaims.

I offer her a smile. "They have their own husbands and leaders. I assure you, they are well-versed in the art of war and know how to use this terrain to their great advantage."

Sarah falls silent then, the veil of her own thoughts consuming the dance of her expressions, and I wonder if I haven't missed something. She wept the first time I slaughtered a pig for consumption, and she continues to speak of the cruelties George perpetrates against his slaves. Her distress over a murdered youth makes perfect sense. And yet, there seems to be more.

"Did you go anywhere else?"

She startles out of her mind. "Thistledawn. George and Elizabeth seem to have little joy in their marital bed."

"I am not surprised," I say wryly, another piece of the puzzle sliding into place. Seeing her sister often rattles Sarah. "I have always suspected they may each prefer center stage too well to share it."

Sarah frowns. "I thought she would enjoy the reflected glory."

Privately, I think one of the reasons Elizabeth upsets her so is that Sarah has no ability to correctly evaluate her sister. But I hold my tongue.

"Well, I have hope they will muddle through." I smile. "Did you manage to get new rope from the storehouse?"

Her gaze slides slightly aside once more. "They had none."

When I spoke to Griffith not two days ago, he said one of the local wives was to bring a large supply of the stuff to them within a sunrise. Sarah has lied to me.

THAT NIGHT, I LAY IN BED BESIDE HER SLEEPING FORM, TURNING THAT falsehood over and over again in my mind. If the Powhatan rage prevented her from entering the fort, she could have simply said so. If she had forgotten, I would not have admonished her. I can find no reason in the world why she would lie about that. My thoughts chase each other in hapless circles, keeping me awake. I have only one solution for such a problem.

I transform almost before I reach the tree line nearest the house, human foot leaving the ground and lupine paw striking it next in a burst of power. Wind whistles, and quiet nighttime instincts tempt me deeper. If I can outrun my own mind, sleep may still await me yet tonight.

Paths I know well accept the rhythmic thudding of my paws. My muscles groan and stretch in new forms. I heave great, panting breaths, howl at the half-moon, allow my mind to become that of the beast. When I am him, matters like lies seem far smaller. Sarah is my mate. She returned to my den, and truly, I can ask nothing more of her.

I return to the house, exhausted but soothed. When I look up at the bedroom window I know she waits within, a curtain flutters back into place.

19

FACT-CHECKING

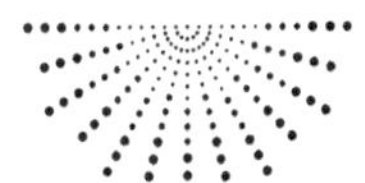

Rafe

THE PEACE OF MY RUN DOES NOT STAY WITH ME THROUGH THE DAWN. I rise early and behold my sleeping wife. No worry wrinkles her brow. The scrape on her palm is nearly gone, thanks to a healing poultice Dinah concocted for her. She looks exactly as she has every other morning I have woken beside her, and yet something has changed. Her falsehood hangs between us like a musket set on a gambling table. One of us must grab for it first, and I would not like to know the results either way.

In my memory, Father chastises me. *Other men can wait for those around them to act. Leaders always move first—it is what coaxes others to follow.*

I have run from one thing in all my life, and had I not, I would not have a life to speak of. A woman with lies on her lips shall not change that number. I dress numbly, inform Dinah I shall be visiting Jamestown today, and go about my morning routine. With distrust heavy in my limbs, I find myself also scrutinizing the grape vines.

Sarah has shown no weakness of ability, no relinquishment of tasks assigned to her, but she has not lied to me until yesterday either.

The vines are growing as well as they might in the heat of summer, and a single weed threatens the dirt, young enough that it could well have sprouted in the time since her last review of them. I exhale slowly. Something has changed between us, but she is still very much the woman I thought I was marrying. Or at the least, she is the woman I met the first night we shared a bed. Perhaps there is a reasonable explanation for this lie, but I can only discover it if I go searching. To town first, and if that yields nothing, perhaps I shall pay Thistledawn a call. With a few instructions to a quite confused Klaus, I leave for Jamestown.

Mr. Spraggins waves as I approach the gate. "Good morrow! How is the lady wife, after her encounter yesterday?"

My gut sours quickly, but I shall not make my ignorance plain to a gossip like Spraggins. "Well as can be expected, though she spoke of it little. Were you nearby?"

"Damn near in the heart of it," Cuthbert says tiredly. "I thought young Spraggins might dive into the crowd headfirst after her."

"Would you not have?" he objects.

"And incite that mob?" Cuthbert grimaces. "I thank you for your kind words to the governor, Mr. Stone, but it is looking like a military man might be just what Jamestown is going to need at its gates in the coming months."

I nod at the two men, my thoughts spinning as they open the gate. Whatever could have induced Sarah into the crowd? I know she counts the trader Matatishe a friend, but a dear enough one to risk violence? Cuthbert salutes me as I pass, his gaze haggard. Perhaps the old soldier is quick on the trigger, seeing war in trouble's shoes. Sarah did not say the Powhatans were armed—but neither did she say she spoke to them at all.

The gates thud closed behind me, and I find myself on a shockingly crowded main road. It looks as if the church bells have just rung, rather than that a weekday dawn still colors the sky behind the sun. I stride up to the first group I recognize a member of, Mr. Jasper Ingram.

"They say it is the ghosts of this place. The very New World is haunted!" a young, credulous planter named something like Shillingford declares.

Mr. Ingram scoffs. "And how would a ghost drain a body of blood?"

"Is that the rumor?" I ask as I step into the circle. In addition to those two, a wide-eyed indentured woman and an older gentleman who joined us too recently for me to have learned his name look to me.

Shillingford—or perhaps Sheffield—nods. "I heard it from Miss Cecily, one of the new crop of wives, who said she heard it from Sir Thomas himself."

Sarah is an extremely observant woman, sometimes to my own downfall. I cannot push myself an extra hour in the fields without her noting my aches the next day, nor can I neglect my rest in favor of reading but she tells me I have been rubbing my eyes raw. If she stood amidst the Powhatans, spoke with Matatishe or some other of them, she knows the body was drained of blood and left the detail aside. A symptom of a delicate constitution? Doubtful. Though she wept when the pig was killed, she did not flinch when I requested her hand with the butchering. The pain had ended, she said.

"And what is this of a ghost?" I ask.

The gentleman-stranger shakes his head. "Old Warren has been hectoring about it for months, ever since the first deer. I heard him call it a ghoul, but otherwise, the lad has it correct."

"Ghouls eat, Mr. Hines. They do not drink blood." Mr. Ingram crosses his arms. "And I cannot believe so many educated people are holding Warren's nonsense in any regard."

"'Tisn't nonsense." The indentured woman's voice lilts with brogue. "All lands have their own Fair Folk, and we haven't learned these rules yet."

"Don't indulge her," Mr. Hines says flippantly, cementing my opinion of him as barely worth the air of speaking to. "Mr. Ingram has the right of it. We would be better off pointing fingers where they belong—the savages on our doorstep. It would be quite lucky for them if we had a ghost to fight, wouldn't it?"

I bow and take my leave of the conversation before I fall ill of whoever may enjoy the company of Mr. Hines by knocking him about the head. Everywhere I look on the street contains groups exactly like that which I just left: strange configurations, heads bent, fearful whispers blending with brassy contradictions. The death of the Powhatan youth and the people who came to seek redress is on every mind, though no one else seems to know anything of Sarah's involvement, and I quickly learn the Powhatans did not breach the gates. Mr. Warren's theory about the ghoul and the haunted land seems to have taken root in many heads, though just as many dismiss him as a crank. For the sake of my own reputation, I do not point out that there is only one creature of presumed legend known for draining its victims of blood. If the word *vampire* has not occurred to others, I see no need to speak more paranoia into existence. Those monsters exist only in Europe.

The storehouse yields only more questions. Griffith, behind the counter, trades me a length of rope without a heartbeat's hesitation. When I spare an additional moment to ask about the rope's arrival, he looks at me strangely.

"Two days past, as I said it would be."

"And Mistress Stone, did she ask you for it yesterday?"

"Mistress Stone did not set foot here yesterday." He drags his gaze over me, evaluating. "Are you quite well, Mr. Stone?"

"Rafe," I correct tiredly, having no other answer for the young man.

With the rope in tow, I leave the storehouse. Sarah never even so much as entered the place. She asked nowhere else for rope. But what reason would she have to hide her movements? Is it simply that she feared her interaction with the Powhatans would distress me? That seems an unusual level of worry for a woman I have come to rely on for frankness and honesty.

"Brother!" George bellows from the opposite side of the street, for once without his carriage."

I swallow a sigh and cross to meet him. No individual on this Earth may be less beneficial to clarity of thought than George Moore.

"How does this day find you?" I say, taut with mandatory politeness.

"Better than the Indian lad." He barks a laugh. "And you? The lady wife?"

"Well as can be expected." My irritation grows as I realize I do, in fact, have business with the man. "I wish to purchase a man called John off you, whenever such a deal can be arranged."

"You are going to have to be more specific." He smirks. "I have more Johns than I have fingers."

"An African." I cast my memory back through Sarah's description, given quickly over dinner. "Tall, shaven head, working in the front-most field yesterday."

"Him?" George's eyebrows raise. "He is more trouble than work. I can recommend a better one—"

"Him," I say resolutely. In the depths of my mind, I wonder at myself. I am here to investigate Sarah's lies, but the first moment an opportunity arises, I do her bidding. This man John could be part of the falsehood in any number of ways I cannot see.

But she has given me an opportunity to free a man from captivity. Whatever musket lies between us, I cannot abandon such a chance. Frankly, it shocks me that I have not pursued such an option sooner.

"We can work out the details whenever you like." George claps me on the shoulder. "I should be paying you. The last thing I need around the plantation is more trouble these days."

"Oh?" I take in the bags under his eyes, the additional falsity of his grin, and remember what Sarah said about his relationship with Elizabeth. If he begins confessing his woes to me in the street, I shall abandon all rules of propriety to escape.

"We've had this rash of deaths." He shakes his head. "Animals, thankfully, but to a one they're drained as if for slaughter. No explanation for it, and not a pen I've put up has changed things a whit. Have you any of the same troubles or advice for one who does?"

My gut sinks as if I've swallowed a rock. Animal senses usually dulled to me in this form prick—those which tell me I am watched, not the only predator in a sea of prey.

"When did this start?" I ask faintly.

He blows out a long breath. "Near on two months ago."

Just after he wed Elizabeth. Which, coincidentally, was just after animals stopped appearing at the gates of the town in the same state.

Father told us all stories of vampires. They came from the east, he said, and they were evil. Hunger made flesh, a human soul twisted until it could do nothing but destroy that which reminded itself of its old shape. He spoke of the blessed stakes, electrum blades, and raging fires which could kill them. I have never met a vampire to my knowledge, but I was raised knowing them. They are monsters.

Abruptly, I remember the first moment I met Sarah. When I heard her in the forest and, assuming she was an animal, turned to look, revealing how acute my hearing was. She was already looking at me, though she should not have even been able to see me at that distance.

Other memories come quickly. How little she eats. The disappearance of that scratch on her hand which, if I accelerate the healing process, could well have been a slash from a blade or whip. How quickly she completes tasks when there is no one to watch her. The strange way nearly all in Jamestown seem to have avoided her from the start, though dullards were more likely swayed by the opinions of those more intuitive, if George's choice of wife is any evidence.

"Good day." I fumble a bow to George and speed away before he can expect any further pleasant conversation. I must speak with my wife.

The path home disappears under my feet, though I wish it was lined enough with trees that I might transform and move that much faster. My heartbeat is a wild thing, untethered from any natural rhythm. Elizabeth and Sarah are vampires. I do not know which of the two murdered Manteo, though I certainly have my suspicions, but the very fact makes my skin feel as though it is about to burst. I have slept two months beside a vampire without so much as noticing.

Her constant trips to the forest—has that been how she feeds?

I scent the air as I approach the house. Finding Sarah by human means seems little more than a waste of time. Her smell guides me to the small grove of mulberry trees, where I find her blessedly alone. My hands quiver with barely restrained intent, though I do not know what I intend.

"I have been to town," I say.

"How was it?" There it is, that note of deceit in her voice. How could I have missed it?

"Everyone is talking about the murder." I clench my fists. "Apparently, the youth was drained of his blood. Just like those animals some months ago. Do you remember?"

She hums as if thinking while refusing to look at me. Sick, sour betrayal oozes through me.

"I don't believe I do." She plucks a dying branch from the trunk. "That sounds awful."

I fly the last few steps toward her. Inches between us, I tower over her. Fear once again fills her blue gaze.

"Are you a vampire?" I ask. There is truly nothing more to say, and I grow tired of these games.

"Those are not real." Her voice shakes, and indecision mars her face.

"Do not lie to me!" I bellow.

Sarah flinches. Something in my chest cracks. After all I swore yesterday, now I am what frightens her. But, in truth, this deep of a falsehood frightens me. If she is such a perfect manipulator, even I may be in danger.

"I...think so."

My breath catches.

20

THE TRUTH SHALL SET YE FREE

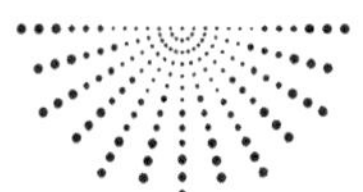

Sarah

A SINGLE BEAD OF SWEAT DRIPS DOWN MY FOREHEAD. MOSQUITOES buzz. Rafe's green eyes widen until I think I might be able to fall into them for all my days and never reach bottom. Until there is nothing but the words I have not yet spoken to any but Elizabeth and an expanse of emerald. A questioning, judging expanse. I wish I had a frog's tongue, so I might snatch the words back as easily as they capture flies.

When he flew at me, Rafe looked wild, possessed, as if he were all the fury of a cyclone bound up in a single body. And, if I might take the strings of life's tapestry and weave them in whatever order I wished, I would take that anger in a heartbeat before I would this frozen nothingness. I did not recognize my husband in his anger. I do not recognize humanity in the statue in front of me.

Perhaps that is for the best. I have not recognized humanity in myself for half a year now.

"Please—" I take a step forward.

Rafe's shoulders tighten, not with fear, but with the incipient violence of a predator about to strike. My undead heart gallops.

There is no way to run any longer. Months of fear boil off into simple exhaustion, and I sit in the summer grass. All my life, reverends have preached the values of truth and confession. If I am no longer a creature which walks in God's light, have they any salvation for me?

Have I any other choice, with my husband watching me as though I am one of the snakes we have been so warned of?

"Are you acquainted with Lord Mallory?" I ask.

Rafe blinks, then thaws. He retreats until his back hits a tree, rustling the leaves overhead. "In… In England?"

I nod, and recollection takes my tongue.

"You are mad," I said numbly, barely able to behold Elizabeth in the full blush of her ballgown, still swaying faintly in the doorway. "We cannot attend the ball. Gertie is already penning our apologies."

"You do not refuse Lord Mallory's invitation," she replied, sounding slurred with wine as she had since awakening after last Wednesday's ball.

"You do not put yourself in the way of such great temptation." I took a step closer. My gaze flickered like a nervous hand from the newly alabaster pallor of her skin to the high red spots on her cheeks to the splintered chunk of door frame she clenched in one fist from a disastrous attempt to swing through it as she has been used to. "Father might see you."

"It has been a week." Elizabeth's smile looked like that of a woman dying of fever, but I knew all too well that, were I to lay my hand upon her cheek, she would be cold as ice. Poets would have swooned at her feet, but I could only see the monster my sister had become. "Surely, he would have noticed by now, were he going to."

"In your isolation, you have been unable to…feed," I whispered the final word, sickening on my tongue. "Will you not find yourself too sorely tempted in such a crush?"

She closed the distance between us in a single breath, impossibly fast. When she grabbed my arm, linen ripped beneath her fingers, and my tender skin bruised. "An older sister ought to keep the younger from temptation, should she not?"

"I—" My cheeks boiled with shame. Elizabeth had not said it since she had awoken as one of the boogeymen that populated Father's terse bedtime stories, but in truth, I should have stopped her from going off with the strange man who had transformed her. I had been... I am not certain where, but distracted. If I had not stopped her, I should have recognized the symptoms of transformation during her illness on the carriage ride home and taken her promptly to the herb garden for a cure–if that were even possible. Instead, I had shirked my duties. Her death and rebirth were my fault, so it was only right that protecting her from the consequences thereof would fall at my feet.

"You shall go ready yourself?" Elizabeth said coaxingly.

I nodded.

As the sun set, we trundled toward Mallory Manor. It was as the rumors described it. Every window glowed with a candle or three, lighting it nearly as bright as London itself. Music poured down the path like honey and caught feet that had not yet even stepped inside. Silks and brocades glittered like jewels. Lord Mallory hosted the sorts of balls at which lives were made and broken, and as we drew to a stop in front of the door, I understood why the best of the city still attended them.

Elizabeth seemed enraptured, the sharpness of her coloring slightly muted by the dark but her awestruck grin impossible to ignore. I took her hand firmly in mine.

"William shall be here tonight," I told her. "I shall need to spare him at least one dance, or he shall be quite hurt."

She nodded, her gaze still on the party. I would ensure she heard me before joining my betrothed. If her temptation was mine to guard, I intended to guard it as the angels guarding Eden.

"Betrothed?" Rafe asks, his voice rough enough to jar me from the haze of memory.

"Lord William." I swallow, burning once more. "He is deceased, but I still ought to have told you."

He nods slowly and says nothing further, returning to a statue of himself. With a deep breath, I plunge once more into the depth of my tale.

Inside Mallory Manor, the idea of Eden rang even more strongly. No earthly pleasure had been forgotten, even a few that wrinkled my nose in offense. Smoke filled the air, blotting out the warm smells of food and bodies. If ever one did not enjoy a song, one merely needed to cross to the next room, and they might hear another. Quickly, thoughts of Eden became thoughts of Sodom and Gomorrah.

William appeared out of the crowd, his smile soft and warm.

"My dear." He kissed my hand on a gallant bow, then greeted Elizabeth with a wrinkle of worry around his mouth. William could see the strangeness in her coloration, so others must. "Are you well?"

"As can be expected." I wove my mouth into something like a smile. It did not allay William's concern.

"Go and dance," Elizabeth chirped. "I shall gather us punch and return."

My every muscle iced over at the idea of losing sight of her, but she gestured to the table in the same room as the nearest dance floor. At most, I might lose her for the length of a spin. Unless I were to chain her to my very wrist, I could not keep her much closer. William extended his hand, and I offered him mine. We joined the whirling couples.

Elizabeth stood at the table. She poured cherry-red punch into crystal cups and lifted it to her mouth.

"Sarah?" William said.

"Hmm?" His expression shrieked his concern across the ballroom, and I realized my mistake. I would check on my sister occasionally, or I would never have a life of my own. "Apologies, Elizabeth is in one of her moods."

With a nod and a smile, William threw his spirit into the dance. He was well-trained but lacking in elements of rhythm which made him enthusiastic if occasionally inexpert. By the end of the song, I had even managed a laugh. We returned to Elizabeth, who seemed perfectly un-tempted, and I drank half my glass of punch in a single sip.

After that, I only remember the night in flashes. Elizabeth threw her head back, golden hair shimmering like a waterfall of wealth, in a laugh. We danced together, hapless and graceless but still nearly two of the most put-together upon the dance floor. William escorted me to the garden when I complained my head had kept spinning even though I had stopped dancing, and the evening air whispered past us, scented with primrose and the nearby moors.

Smells—those, I remember clear as crystal. The main meal was rosemary-brined boar and thick slabs of hot bread. One man had a tobacco from the Far East which stank of spices I could not name. Lady Amabel wore a reeking French perfume like a thousand dead violets crushed into a single jar.

And then, morning was upon me. My own familiar canopy winked down at me, promising I had discovered a way home. Had the punch been laced with some strong wine? I didn't believe I'd had that much. I moved, and my body reacted like an ancient oak being asked to step aside. Every inch of my skin moaned, as if I had dragged myself through a briar patch. My mouth felt as it did the one time I had sampled some of Father's hard tack without softening it first— desperately dry and as sore as if I'd bitten a rock. I had never been hungrier, thirstier. My gums, in particular, lodged a series of complaints against my behavior.

I started to sit up, and Elizabeth appeared beside me, her blue eyes intent as she took my face in her hands. The iron grip I had grown used to over the past week felt more like strong wood cut thin—powerful, but not unbreakable. Ice tumbled sluggish through my veins.

"Do not look anywhere other than my face," Elizabeth said.

Obeying was simple, far simpler than thinking the thoughts that threatened at the edge of my fogged consciousness.

"The vam—man who reached me at last week's ball must have attended Lord Mallory's last night." Her voice was lower than I thought I should have been able to hear, a mere vibration in her throat, but I knew every word. My stomach cramped around nothingness. I wanted to be sick, but there was nothing to expel.

"Do you think Father's wor—"

"Hush," she hissed.

I flinched at her volume, a shred louder than before and painfully too loud. My own half-normal voice had sounded like a scream.

"I have secured us passage to the New World." She released my head and pulled me slowly off the bed by my hands. "It leaves today, if we can pack in time."

I stared at my sister, limned in sunrise like a saint in the window of a Catholic church, and wept.

WHEN MY STORY ENDS, I EXPECT RAFE TO THAW ONCE MORE. TO BURST like lit tinder or melt away like the last snow. I do not expect the same stillness.

"If you have concerns about the Powhatan youth and my diet," I say, as fragile as a glass bell, "I can assure you I feed only on animals I can hunt in the forest."

He remains a stony recreation of himself, those eyes still heavy on my face as if searching for something I've failed to provide.

"I have never killed a human being." I pluck a blade of grass and twist it between my fingers. "With intent."

"With intent?" His voice is a whetstone against a dull blade, sharp and painful.

Rye-colored hair. Soft smiles. Elizabeth's hands on the side of my face, preventing me until the very last moment, when I risked a glance back, from discovering what the weight I didn't want to feel on the other side of my bed truly was. I snap the blade of grass and pick another. Confession has yielded me nothing. I have no more of it left, and certainly not that most painful part.

I set a hand on my stomach. "In becoming what I am, I lost all ability to produce a child. Any I might have borne lay dead within me."

That shakes him from his stupor. He sinks to the ground and sits with his back to a mulberry trunk, then closes his eyes. The rustling leaves sound like laughter now—look at the foolish monster who thought offering up her monstrosity might be her salvation! Now, she shall have what she has always deserved: nothing!

Long minutes pass. I fancy I can watch the sun cross the sky past Rafe, though that may merely be a trick of the eye. He has not begun whittling a stake, nor has he yelled for the laborers. Despite my strength, I am certain they could restrain me if they chose to work together. Perhaps he has developed just enough fondness for me that he might only send me away in shame instead of killing me. While I wait for some answer, I decide that I will join the Powhatans if he does. I shall have no life in town, and I shall have no peace with Elizabeth. Matatishe is my only hope. Perhaps I can protect them from any further incursions.

"Very well," Rafe says with the quiet finality of a door closing.

I study him, shocked. He seems terribly tired, years older than he was mere moments ago.

"You are my wife," he stands, "whatever else you may be, and I believe that holds meaning."

"Oh." Relief knocks me breathless, but there is no excitement in Rafe's tone.

"In exchange for this kindness, I expect your lenience in the pursuit of my heir."

I know, abruptly, what it is to be a sword on a blacksmith's anvil and watch the hammer come down. We are to be man and wife in name only. He is allowing me my life, the name he has already granted me, and nothing more.

Still, I nod. I owe him that courtesy. And I do not believe any words would have come to my tongue, were I to try to argue. Every word seems bound up in the story of my transformation, Elizabeth's transformation, the many failures that have led me here.

Rafe leaves the grove. That evening, he does not speak to me when we sit together after supper, and he goes to sleep in the garret alone.

21

BENEATH THE FULL MOON

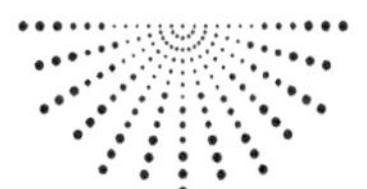

Rafe

THE NIGHT THAT SARAH CONFESSES THE TRUTH OF HER PAST TO ME, I lay in the garret cot, chasing sleep like a puppy after a deer. I haven't a hope of catching it, but instinct demands I continue to try. I turn, straw crunching, and think mournfully of the featherbed below.

Away from her, my anger ebbs. She lied. I cannot escape that, and whenever I allow myself to think those words, I threaten to boil out of my human skin. Perhaps the marriage vows do not include an oath of trust, but I did not think it needed to be stated to be understood.

However, when I suck down breaths of sweet night air and cool my head, I remember that I have not been completely truthful with her myself. The exact reason Elizabeth felt they needed to leave London at the moment they did remains unclear to me, but it is very clear that there was some imminent threat. They had reason to fear for their very lives. And if there is any falsehood on this Earth which I can find defensible, it is that sort.

Certainly not, constable, Esther says in my memory, voice still high and sweet. *We've seen neither hide nor hair of so terrible a wolf.*

I roll over once more, scowling at the ray of moonlight that paints my face and my mind. It is not as though I need to be reminded of my own history. With that scowl firmly in place, I chase all thoughts of Sarah and my lost family from my mind until nothing may fill it but sleep.

I rise earlier than usual, earlier even than Dinah, and get my own breakfast while sleep still hangs heavy in my limbs. In the morning half-light, the kitchen looks far too like that which I left behind in England. Mother supervises the cook in the corner of my vision, her arms crossed but a soft smile on her lips. Crispin lurks behind a corner, waiting for a moment to snatch hot pastries and abscond, swallowing butter and laughter in one mouthful. Father—

Father stumps into the room where I, then a fuzz-cheeked youth, prepare a simple tea for myself, and sighs. In a heavy tone I hadn't heard before that moment, he tells me that Digory Binder has been put to death. The constable must have some outside help because he knew to use silver.

I shake my head. Work awaits; I haven't time to be haunted by these ghosts of my past, ghosts I laid to rest long ago. The destruction of Moorhurst has little to do with what Sarah has done. I have done all I might by carrying her secret, keeping her my wife. Were I to march into Jamestown and declare her a vampire—or simply a witch —her death would follow without question. Now, I must turn my thoughts to the future and how I will achieve the heir I require rather than dwelling on either of our pasts.

The bedroom door creaks open upstairs. I suppose there is no point to her hiding her preternatural abilities now. My own advanced capabilities are all I need to stay ahead of her, however. I gather my breakfast and leave for the fields.

"LITTLE SLEEP?" KLAUS ASKS ME WHEN I SLOW FOR THE DOZENTH TIME the next day. "You look like a rabbit three days dead."

I can only nod. The garret cot is far from comfortable, but I passed two weeks on it without issue before. What is keeping me awake now are the dreams.

Esther's husband, Samuel, bursts into the manor with blood on his hands.

I embrace Adam's sobbing wife.

A secret door closes between Mother and myself, both of us believing it will be the last time we see the other and neither being truly wrong.

"There are charms for that, you know," Klaus offers as he bends to pluck a sucker shoot off a knee-high tobacco plant. "One of the newer women makes them."

I dab my forehead with the handkerchief Esther embroidered, its own sort of charm. "Which?"

"Bridget, I believe." He shades his eyes and looks across the field. "Dark hair, thin."

I nod, the information already slipping from my mind. It crowds with far too much thought, past and present folding over each other like fine steel. Last evening, Sarah and I ate dinner across from each other without speaking a word. Until her confession, such a night would have been an anticipated pleasure. Now, even her silence has soured. It is as if I have grabbed the musket of her secret, turned it upon her, and she has produced her own flintlock. The two of us stand in uneasy deadlock. I know not what Sarah thinks, but I find myself wondering not simply which will pull the trigger first but if we may ever set these weapons down. A lifetime armed seems worse than any fate I imagined for myself after throwing my lot in with Sir Thomas's scheme.

"My indenture comes due in September, you know," Klaus says.

"How could I forget?" We shall lose him for the harvest and drying, when clever hands are far more valuable than many hands.

"If you are so troubled, I had considered offering my services—for hire—through this season."

"Twice the usual rate," I reply without a second's thought. Klaus's offer is no trick or pity; I intended to make the same, had he not broached the topic first. And it offers a grateful raft away from my own mind, in which I find no solace at this time.

He guffaws. "For that, I might offer a second season."

I clap him on the shoulder. "As long as you want work, it is here for you."

"If I had known you were this soft, I would have waited until you were far more desperate."

I start to smile, but a trick of the light turns Klaus's fair hair to Crispin's ashen black, and my stomach turns. The last I saw my eldest brother, he told me after Father's execution that he would be attacking the constable in his bed at midnight, and I needed to take whoever else remained and run.

That night still tastes of smoke in my memory. The thick, acrid smoke of Moorhurst burning, to the trembling chorus of human and lupine screams.

"Rafe?" Klaus frowns at me.

I shake my head. "What was the woman's name again?"

"How grows the tobacco?" Sarah ventures after an hour of silent work beside each other the next evening.

I grunt vaguely in return. Anger has all but left me; I can look at her with no rush of heat or violence. What remains is a sting I can only name betrayal. It is neither fair nor reasonable to expect of her what I will not do myself, and yet I cannot stop. She is my wife. The first soul I wished to know since escaping the blackened husk of Moorhurst alone. That she could have hidden—that I could have missed—such a large part of her pricks like lemon juice in a cut, no matter how I try to forget it.

She stiffens and turns back to her work, one of the only fine pieces I have seen her turn her hands to. Springtime animals dance over the collar with a grace and elegance I would not expect from a woman who I have nearly only seen darn and knit. It nearly rivals Esther's.

FIRELIGHT FLICKERED OFF THE STONE WALLS OF THE PRIMARY SITTING room in the manor. Crispin, Adam, and I played cards at a small table while Mother and Esther worked in chairs before the fire. Father penned a letter on Mother's left, paper pinned with his elbow so he might hold her hand as always. It was a quiet evening for us, no guests or festivities, but I was winning at cards, so I didn't much mind.

"Mr. Binder to see you, sir," the butler, Higgins, announced.

Father sat back, brow furrowed, but gestured for him to be allowed in. Everyone perked to attention. Digory Binder was one of the many citizens of Moorhurst who belonged to our pack—more than half the village, at that rate—and as its Alpha, Father must have been willing to hear from him at all hours, as I would be when I inherited his position.

Digory stumbled in, hair wild and pants mud-spattered. I would have thought him drunk, if not for the sharpness of his gaze. "The new constable," he gasped.

Father gestured for Higgins to get Digory a drink, then led him into a chair. "What of him?"

Digory slugged the glass of wine Higgins brought. I watched his pulse jump in his throat. Though Digory was not always the steadiest hand, I had never before seen him so shaken.

"He caught me in the woods tonight."

Adam's dropped cards sounded like an avalanche in the silence that followed. Father had taught us all many things, including what a constable's attention meant for shifters.

"What do you mean, 'caught'?" he asked.

Digory set the wine glass down with trembling hands. "He was hunting and spotted me in my wolf form. I ran, thought I had lost him, shifted, and… he caught me at the edge of the wood slipping into my clothes. Asked a great many questions about why I had come out, had I seen the wolf, and so on."

Crispin slumped like an unstrung marionette with relief. I knew what he thought—Digory hadn't been truly caught, merely suspected —but I did not share his solace. Suspicion was the first step.

Father laid a hand upon Digory's shoulder. "A new constable shouldn't be much trouble. We shall face this as a pack."

I STAND ABRUPTLY. "I AM GOING TO BED."

Sarah nods without looking up at me, and I flee the memories that have pursued me since her confession yet again. Father's last words sound like a dire prophecy now. The pack did face the might of the constable, and we lost, nearly to a man. Had I not escaped to the colonies, I might have been hunted to ensure the job had been finished. Digory's simple mistake, one any of us might have made, was the spark that set Moorhurst ablaze.

With these thoughts rattling through my mind, sleep is once again elusive. Everywhere I turn, another painful memory awaits. The testimonies at Father's trial, the *crack* of the ready constable's killing shot through Crispin's heart, the slick mud covering Esther's shallow grave. I throw open the window and stare up at the sky.

A full moon stares back down at me, bright and welcoming enough that my decision is made before I truly know I am making it. I creep from the house, enter the forest, strip off my clothes, and let my inheritance take me.

The symphony of night noises fill my lupine ears. My paws pound familiar earth. Friendly wind rustles my fur. In this, I leave my thoughts behind. I push myself faster, then faster still, until I am little more than noise myself.

A strange smell catches my nose, not exactly hot, fresh blood, and I wheel on simple instinct. I did not intend to hunt, but the simple satiation of fulfilling my purpose may help me sleep. Ferns whip my muzzle. Trees disappear in my wake.

I skid into a small clearing and recognize the smell alongside my mistake. Fresh blood mingles with old blood and the scent of rosemary as I look at Sarah, crouched with her mouth to the throat of a stag.

Time crawls. I take a step back, but she lifts her head. A single line of crimson dribbles from her lips to her chin. The faint tips of fangs dent her lower lip. I pray she sees a simple wolf, another predator on the hunt, but my prayers have long since ceased being answered. In the silver light of the full moon, realization contorts my wife's face.

Every wolf shifter keeps one thing between both forms: their eyes. And Sarah has recognized mine.

22

SECOND FIRST MEETING

Sarah

I STARE DOWN THE WOLF I ONCE SAW FROM MY WINDOW, UNABLE TO comprehend Rafe's eyes in its face. Am I simply so lonely from these days of avoidance that I am imagining him where he isn't?

Rafe answers the question before I have to ask it. The massive wolf before me folds into itself, shrinks. Hair shoots back into skin like rope being wound. Pointed ears and hungry snout melt into nothingness.

He stands, nothing but bare human skin in the moonlight. My husband, the…wolf?

"Werewolves are not real," I say foolishly.

"They are not." He holds up his hands defensively, as if I am the threat.

"What?" My mind tumbles over and over itself, a sheet caught in a washing drum, but no sense escapes.

"I am a wolf shifter," he says slowly.

"You are…." For once, I am completely shaken from the meal before me, the deer only half-drained and oozing valuable life into

163

the grass. It hardly matters, and neither does the hunger with its claws sunk into my throat. There is only Rafe, and the wolf, and Rafe who is a wolf.

Rafe who is not human.

That, I can make sense of, with a burst of blazing rage that sends me shooting to my feet. "You have been avoiding me for days."

His gaze slides away from mine, guilty as a boy caught passing notes in church.

"You were so furious." I advance toward him, my nightgown fluttering in the breeze. "You said all those things—and all along, you were no more human than I? Surely, you understand why I would have left some information aside, as you did."

He does not answer before I reach him, so I brace my hands against the muscles of his chest and shove. Despite every ounce of demonic strength I expend, he only sways like a tree in a breeze. Abruptly, I remember the moment he crushed my fingers as we danced. He has always been stronger than me, even when he was sloppily attempting to disguise the fact.

"You accused me of lying." My voice builds to a shriek. "What does that make you?"

He flinches but does not move.

"Had you been new to Jamestown, the wife bought and paid for," I yell in his face, "you would have done exactly as I did, and yet you put me aside?"

"You are right," he rasps, grabbing my wrists as I rear back to shove him once again. "I apologize."

He has not touched me since the mulberry grove. The warmth of his skin on mine saps the energy of my rage, and what remains simmers when he meets my gaze. Shame and apology dance in the green eyes which so recently belonged to a great, dark wolf. He has been avoiding me, at least in part, because he is aware how unreasonable his upset is.

Were I faced with his dilemma, a demon unknowingly shackled to a monster, I do not know that I could have reacted in any more logical manner. I deflate, lean into his hands.

"Might we return home?" he asks. "I would like to discuss this where we can be more certain there are no listening ears hidden in the treetops."

I glance at the deer. Without anger clouding every sense, its scent nearly overwhelms me.

Rafe releases my wrists in silent permission. His gaze is heavy on my shoulders as I kneel once more and place my mouth back to the punctures in the hide. Lifeblood flows past my lips, slower than if I had not paused. The animal's heart is fading—I have left it a far more painful death than usual. In my own apology, I drink the remainder quickly.

Cheeks burning, I lay my hand on the spent deer's chest and murmur, "Thank you," as has become my custom.

Rafe makes a small noise in his throat, but he is expressionless when I look up at him. Without a word, he turns into a wolf once more, the process repeating itself in reverse, and takes off toward Bluebonnet. I climb to my feet and follow.

He is fast, but it would be easy to outpace him. I decide not to at this moment, for the same reason I believe he allowed me to finish my meal. The brief touch of his hands on my wrists, the rasp of his apology is fragile as glass. We dare not prod at it.

Inside, Rafe dons a pair of breeches, then pours two glasses of whiskey from a barrel which I have only seen him touch once before. He offers the smaller to me, and I accept it. Though Father's whiskey always turned my stomach, I can smell far more complexity in the amber liquid now, enough to tempt my palate.

"Werewolves are not real," I say as I settle into my chair before the banked fire. "But you are."

"I am a wolf shifter." He repeats, taking a deep draught. "Werewolves are a scary story told to make us seem like monsters. We are not beholden to the full moon, we are not destroyed by the transformation, and we are not made by bite."

"You have no blood-fury?" I barely manage to ask.

He gestures at the brilliant moon. "If the legends were true, I could not have this conversation with you now."

I frown. "How are you… made, then?"

"By birth." He offers a bittersweet smile. "I grew up surrounded by shifters, one of five in my family alone. The whole pack comprised forty wolves at our strongest."

A pack. Forty wolves. I sip the whiskey, and it burns down my throat like over-hot tea without the pain.

"Where are they now?" I ask. "Your pack?"

"Dead." His smile dies with the word, and he looks away. "Slaughtered for those damned legends when we had not hurt a soul."

Forty souls destroyed. His whole family. And here I believed I had lost so much. Suddenly, abandoning my life, losing William, and destroying any relationship with Father feel like small prices to pay.

In my reeling, Rafe sees his opening. "Since we are putting the full truth between us, I must ask: What did you mean, you have never killed a human being with intent?"

Just as suddenly, the price feels quite large once more. Rafe is not human, but neither does he seem the sort of ungodly monster I have been cursed into. Upon my very wakening, I lost my soul. Perhaps that equals out to forty losses, or perhaps the whiskey clouds my judgment.

"Must I?" My voice breaks.

He sighs. "No, I suppose not. But you are the creature of legend. I have much more to fear of your bloodlust than you of mine—I can happily sate myself on mortal food for the rest of my days, whereas you seem to choke down a few mouthfuls at mealtimes."

He is not wrong. I worry my lower lip between my teeth. Confessing a loss is painful; confessing what I have done makes a person sick with shame. I have been sick with shame since the moment I discovered it.

"Tell me one of your regrets," I say instead. "A great one, please."

Rafe looks at me strangely. His eyes—so inhuman now, yet still so natural—shimmer with low firelight such that I cannot read any emotion within. I cannot imagine how I look to him. When I flicker with flame, does he picture me burning? I withdraw into myself like a turtle pulling into its shell and pray that he might speak soon.

"Though I was not the eldest, I was heir to the pack," Rafe says slowly. "When it became clear that we were being targeted, exterminated, my older brother told me the plan that I might escape with as many of our pack as I could." He turns back to the hearth as though he cannot face me when he says this. "I thought his plan flawed, and I knew Father had chosen me, but Father was dead. Crispin seemed so sure...." He shakes his head. "I will regret until the day I die that I did not so much as amend his plan, even gather our survivors, before he struck. The rest of the pack died, as did nearly every human living in our village when the constable burned it to the ground."

Once again, the weight of Rafe's pain strikes me with the dull thud of a club. The scale of his loss is so enormous. Grief bows his shoulders, and shame twists his mouth into a grimace. This is perhaps his greatest regret—and still, I fear I have worse to confess.

I place my hand on his knee. He looks at me, abrupt and startled.

"You did all you could," I say. "I know you did not wish them to die."

Pain contorts his face, and he looks away once more, but he covers my hand with his own. My own truth boils behind my lips, dangerous as a cauldron of oil, but I cannot refuse him now.

"Do you remember how I told you of Elizabeth holding my face upon my wakening?" I stare at our layered hands, what I hope is a promise that there may be a way past this where I do not live the rest of my days with a distant stranger.

"Yes."

"She was... blocking my view." Emotions knot in my throat—shame, fear, whatever grief I am allowed after what I have done. "Another body lay in the bed beside me."

Realization blinks across Rafe's face, but he hides the expression as quickly as it arrives, waiting for the end of my tale. How can I speak the words, though? I never have before. Even between Elizabeth and myself, we have never said the truth of what occurred.

He tightens his grip on my hand, a breath of comfort in the wilderness of my own emotions. "Tell me."

❧

MY HANDS TREMBLED AS I SHOVED THE FOLDED SKIRTS, BODICES, AND chemises Elizabeth handed me into our bags. The rustle of fabric deafened me. My skin screamed. Every ray of sunlight through the windows lanced across me like a hot iron, leaving me shocked I did not sizzle in its wake. Every symptom matched what I knew. Elizabeth had spent two days abed after her own transformation, thankfully a common enough event after a ball that Father hadn't asked. I felt as though I might shake loose from the envelope of my body at any moment, and yet we had to pack.

"Are you well?" Elizabeth huffed a laugh. "That is, well enough?"

I nodded mutely. Whether I had lied mattered not. The weight in the bed beside me tortured my mind. She would only have touched me as she did, spoken to me as she did, if the weight was what I feared: a body. I hoped I had fallen upon one of our rare animals when Elizabeth and I returned, but I doubted my luck. In the pandemonium of Mallory Manor, I might have stumbled across any soul.

"Dear Lord—" I broke off my murmured prayer of absolution as my tongue shrieked with indescribable agony, crackling from that muscle down my throat and into my very spine.

"Hallowed." Elizabeth patted my hand comfortably. "You shall get used to it."

Of course. I knew that. I closed my lips around the pain and packed the last few garments. Soft footsteps and clattering had begun to reach my ears; the house was awakening, and it would not be long until my maid attempted to wake me.

As soon as the body was discovered, Father would want to kill both of us.

I fought the clasps of my own portmanteau while Elizabeth snapped hers neatly shut.

"Remember"—she took my hand and stood—"keep your gaze always on me, and we shall put this behind us."

I struggled to my feet and nodded. Hungry claws of memory

snatched at me, offering snippets of the night before, all coated with the same haze. So many faces—which did not greet the dawn?

Elizabeth was correct. I would be happier if I did not look, if I never knew. That thought powered me from the dressing room, past the fireplace, until she laid her very hand upon the knob. Then, ice caught me by the throat. If I never knew, I would never be able to repent. I would never understand the depth of the wound I had dealt the world. And so, as Elizabeth opened the door, I turned back.

Rye-colored hair. Long, elegant limbs. Half a smile still curling familiar lips. Blood in rivulets down his neck. Dark eyes empty of the life I had so loved in them. William lay propped on a pillow as if settling down for sleep, stone dead.

The sound I made wasn't human—it was that of an injured animal.

Elizabeth covered my mouth harshly, nearly louder than my cry. "Father will kill us if he learns of this before we are gone."

I left my home with tears in my eyes, swallowing sobs more than air.

Rafe's grip loosens. "William, your betrothed?"

I nod miserably. He shall leave now, and he shall be right to. I am not an exception to the stories of my kind—I am archetypal.

"How are you certain you killed him?"

I blink up at Rafe and find his brow furrowed in concentration. "He lay in my bed. I had just been transformed, and I was not ravenous as Elizabeth had been. What more do you need?"

"But you do not remember it?" He leans forward, gaze intent.

"I do not remember returning home, and yet I did." I lean back, unnerved by his reaction.

"That lapse in memory, it began after the punch, yes?" he continues.

"I... suppose." There is a hunger in his gaze that frightens me. I do not know what he wants, but I know none should respond to the story I have just told in this way. "I wouldn't like to speak of this any longer."

"But what if—"

"Please." His hunger makes sense now. He does not want a murderer for a wife, so he is attempting to discover a way in which some villain might've crept into my very bed and befuddled me so. But I know the feelings I woke with. I know the look of William in my bed. My soul was destroyed that night because, in the fugue of transformation, I took a sweet, honorable life, and there is nothing more to say.

Rafe seems to read this in my face. His intensity softens, and he cups my face with his other hand. "Thank you."

I look away. He may cling to this delusion for himself, but I cannot further it.

"Listen to me." He pulls my gaze back. "Nothing that occurred in England matters here. We have our fresh start, to make with what we can. And I intend to make a place in which you may feel safe."

My heart flutters. He means every word, and I wish to believe him.

"I love you," he says.

A rush of warmth envelops the old memories, not washing away their pain but dampening it. He loves me, even with the whole truth before him, as I thought none ever would. His whole truth no longer frightens me either.

"I love you."

His face glows with a smile as he leans in to kiss me.

23
WEDDED BLISS

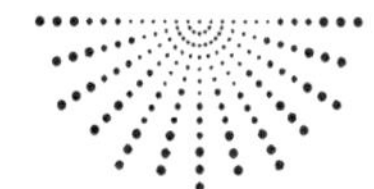

Sarah

WILLIAM AND I SAID MANY THINGS TO EACH OTHER, BUT WE SPOKE OF love only in idea. I hoped I might love him, and that he might love me. Happiness was assured; love, a far loftier goal.

Thus, when Rafe slides his hand from my cheek into my hair and pulls me to his mouth, it is something like a miracle. My first kiss from a man who loves me and one I love. A heavenly host choruses my bliss. I reach for his bare chest and trace the furrows of his muscles with careful fingers. In these past few days, I have believed that the last time Rafe and I lay together would be the final time. If the sun rises, and he discovers he has made some terrible mistake, I do not intend to forget this.

I doubt he will, however. He touches me, not as if I am fragile glass, but as if I am precious. Worthy of gentleness regardless of what ungentle hands might do to me. Perhaps that is the miracle. Or perhaps that is the love.

Our bed is so far away, and it is much too late for any of the workers to be about, so I quit my chair and join Rafe in his. My legs part over his lap, welcoming his warmth and burgeoning hardness. I run my thumb along the line of a scar across his ribs and wonder if it came from the constable or his brother in a childhood accident. The idea that I might ask and be given the truth pulls my lips into a smile so wide it breaks our kiss.

"What is it?" Rafe asks, his own indulgent smile echoing mine.

"I love you." There is simply nothing else that summarizes the feeling so succinctly. After months of shame and loathing, of believing I was to be alone in this world with Elizabeth as my only true companion no matter her sins, everything refracts through the lens of that simple truth. My monstrosity does not drive me away from my husband; it drives me toward him. We are more alike in our inhumanity.

As he rejoins our mouths, a new future unfolds before me. With Rafe alongside me, I am certain we can invent a safer, more humane solution to my current feeding. It is easier to consume mortal food when I am rich with blood, so visions of myself setting a Christmas table and enjoying it with the rest of our guests dance through my mind. I may not be able to have my own children, but perhaps there will be other children which have no parents to care for them. Perhaps some of the indentured women will fall pregnant and not wish the trouble of work and infants. My Christmas table populates with one child—two—enough that I can no longer count them for all their running around. In my mind's eye, Rafe smiles that same indulgent smile as he carves, and the children all bicker over the best pieces before I declare they go to my husband for all his hard work.

Cool air caresses my thighs, and I jar out of my thoughts as Rafe slides a hand beneath my nightgown. Future happiness is subsumed by present delight. I throw my head back, hair wild, and cling to him with all the strength I have been restraining. He makes a low, ravenous sound which almost sends me to the heavens before I have even felt his cock as anything more than pressure between my legs. When I look at him, he is already watching me, gaze hooded and reverent.

"Beautiful," he murmurs.

His clever, dancing fingers distract me before I can blush or worry. I can hardly shape words, or I would tell him what I think of his handsomeness in turn. He looks like he stepped from the very bark of a tree, like a nature spirit of old. Perhaps he is, in some ways. I map every line of his body, from broad shoulders to narrow waist, from barely stubbled chin to wiry hair trailing past his breeches.

"Let us pretend," I say as I free his cock, "that we are starting our family."

His smile is bittersweet the heartbeat before he buries his face in the crook of my neck. Are his teeth sharper than before, a sliver of wolf in the man? Regardless, I shiver with their scraping threat and position myself over him.

Rafe slides home like the hasp of a lock clicking into place. Perfectly fitted. The burn of stretching around him has all but disappeared. I cling to his neck and roll my hips, imagining our first baby. A bouncing, beautiful boy, I decide, to inherit the plantation and his father's eyes. A little wolf puppy for me to coddle silly while his father makes him tough. A tiny proof of our love that the whole world might admire.

The height of pleasure startles me. I cry out and quiver around Rafe, who holds me through the storm like he wants nothing more than to protect me.

WE REMAIN AWAKE PAST SUNRISE, TALKING AND TOUCHING, SO WHEN sleep finally separates us, it does so violently. I open my eyes to find the sun so high in the sky that its rays through the window are swiftly creeping toward my exposed foot.

With a yelp, I scrabble across bedsheets and reach for the shutter I opened when I left last night. The commotion wakes Rafe, who leaps from the mattress with the grace of a dancer and shuts the sun away before I have even gotten to my feet. I smile sheepishly at him.

"Apologies."

"Ask it, and I shall remove the windows from the room." He kisses the tip of my nose.

I shake my head. "Though a way to close the shutters from the bed may simply be clever."

"Anything for you." He rolls back into bed with an ease I have not seen in him since our confrontation—an ease I didn't even realize he had gathered around me in the months of our marriage until it disappeared. Though he is perfectly cordial in town, he is never at ease. This man is mine and mine alone.

I pull him into an indolent kiss with no real intent. Soreness gathers between my legs, though nothing I could not overcome. He matches my honeyed pace as if we have all the time in the world.

"Should you not be in the fields?" I ask, leaning away abruptly.

"One day shall not the difference make." He smiles. "Klaus knows the land nearly as well as I."

An answering smile dawns on my own face. "Do you mean that you have nowhere else to be? No further draws on your time?"

He grazes a hand up my bare torso, leaving ghostly fire in his wake. "Why do I suspect I already know why you ask?"

I swat him gently—then again, gently according to the full power of my strength. I needn't restrain myself with him any longer. He merely chuckles.

"Answer my question."

"You are correct." Rafe peppers kisses along my rib cage, almost light enough to tickle. "Now, may I ask why?"

I wave my hand permissively.

"Why, your majesty?" he asks with a laugh.

"Because I have missed you." The honesty still throbs, raw as an open wound, but I do not intend to cede the ground I have gained to mere daytime. I card my fingers through his ink-black hair and separate the tangles. "I would like to spend a whole day at your side, as if it were the Sabbath—oh!" I sit up, and Rafe follows me with concern in his gaze. "I know not if there is anything we might do about this, but I ought to tell you that attending service is terrifically painful for me."

He barks a short laugh. "I would not describe it as such, but I would not say I have the pleasantest experience there myself—nothing to do with Father Buck's sermons."

His distance on our wedding day, his sluggishness after service—pieces of the life we have been leading slide together like tiles in a mosaic to form a picture I should have been seeing all along. We should discuss the church, I know, but all I can do is kiss my husband before the chalice of love in my breast overflows so awfully that I am drowned in it.

We spend another hour in bed before finally rising.

"I'll tell the lads you've survived the night," Dinah crows when we enter the kitchen hand in hand. "Troubles over, then?"

I glance at Rafe surreptitiously.

"Tell the gossip who said my wife and I were experiencing anything but wedded bliss that they ought to mind their tongue," he says blithely. "And if it was Klaus, tell him my offer is now one and a half."

Dinah laughs, and I join in, knowing there is no heat behind any of Rafe's threats. Though I do want the children I envisioned last night —most of all that green-eyed little boy—in truth, we already have so much of a family here. Rafe has rebuilt his pack, though there is not a wolf among it any longer save himself.

"I was readying supper," she says when the laughter dies down. "You can either eat readied goods for breakfast or make your own."

"Read—"

I squeeze Rafe's hand. "Let us cook."

"I did say anything." He shakes his head at Dinah. "I should warn you, I am less than useless."

"Then I shall simply have to whip you into shape!"

A WHOLE DAY PASSES IN THAT SAME DELIRIOUS HAZE OF HAPPINESS AS IF we are newly married once again. Rafe is less than useless in the kitchen until I set him to chopping, at which he is fast and accurate despite his playful complaints. We eat lawlessly, curled in the same chair in the sitting room. When breakfast ends, we each go about our own tasks beside each other. I pick up a hat I am knitting, but Rafe captures one of my hands before I can start and refuses to release it for anything. He simply insists I must take up reading—as his mother did–to hold his father's hand.

The following day, I expect reality to return, but it only sets a single foot inside the door. Rafe leaves bed early, but he kisses my brow to waken me first. We both take lunch with the hands and endure their teasing. The field he assigns himself is far closer to the house than usual, and I find myself drifting out to visit him often. It is as though we were previously separate paths which crossed occasionally, and we are now a pair of magnets pulled occasionally apart by some patient scientist. My cheeks ache from smiling before the sun sets a second time.

A few days later, I approach the cypress Matatishe does all her trading under. "Hello?"

She rustles out of the brush, looking haggard. "For you alone."

The ignition point of my happiness, her brother's murder, returns to me in a rush, and I burn with humiliation for my smile.

"How are you?" I take a step closer, and she honors me by remaining in place.

She scowls at the dirt. "How can you ask me this?"

"I apologize. Of course, you feel awful." I set down the basket I brought for the produce I intended to trade for and open my arms. "In my culture, an embrace is comforting."

She eyes me for a long moment. Then, as slowly as if one foot is dragging her forward and the other back, she walks into my arms. I fold myself around her and squeeze. For all I have been so happy, there has been much grief in the air. Rafe's pack, William, Manteo. Elizabeth, perhaps, though I truly have not thought of her or the murder she committed since Rafe nearly accused me of it. Yet another selfishness for which I shall have to atone.

After a heartbeat, Matatishe hugs me in return. She trembles like a leaf in the breeze, but tears do not wet my shoulder.

"He made us laugh," she mumbles. "Were another dead, we would laugh with one eye and cry with the other. Without him, we only cry."

I squeeze her tighter, vowing to make this right. My friend shall not suffer with no recompense. "I know a few jokes, if you would like to hear them."

She frees herself from my embrace. "Chawnzmit's people have no humor."

I pretend to be offended, a hand on my heart. "I assure you we do, if you would only let me show you."

Matatishe narrows her eyes but nods.

"Once, a fool desired to see how he looked as he slept." I smile at her. "Thus, he stood before a mirror with his eyes closed!"

She shakes her head, but I can see a flicker of amusement around her lips. We pass most of an hour in this way. I scrape the crevices of my mind for any scrap of humor left behind, and she begrudges me a smile or two, perhaps a snort. Still, her gaze is less leaden when I finally admit defeat.

"I am surprised you laugh," she says, braiding three pieces of grass together.

"Why?" I lean up on my elbow from where I have lain down.

"One of your youths is dead now." She looks at me. "Perhaps this matters less to you."

My body buzzes as if I have leapt from a warm bath to an ice-cold river. Another dead in less than a week. Another youth, as though Elizabeth is choosing them specifically.

"Are you certain?" I demand.

"No. Your rumors come crookedly to us." She glances at the sky, then climbs to her feet. "We must trade. I am needed elsewhere."

I falter through the exchange and race home just as soon as I am certain she will not see my unnatural speed. My heart patters as fast as my footfalls. Two murders since the last Sabbath. Elizabeth is losing control—if Matatishe is correct.

Dinah looks up as I burst through the door, and her expression alone tells me how wild I must look.

"Have you heard of another death?" I ask.

"Haven't been to town." She glances over my shoulder. "Rafe should be returning from there soon, though. Come, sit."

I allow her to fuss over me until I hear Rafe's steady gait on the front path. A mortal run feels no faster than a crawl, but I force myself. I cannot bear the weight of Elizabeth's crimes.

One look at his face tells me all I need; anger and sadness blend into a potent cocktail of clenched fists and furrowed brows.

"I must go speak to Elizabeth." I stride toward him.

He grabs my wrist, then turns my palm up. "Last you spoke to Elizabeth, you nearly revealed yourself to her foreman. You cannot control yourself around her."

"She cannot control herself!" That ember in my breast burns hot and bright. "And I shall not allow her to escape consequences."

"She shan't." Inexorably, despite the blazing heat, he gathers me to his chest. "I shall speak to Sir Thomas, Governor Yeardley, whoever else you like. We can handle this from a distance."

Instinct shrieks through me—Elizabeth likes little less than distance. She loathes to be rendered invisible. Attempting to stay away will only agitate her.

But she will grow agitated at me. Though I know human blood will strengthen her above my own diet, I am more equipped to handle her than any other in the colony. Especially, as the siren song of Rafe's embrace assures, with a wolf-shifter at my side.

With a sigh, I nod. "For now."

"For now."

2 4

LOVE THY NEIGHBOR

Rafe

A FEW DAYS AFTER THE BODY OF YOUNG CHESTEN MCBRIDE IS FOUND outside Jamestown, I stride up the path toward Thistledawn Plantation. I have not visited the place since George and Elizabeth's wedding, nor had I before that day. As July melts into August, it shimmers into view at the top of the road like an oasis. Mosquitoes buzz in thick clouds I am grateful not to be troubled by.

George is a boor. A braggart. A king's son born too low and determined to take the difference in presumed station out on the world. And yet, I have spent six years as his neighbor. He arrived with De La Warr's ship, skating the worst of Jamestown and arriving just soon enough to snatch land while it was plentiful. There are some, mostly those who endured the Starving Time alongside me, who still resent those that arrived after. They don't count George Moore and his ilk as truly *of* us. I do not begrudge them the feeling; I certainly indulged it, in their earliest days. But when George is threatened, I find myself unable to sit by.

179

I rap on his front door. Dust smears the fine varnish Elizabeth so bragged about, last she visited Bluebonnet, creating a stark line between the shining perfection of the top and the hazy mundanity of the bottom. My doors may not be varnished—a silly waste of time and money, I think—but when the bottoms grow grubby, they do not look half one color and half another.

Finally, the door opens. A woman whose name I do not know dries her hands on her apron.

"Mr. Stone." She curtsies. "The master is in his study. Is he awaiting you?"

I shake my head. "I wouldn't expect this to be a particularly long visit."

After another curtsy that reveals the raised scar tissue of a whip strike crawling from the neck of her dress, she hurries away and up the stairs. I find myself alone with one of the most garish settees I have ever beheld in my life and nothing to think about than that scar on the woman's neck. When the African, John, arrived the day before last, he was traced all over with them, each one fresher than the last. I am no wide-eyed innocent; I know the methods by which my fellow planters coax obedience from their workforce. On occasion, a switching is even the correct course of action for a recalcitrant laborer or child. But there is no call for the sheer scope of what I saw on John, what the faded slash on the woman implies.

George thunders down the stairs, and I am forced to remember I came all this way to endeavor to save his life. Should he die, his indentures...would pass to Elizabeth. I stand, straighten my clothes, and wonder no more about whether this is the correct choice.

"Rafe." He clasps my hand genially, though confusion mars his brow. "Is John not working out for you then? I did warn you."

"We have no such issues." Since being granted his freedom, John has taken one day in bed to heal from his most recent wounds at Sarah's urging then folded into the workforce as neatly as any other. "I merely wished to speak to you."

"That so?"

Confusion turns to utter befuddlement. It is difficult to believe I am saying the words, though it speaks better of his perceptive skills than I thought for him to have noticed the discrepancy. I assumed he did not notice my endless street crossings and polite puttings-off over the years.

"We are now brothers," I say half-miserably. "Oughtn't we know each other better?"

"All right." George turns slightly toward the kitchen and bellows, "Thomasine!"

The indentured woman hurries back out with another curtsy. "If it pleases you, sir?"

"Lunch and ale for Mr. Stone and myself, to be taken in my study." He nods in sharp dismissal, and Thomasine bustles away. Without a word, he leads me up the stairs.

"Sturdy make." I knock my heel against the boards. "I haven't seen wood this dark in Virginia."

I do not need to see George's face to hear the cocksure grin around his words. "I had some fine walnut shipped from England. Only the best."

My vaguely affirmative mumble seems to smooth whatever waters my appearance has stirred. He happily points out other treasures we pass—furniture, artworks, a few hangings even I must admit add a certain charm to his whitewashed walls. Sarah is a frugal soul herself, given to usefulness over beauty, but perhaps she wouldn't mind a piece of art or two. Finally, however, George admits me to his study. The tour took long enough that Thomasine is on our heels. She sets plates laden with breads, cheeses, meats, and even fresh fruit on the edge of the desk, curtsies, and departs.

"Apologies." George takes one plate and the tall chair behind the desk. "Elizabeth occupies her room on the ground floor, and she loathes to discover I am entertaining without her."

Perhaps there is a kindly god, watching over my endeavors. I take a bite of bread, hot from the oven, then say, "Are things well between you and she? I heard from Sarah that you may be experiencing some difficulties."

"Oh, all Elizabeth knows is experiencing diff—"

Thomasine re-enters with two mugs of ale and leaves once more. I cannot help but notice the way George's words die on his tongue the moment the door so much as whispers movement and do not return until the kitchen door closes downstairs. He does not know what Elizabeth is—he hasn't the patience to do anything but attempt stakes and fire the moment he discovered the truth—but he has learned some of her abilities. My gut knots about the implication tied to his silence.

Yesterday, I asked Sarah if a vampire might quaff blood without draining the body dry. In part, I wondered if my own life might sustain her. Her simple answer is all that keeps me from searching George all over for bite marks, no matter the social impropriety: not without making another like themselves.

"Then there are troubles," I say slowly.

"More than enough." George swigs ale until it dribbles into his beard. "I've never met a woman less likely to turn her hand to a task. Do you know who last darned my socks?"

"You?" I venture.

"Your little wife." He sneers disgust at his desk, as though it is to blame for the state of affairs. "More than that, I never see her but that she has a request on her lips. The jewels, furniture, fabrics, I am all happy to indulge."

"What else does she ask for?" Thomasine must cook every morsel of food in this house, so Elizabeth cannot be asking for a modified diet. Shovels, though? Undisturbed patches of ground? Two bodies have been discovered, but Sarah eats every three days. There is no knowing how many more might hide on the grounds of Thistledawn. The occasional disappearance has long been a fact of life in Jamestown, especially for those outside the fort walls.

"She wishes me to cease snoring. Cease taking the horse to town without informing her ahead. Cease wearing the spotted suit I am so fond of." He gestures with bread soaked in fruit juice, spattering pink over his papers. Privately, I think Elizabeth may be right about the spotted suit. It makes George look like a great pox. "Cease interrupting her at her own business, cease leaving her alone, cease bothering her about things which she said she would do. If you name an activity I might have done in the past four months, she wishes it ended. Here alone do I have my peace."

I glance around the study. Two bookshelves flank the door, both nearly full with tomes I sincerely doubt a man such as George Moore has so much as opened but which I would endure another visit to Thistledawn to borrow. His desk consumes the whole floor, leaving space only for a chair behind it and one in front. A plush, intricately woven carpet cushions the floor.

"Perhaps that is not all the worst," I say. "Perhaps the two of you ought to spend time apart. Have you a lock for this door?"

Of late, Sarah has been teasing me about which of us is truly stronger, though we have not tested it yet. I can break through most anything Symon, our blacksmith, attempts, but Sarah and Elizabeth may not have the ability.

George laughs at me, a sharper, more acrid sound than that he booms in public. He does not even throw back his head to draw my eye.

"Spend less time with her? I am already fighting for inches in my own bed. If I begin to lock myself away, there is no hope of an heir to carry the Moore name into the future." He scowls at the drops of fruit juice. "She has not fallen pregnant of yet, as I am certain all Jamestown has noticed."

For a moment, I consider that telling George she never will may be the greatest kindness I can do him. Then, I see the smoldering in his gaze. Were he to be sure of that, I truly believe he would seek to divorce Elizabeth, and I will merely have started the cycle again.

"Neither has Sarah." I keep my words even, cautious. "It has not yet been half a year. Such things are common after long sea voyages."

"Do not coddle me with comparisons to your wife." His ire flashes onto me, hot as a brand but toothless as an elderly cat. George hasn't the spirit to be truly angry with me, at least while I sit before him. "She is a pliable woman. I am certain she does not chase you from your bed."

The days I have chased myself out float through my mind. "Perhaps not, however—"

"However, she is a skilled and dedicated worker? Lovely enough never to make a man wince? Well-mannered? Tolerated rather than ill-liked?" George throws his hands up. "I would not need to entertain without Elizabeth so often if she did not insist upon irritating every soul who sets foot in our house!"

The door crashes open behind me.

"Irritating?" Elizabeth stands in the doorway, eyes lethal as a blizzard, chest heaving with hardly sustained rage. "I would look in the glass, little husband, and see whose name is truly spoken with more ire."

"I had a fair phalanx of friends before our wedding day." George stands, uncowed by his wife somehow. "And you?"

"I shall take my leave." I begin inching toward the door, though neither seem to notice me.

"In London, I could not go a *night*"—it is impossible not to notice how she lingers over that word and its every implication—"without company."

"Forgive me," he sneers. "I had forgotten your time as a lady of ill repute."

She looses a wordless shriek and prowls into the office. After I caught Sarah in the woods, when she returned to the deer that was her supper, she moved with the same leonine grace. A predator, uncloaked from its disguise as prey.

I stop my crawl toward the door and freedom. Elizabeth's anger certainly lacks the careful aimlessness of George's—if I draw her eye, she will turn on me just as easily. But George cannot bear up before her in anything but spirit for longer than a heartbeat. For the sake of the six years I have known him and the hard winters we have shared —for the sake of the men and women beneath his dubious care—I shall stay.

"Say that once more, to my very face." She leans over the desk, striking distance from him. "Tell me you believe you have a whore for a wife."

George's skin reddens. "I—"

"You wouldn't dare!" Her whole body knots with barely restrained power. "I know you all too well, George Moore. By the Lord, I know you."

What was a fight quickly melts into little more than a tantrum. She screams all the complaints George alleged back into his face while he stutters out a syllable at a time. On occasion, he looks at me. I do him the pitiful honor of averting my gaze.

"And to compare me to my very own sister, as though I were the lesser half of a cattle trade—" The words seem to catch in her throat, too plentiful and virulent to escape.

I see a rare opportunity. "Fear not, sister, I arrived to commiserate with your husband."

Her single laugh lands like a stone at my feet. I brush past it.

"We have not yet fallen pregnant," I say. "And Sarah wearies quickly of the effort. She is terribly isolated and unhappy with me. I find her...workaday, at times. A wife was intended to bring some excitement to my days."

Elizabeth cuts her frozen gaze at me. "Sarah has always been dull. Her worrying must prick at you as well."

"How could it not?" I swallow a wince at the falsehood. Sarah will forgive me; she will understand the lives on the line if her sister's temper is not restrained. When I return home, I swear I shall tell Sarah her eye for detail and precision frees me from cycles of my own worries. "I have never met a more nagging woman."

"You see?" Elizabeth flips a hand at me, though her attention turns back to George. "You are not uniquely abused by God to be my husband. This is merely what a marriage is."

Thus settled, she storms from the room as quickly as she entered it. The house seems to echo with her absence. Familiar noises filter back in slowly, like animals creeping from hiding in the wake of a sudden shower.

I step to the very edge of George's desk and bend close, lowering my voice as much as human ears can perceive. "A lock, George. Consider it."

He sits back with a cocky grin that strains around the edges like a shirt that has seen too many seasons of wear. "If you wish to fear your little wife, Rafe, you may. I know how to handle a woman."

As I leave, I pray Elizabeth is still enough a woman that George might be right.

2 5

NEW HORIZONS

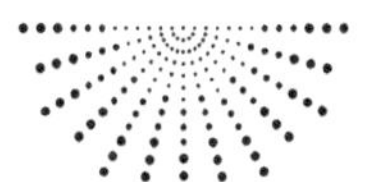

Sarah

"Perhaps it was foolish," Dinah says, caked up to the elbows with yellow corn flour as we knead dough side-by-side. "But I stood there in my fine dress, all my family, all his family, the priest who baptized me looking at me like the saddest thing they'd ever seen, and I simply couldn't stay."

"So you sold yourself as an indenture?" I ask breathlessly, as though I did not leave London with all the same haste.

She nods, smiling ruefully. A bead of sweat traces down her round cheek. "Haven't much regretted it neither. Had Clement come to the wedding, I would be doing much the same, only with wheat flour and a passel of children about my knees."

I drive the heels of my hands into the dough. In truth, the picture Dinah paints is not objectionable to me. The longer I spend with Rafe, the more evenings I enjoy in his arms, the more I wish I did not lose all chance at motherhood. Since I discovered his truth, he has not mentioned the idea of having a child with another woman, but I know he looks at this plantation and sees his legacy. I know he shall

187

someday desire to secure that legacy more than he desires to please me. Sometimes, I fear that day may kill me. I would raise another woman's child as happily as I might raise my own, but I do not believe I could raise his child with another. I would forever be picturing the night he shared with a stranger.

"What of you?" Dinah asks. "Gentlewomen don't much come to the colonies without their own story."

My tongue grows metallic, as if I've hidden a coin beneath it. I swallow. That has begun happening of late. I believe, though the gnawing has not yet truly started in my gut, that it is simply an early sign of hunger.

"Would you believe me if I said my father believed my best prospects were here?"

She looks me up and down. "As easily as I would believe that Lady Elizabeth came here when she had any other choice."

A laugh bursts from my lips, unbidden. I did not realize Dinah had taken such an accurate measurement of my sister in her few visits.

I pick my hands from the dough and turn to give a more passable explanation. The room hazes about the edges, as if morning fog has crept in from the August afternoon somehow. My knees turn all to liquid, and I sway.

Dinah catches my elbow. "Sarah!"

"I am fine," I mumble, in no way certain I speak the truth. "Merely the heat."

"Oh, of course." She wraps one flour-coated arm about my waist and leads me from the sweltering kitchen to the sitting room. Perhaps it is the heat; there is little relief to be found from it anywhere in the colony, but the gentle breeze pouring in from the windows and the empty fireplace create the illusion of coolness. I allow her to settle me in my chair and rest my head against the back while she brings me a chilled drink.

As quickly as the swoon came on, it fades with a few sips. Still, Dinah's face pinches in worry, and she refuses to allow me to return to the kitchen.

"Your constitution is too fragile." She lays a hand against my forehead, testing my temperature. "The height of summer is no time for you to work."

"I am no flower," I protest, but there is no talking Dinah around, as I've well learned. And, though I feel much steadier, I wouldn't like to be proven wrong. If I were, she would send for Rafe, and I would be lucky to find myself out of bed for two weeks while the whole house fell to worrying over me.

She leaves, and I take up my knitting instead. It is a funny thing; I ate only yesterday, and I have not yet swooned since my transformation. I assumed it was yet another ability I had lost, and one I was not sad to see go. Perhaps even demonic strength is no match for a Virginia August.

When Rafe returns an hour later, grubby with the first tobacco harvest of many, I feel much stronger. Still, his emerald gaze roves over me, sharp as a knife.

"Something is wrong."

"Did Dinah say something to you? Because it truly was the heat."

He takes a step closer, eyes narrowing. "She did not. What happened?"

Drat. I smile, even as that metallic taste fills my mouth once more. "A tiny faint. Apparently, I have too delicate a constitution. I did not inform Dinah how often we have proven that false."

Heat fills his gaze instead, but it does not fully replace the worry.

THE NEXT DAY, WHEN I AM QUIETLY SICK FOLLOWING AN ATTEMPTED lunch, I decide that perhaps there is a grain of truth to the others' concern. However, I would still not like to be imprisoned abed like an invalid. There is one woman in twenty miles in whom I can confide and trust she will respect my freedoms.

"I am off to the forest," I tell Dinah brightly. "We are almost out of blueberries."

She waves me goodbye, and I am off.

Long gone is the rough map Mistress Forrest sketched me soon after arrival; I know these woods as well as I once knew my very own in England. A paste Matatishe concocts herself wards mosquitoes from the rare patches of my exposed skin. Ferns rustle their own greetings. Bright bundles of wildflowers wave in the scant breeze.

"Good morning, cypress." My fingertips trail over the trunks of welcoming trees. "Good morning, hickory, pine, and oak."

They do not reply in words, but I hear it in the fluttering of their leaves. Hot, wet air leaves my kirtle clinging to my skin, but I do not stumble as I did in the kitchen. How very strange.

"Matatishe," I call upon arriving at the base of the Trading Tree.

She steps from the brush. As a concession to the heat, she has abandoned the sling of leather across her chest entirely. The first time I saw her without it, I was scandalized. After weeks of enduring this weather myself, I am far more envious. Would that it were easier to strip to the waist, in her presence at least.

"It has not been long," she says.

"Have you any blueberries?" I say by way of answer.

She raises a single, dark eyebrow. "None that I did not pluck from bushes a much shorter walk from your door than mine."

Thankfully, Dinah did not think to wonder the same. "You have called me out. I craved your companionship."

"It has not been long." This time, she says it with a faint smile that promises she does not resent my repeated visits.

"How are you keeping?"

She lifts a black-brown feather braided into her hair. "A vulture visiting Manteo left this behind. It is a good sign."

I touch her hand in comfort. In the weeks since her brother's death, I have learned that the Powhatans do not inter their dearest dead. Instead, they are laid upon great wooden scaffolds, where they are picked apart by animals until naught but bones remain. These bones, Matatishe and her family will take into their home. In some ways, I cannot imagine watching Mother degrade. In others, I wish dearly I had a packet of her to carry with me through my days. There would be an honor in watching her feed the world.

"It is lovely." I sit in a twist of roots very like a seat, then bounce back to my feet. The uncultivated chair in which I can normally rest for hours bruises my skin instantly, as if I were no hardier than an apple.

Matatishe eyes me. "There are no nettles in the roots."

"I have been feeling…odd of late." I lower myself to the grass instead and find its soft embrace far more comforting. "Rafe worries far too much. I did not wish to talk to him of it for fear he might overreact."

She nods knowingly. "Chawnzmit and Chawnrawlf were always like this with our women."

John Rolfe, the wealthiest planter in the colony by orders of magnitude and a man with such prestige about him that he rarely, if ever, sets foot within the fort, is a name I have only heard spoken. Rafe says he once knew the man well but compared him without much warmth to Sir Thomas.

"Tell me." She says, taking the root-chair my body rejected.

"It is only little things." I straighten my skirt around my legs, half-terrified Matatishe will tell me I have some Virginian wasting disease that eats even monsters like myself whole. "My midday meal returned, but only today. I find my mouth tasting of coin—of metal. It leaves quickly and seems to have no origin, just the same as the swoon I fell into yesterday." I smile self-reproachingly. "Perhaps this may not surprise you, but I am not a woman who often swoons."

"Swoon." Matatishe tastes the word thoughtfully. "What is this?"

"Faint?"

She shakes her head.

I bite my lower lip. "It is as if you are falling asleep, but suddenly, often without cause, and often while standing. Genteel ladies find themselves most afflicted with it."

"This I know." She eyes me, dark eyes sharp as a knapped blade. "Your chest is sore?"

When I look at her in confusion, she grabs one of her own bare breasts. My face burns. The stays have been digging in particularly this week, but I merely thought my fingers had grown clumsy with my other oddnesses. I nod.

"When are you next to bleed?"

I cast my gaze at the vibrant grass. Though I count her my dearest friend, we have never before spoken this frankly. "Within a few days. It has been unreliable for the last year."

Ever since I woke like this, I only have my monthly bleeding if I have eaten well enough, which I rarely have. Elizabeth has nearly never missed it.

"I know what is happening." She smiles at me, celebration and sorrow a potent brew on her face. "You are with child."

"No," I blurt. My skin tingles. The sounds of the forest dampen, then roar back to my ears. "That is not possible for me."

Matatishe merely shrugs. "What you believe is possible matters little in the face of what is. Do you not wish for a child?"

"I do." I cup an arm around my belly, struggling to fit her words into anything like sense. "More dearly than anything, but you don't understand, I cannot—"

"You have." Matatishe lays her hand over one of mine. "Thank your god for the miracle and ask no further questions. Miracles are short-lived in this time."

That is simple to believe, at least.

When I am through with Matatishe, I walk at a reasonable, even pace back through the forest. That is, until I catch Rafe's scent on the wind, sweat-soaked and tinged with fresh tobacco. My heart leaps and spins. My husband—the father of my child!

Each footfall lands faster than the one before until I am tearing through the feet between us. It takes every shred of control I have ever mustered in my short life to slow to a human pace when I reach the tree line. Even then, I am not certain I've achieved it. The wind still tugs at my loose hair and yanks my skirts against my body. All I know is that I am nearer something human, at least at something plausibly deniable, even as each inch of my being sings for him.

"Rafe!" I yell as soon as I feel the first acid-scream of sun against my exposed wrists.

He lifts his head, and the knot of tension in his shoulders promises he heard me coming long ago. Were it not for the many watchful eyes and ears, he might have shifted and met me in the very forest. I laugh, delighted by the sheer fact of seeing my restraint mirrored in him. Our lives may never be easy, but they shall always walk parallel paths.

When he sees that, he throws down the razor-sharp knife he was using to harvest ready plants and sprints toward me. The fields, the laborers, even the burn of the light fades from my attention. There is only Rafe and his glowing green eyes.

He catches me by the forearms, and we spin with our combined momentum. My skirts flare around us.

"I believe I am pregnant," I gasp.

"No." His eyebrows shoot so high I wonder they don't take wing and flee his face altogether. His mouth falls slightly open. He studies my face intently, as if searching for the humor in my words. Finding none, he simply murmurs, "How?"

"I have no idea." A laugh as clear as a spring brook bubbles from my lips. I picture the passels of children Dinah escaped, the Christmas dinner at a crowded table. Perhaps this is a miracle from some kindly god—I know the Lord looks over me not. But a miracle that comes once might come again, and we have a house to fill. "And that makes it no less true. I suggest we do not question it."

Wonder breaks over his expression like a wave, consuming all else in its path. He releases one wrist and drops his hand to my still-flat stomach. "Pregnant."

I pull him into a kiss, and he folds himself around me.

Around us both.

2 6

OLD WOUNDS

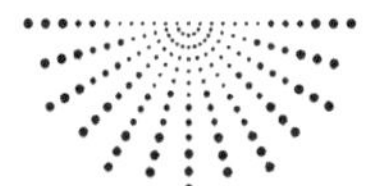

Sarah

THE FOLLOWING MORNING, I FEIGN SLEEP UNTIL RAFE GRAZES MY shoulder with a kiss and leaves for another day in the fields. The moment he departs, I sit up in bed.

I hardly slept. After he and I fell into each other, delirious with celebration, he rolled to the side and relaxed into easy sleep. Most nights, his even breathing lulls me quickly after him. Last night, I stared up at the ceiling with my hand on my stomach.

A tiny life sprouts inside me, fragile and mine to care for. I must protect it with everything I have, everything I am. The world I offer this baby of mine is a dangerous one; disease lurks around every corner, war threatens more often than any would like, and I can still see in Rafe's eyes the ghost of starvation not uncommon in these colonies. So little of that can I protect my child from.

What I can put to rights, however, is the endless parade of Powhatan and English bodies appearing in the no-man's-land between each. Elizabeth's appetite grows, the evidence of it gnawing at me no matter how Rafe tries to protect me from it. I will not have my baby grow up scared of their very aunt, hunted by her in the night. And my window for resolving this closes by the day—animal blood and human blood grant such different strength that, should Elizabeth keep drinking this diet at this pace, I will have no hope of approaching her within the month.

Rafe wormed that detail out of me during a midnight talk, before I realized what it might imply. Ever since, he has been adamant we discover another way to handle the problem of Elizabeth. This child in my womb erases what little time we had left to do so without blackening our souls to nothingness. I wrap myself in a robe, pinch my nose pink, and shuffle downstairs.

"Oh, Sarah," Dinah exclaims before I have even sniffled a breath. "I knew that faint was no mere reaction to the temperature. Get yourself abed, and I shall bring you some porridge."

"No, I—"

She grabs me by the shoulders and turns me about. "Get."

I hide my expression in the collar of my robe and return. While she readies breakfast, I dress in simple, lightweight clothes, then tuck beneath the covers. Falsehood sits uneasily on my tongue, but there is no line I shall not cross for my baby. Even as Dinah worries over me like she is my own mother, I do not falter. The door shuts behind her, and I rise.

The stable hands taught Elizabeth and I to tuck our skirts into pants, that we might sit astride a horse in privacy. My fingers dance through the folds now. Mere moments later, I am sliding out the back window. The studs of the house provide just enough grasp for my unnatural fingers. I scramble down as if I were a spider, curl around the side away from the fields, and set off.

Rafe shall simply have to forgive me; a mother's instinct throbs in my veins, alongside that of a hunter, and it cannot be ignored.

Men of every color tend the fields as always when I approach Elizabeth's house. There is no sign of the vicious Mr. Burns, but my feet stray briefly from the path regardless. If I learn a few more names, Rafe can free them as he has John.

A thick, wet sound oozes into my ears. My skin ices despite the sun. My feet twist back, inhuman speed coursing along my muscles.

Elizabeth feeds.

I do not waste the effort of a knock upon the door, but no one approaches when I burst inside regardless. The house is dead, except for that sound and the slowing heartbeat it belongs to. I vault that awful settee and leap up the stairs, two in a bound. The door to George's study lays ajar. Hot, rich blood scents the air. Has she always been this brazen?

A low, masculine moan chases all wonderment from my head. I burst the final feet to the tapestry of slaughter that awaits on George's carpet.

One pale hand lays limp—George's broad, hairy-knuckled hand. Elizabeth hunches over him, looking for all the world like nothing so much as a gargoyle. Her nails drive pale dents into his arm, the lower half of his whiskered cheek. Blonde hair curtains his throat, but I do not need something as simple as sight to know exactly what occurs through the thin shield of privacy. The sounds become something between animal and venal. George's blood hangs so thick in the air I can nearly taste it.

My feet outpace my thoughts. I close fingers around her arm, nestle others in her hair, as if she is no more than a dog shredding a hunt—the shock must startle her into releasing her kill. A clever woman might have eaten before coming here, but the hunger gnawing through my gut sizzles as if it were power in and of itself. I do not need blood to save a man's life.

I tear Elizabeth back. A chunk of blonde curls come loose in my hand, and she shrieks, but I am able to toss her across the room. She clatters into a shelf, knocking books free. George does not twitch as they land.

"What are you doing?" She scrambles to her feet.

"You are killing him." I step between her and George, hoping against hope that his thready heartbeat might stabilize.

"You always think me a fool." Elizabeth shoves hair back from her face, though pieces snare in the crimson drenching her chin. "I know the consequences of my actions, Saint Sarah. I merely choose not to fear my very shadow for what it might think of me."

Where that bitter ember once lived in my chest, now lives the tiny life I must protect. The ember, with all its sour certainty that Elizabeth has been changed more deeply by this transformation than even I, suffuses my blood. Heat thrums through me.

"If that is what you think this is, you are a fool," I snarl. "Murder is a mortal sin."

Elizabeth leans left, then right, testing my defenses. "The church abhors us. When will you stop bowing to them?"

"Without the sin, then." I shift to match her. She is a hairsbreadth faster, and I know she knows it by the widening of her ruby smile. "How many lives have you ended?"

"Where would you like me to start?" She laughs, sharp enough to cut. "London?"

Her words strike like a blow of pure winter. "What?"

She takes the moment of distraction to lunge forward, angling around me for George. I throw myself at her, one arm wrapped about my center for whatever protection that provides. Elizabeth is stronger and faster; my only edge is to fight as if I do not matter most, which she never will.

My body careens into hers like a stone, and we both hit the floor. She claws at me. Pain stripes hot across my face—with only her nails, she draws blood.

"Have you never wondered about Mallory Manor? How a strange man might have gotten to you without either of us noticing?" She shrieks another laugh.

I need to take George away from her. It is his only chance. Elizabeth rolls us over, and opportunity slips from my grasp.

"Of course, Saint Sarah would not." She grabs my wrists, pins me in place as though she has forgotten her bleeding husband. "Saint William neither—he did not even question why I needed to speak with him alone after you were laid to sleep."

His name punctures my haze of concentration. "William? What has he to do with this?"

Elizabeth leans so close that I can smell George's blood heavier on her breath than in the air. "Once I turned you, I thought I was owed a bit of fun."

2 7

BONDS OF BLOOD

Sarah

I HAVE NEVER BEEN SO GRATEFUL FOR MY SISTER AS I WAS THE MORNING I awoke, newly transformed. Everything hurt, and I could not make sense of how the world had reordered itself in a single night. Still, when I am lonely, I cling to the memory of her hands about the sides of my face. When I flew to her, upon discovering Manteo's murder, a crevice of my mind grasped to that kindness she did me as a raft upon turbulent seas. I prayed the Elizabeth I had grown up beside, that I had half-raised after Mother's death, did not die the night of her own transformation.

The winter's chill in the gaze before me now promises nothing of her remains. That one gesture I have been clinging to, revealed in an instant to be nothing more than another of her games. William—she killed William! And she allowed me to believe I had done it myself!

My hand slips her grasp and whips out, not with a predator's intent, but with a sister's agony. It cracks across her cheek, as she has struck me so often, and points of rose bloom beneath her porcelain

201

skin. Elizabeth laughs, high and delighted. She does not even move to grab my hand once more.

Her folly. I know one simple method for melting ice, and it is the ravenous fire searing through my veins, leaving nothing in its path. I fist my free hand in Elizabeth's precious curls and tear. With a squeal, she rolls aside. I roll with her. My folded skirts bracket her legs easily. Fire draws my arm back, brings it crashing down in a fist Father taught us both to make and never use.

She is faster than me. Her head whips aside so quickly I believe a human neck would have snapped. My fist crashes into the floor, then through it. She twines her legs about my waist and twists, seizing the higher position once more.

I scream, futile rage blasting from my lips. "Why?"

"I did not wish to spend eternity alone." She pouts, innocent but for the gouts of blood in the air.

How often have I fallen for that very pout? Still, she is the picture of purity. But I have seen the truth of her. She is a monster. Whatever soul she had was lost in transformation.

"What now?" I tear at her gown, hoping to call vanity to my aid. "You cannot kill me. I will not allow you to continue."

"You know, you were quite distracted that last morning." She smiles gaily down at me. "Have you never wondered what else I may have packed?"

"You cannot touch any stake or electrum blade you may have laid to hand," I spit.

She beholds me coldly, no interest in her clothes, and I know she is discovering I am right. Monsters such as we are have certain defenses against those who would—quite rightly—destroy us. Most mortal weapons will not more than scratch the surface of our skin. Blessed stakes, fire, and the alloy electrum alone will end our endless lives, none of which can be handled by another vampire. That is, as far as Father was aware. I have never yet tried.

"Why would I need to deal the killing blow myself?" she says. "One cry of *witch*, a lucky stake in the correct hand…."

Winter wind blows through me. She would kill me, if she could.

My very own sister. The Bible is clear—some monsters should be killed. It is right and just to do so. Elizabeth has more than revealed herself to be one of them. But I cannot make my hands climb her bodice to her neck. I cannot even wish murder upon her—her gaze remains all too human.

I have but one choice. I let the boiling tears behind my eyes, rage and sadness in a cocktail more potent than any brewed, bubble over.

"Do not kill me," I plead through lying lips. "I would do anything."

Elizabeth smiles slowly. "That is more what I had hoped."

I sniffle, pitiful before her, just as she has always preferred me. She dismounts my body, gestures to her prone husband.

"Finish him, and I believe we shall be able to find a way we can enjoy Jamestown together."

With true trembling in my limbs, I climb to my feet. Aches saunter along my skin. Blood clots the air. I cross the room to George and kneel at his side. Half-lidded, his eyes barely shift to take me in. His thready pulse is weakening. No matter what I or Elizabeth do, he will die. Too much of his life's energy resides within her now.

I bend over him, the secondhand on the clock taunting how little time I have left. With my freedom, I ought to be able to outsmart Elizabeth. She is clever, but she has never correctly estimated a true opponent. Her own pride blinds her to others' strengths. Just as it did George's—a few scant months is an admirable amount of time in which to have pushed her to this breaking point. George is a fighter, that is certain.

Realization bursts through me, soft and golden as the first rays of dawn. Upon my wakening in this form, I deemed it a curse. I called myself a soulless creature, looked forward to naught but endless unhappiness, a parasite upon the world I so love. But Rafe has shown me there is another path. I am, somehow, happy. I am with child. Everything I have hoped for lies within my reach.

With my chest between Elizabeth and George, I raise my own wrist to my lips and sink hungry fangs through the skin. The sliver of pain disappears below a wave of nausea. My own blood sickens me worse than before, as if my baby resents it. *One moment longer,* I promise. Then, I put my bloodied wrist to George's mouth. A few droplets trickle into his gasping throat.

Something strange happens inside me. A new bond grows between him and myself. His breathing evens, and he opens his eyes. I offer him what slim smile I have.

"Where is she?" he snarls.

"What was that?" Elizabeth asks.

George flips me aside with the desperate strength of a fresh-born demon. I wheel through the air, protecting my stomach. I need to explain to him—to show what his life can be.

He hits Elizabeth with a sound like a heavy door slamming shut, and she shrieks.

"Sarah!" Her furious eyes, no longer distantly cold but melting under George's fury.

I scramble to my feet. "George, listen to me—"

"I am through listening to you both!" He grabs Elizabeth, hefts her over his head, and throws her through the window as if she weighed no more than a sack of grain.

Before she even hits the ground, he leaps out after her. Heart pounding, I fly after them.

Sunlight eats at my skin. I barely swallow my scream, a courtesy George bellows his disinterest with. There is no time. In legend, one can only decapitate a creature like us with an electrum blade. However, legend deals far too little with us newborn; I cannot be certain George cannot simply tear her to pieces.

Elizabeth is a monster. She must be stopped. But there shall be no more deaths, not while I have the ability to stop them.

Her golden hair disappears into the distant trees. George, blood-slicked, leaves a red trail behind. I cannot spare a glance for those working in the fields, cannot worry what they may be thinking. Any heartbeat of hesitation may ensure Elizabeth's death.

The forest's shadows embrace me. Tears paint my cheeks. I know not whether I ever truly ceased weeping—whether I ever truly will. Too much has been lost to know. For now, I cradle my stomach with one arm and brush thanks to the trees with the other. It would not do to have them turn on me at this moment.

Neither Elizabeth nor George has my touch. They rampage through the brush, leaving wide, broken trails. Were I lacking my impossible hearing, I could track them without issue. But I cannot catch up. Both their footfalls speed with human blood—hers, that which she has taken from him; his, that which remains within him. I need a cleverer way.

Their serpentine path draws me past the Trading Tree. I glance at its high, friendly branches. Perhaps I—

"Sarah." Matatishe's hiss is sharp as a blade, barely enough to slow my run.

I tuck behind a tree. There is no telling what I may look like, and she cannot learn the truth. Only great will convinces my fangs to retract with so much blood upon the air.

"Yes?"

She huffs an impatient breath. "This is no moment to play. Opechancanough tires of your violence. His war party marches."

My soul tears in two. Elizabeth's hummingbird steps pound over dirt, not so far that I ought to abandon the chase for sheer hopelessness. She may die.

And so may all of Jamestown. There is not a flicker of untruth in Matatishe's dark eyes, simply gratitude for the times I have gone against my people for her.

Elizabeth is a monster.

There shall be no more deaths than I can prevent.

"I shall save as many of yours as I can, my friend," I tell Matatishe.

Before her reply breaches the air, I turn and run for Jamestown with warning on my lips.

2 8

WAR CRY

Rafe

I RECLINE BENEATH THE WAVING BRANCHES OF AN OAK IN FRONT OF THE manor, a treatise spread in my lap. It is all too easy, during the early harvest, to forget that leisure is just as valuable to a growing farm as labor. When lunch ended, I looked out over the fields and told all my men to take the afternoon to themselves. There is little left to pick, and the sweltering sun overhead will do none of us any favors. The faint breeze in the leaves and the intellectual stimulation, however, are as pleasant a way as I might imagine to pass the time before evening.

That is, very nearly as pleasant. I would prefer to have Sarah beside me, but Dinah said she is tucked up in bed, coddling some sure side effect of her pregnancy which Dinah claims is a head cold.

Her pregnancy. Simply thinking the words draws a smile to my lips. I did not know how we might handle the matter of heirs, but if there is something miraculous between my anatomy and hers, then she is right; we ought not question it. The idea of a rosy-cheeked son or daughter joining us before the next planting season may be some of the pleasantness which urged me to end the workday early.

A strange, wet footstep sounds on the path, as if a fish has taken legs and begun running toward me. I set my treatise aside, stand, and shade my eyes. On the wind, a scent of rosemary and fresh running water precedes the approaching figure. Could it be…?

Sarah crests the nearest hill, soaked to the bone and sprinting more than a few paces faster than a mortal might. Another smell joins the others—that of blood, old and new, but most certainly human. Every hair on my body stands to attention. I take off at a run, faster than I ought, all thought of watching eyes forgotten. In the wake of the volcanic rage that consumes me, they mean nothing. If someone has laid a hand upon my wife, my child, there shall be no place on this Earth they can hide.

I reach her, catch her in my arms. The water streaming from her kirtle and the ends of her hair chills my fingers. "What has happened? Why are you wet?"

"Wet?" She looks down at her clothes as if confused to find them in this state. Before I can pry for an answer, she shakes her head and the topic aside. "I jumped in the creek—but oh, Rafe, the Powhatans. Opechancanough is tired of Elizabeth's actions. They are raiding Jamestown."

"They attacked you?" I snarl, twisting toward the forest. When Opechancanough is not raiding my town, he stays in Werowoco-moco, deeper in the forest. I know its location. With the element of surprise on my side and their strongest away at war, I can destroy every timber.

"No." Sarah's breath huffs and puffs from her chest, a level of exertion I have never before seen from her. "That matters not. All that does is that I have warned the fort, but the parties will reach Bluebon-net, and they will not hesitate to seek their pound of flesh here if they cannot find it elsewhere."

Abruptly, I remember Mother, rain-soaked, telling me to leave Father in the gaol because there were others who more dearly needed my help. I ignored her and spent useless days petitioning the constable. It's a mistake I shall not make again.

"You will tell me everything." I kiss her on the side of the head. "For now, I want you inside."

Her face twists. "I can fight as well as you, better than any other man we have."

I stare down into eyes as blue as the cloudless summer skin, the high pink patches of burn on her cheeks. That twist in her face is all stubbornness; I know not what she has already survived this morning, merely that it obliged her to lie to Dinah, but I suspect it may have convinced her there is no danger she cannot face. Her expression twists my heart just as tightly. I cannot lose her. "But you cannot fight and keep yourself safe— your secret safe." I place a hand, gentle despite the violence hanging thick in the air, on her stomach. "You would both be destroyed."

"I can fight from the shadows." She looks about the brilliant August day, a note of doubt in her tone. "I am no delicate flower."

"I know this." I wrap my arms around her and pull her to my chest. Perhaps she can hear the gallop of my heart; perhaps it will convince her of the truth of my words. "If it pleases you, let us say that I am a delicate flower. My heart is too fragile to consider losing you. I would be destroyed."

She melts into my embrace, stubbornness disappearing in a single breath. "And if I cannot lose you?"

I bury my face in her hair. "Then watch. If I am ever in too much danger, you shall know what to do. I trust your judgment."

Sarah pulls back and looks me in the face. She searches every inch of me—memorizes it, as if she truly is as frightened as I am that this may be our last embrace.

"I promised Matatishe," she says, "if you can fell them without killing, please do."

A smile breaks across my lips as delicate as a newborn foal. My Sarah. In this, which may be our last moment, her heart is still too large to think only of us. "I shall."

She kisses me once, a burning kiss in which I can thankfully taste only herself and a scrap of old blood, then leaves for the house. I square my shoulders and go to a shed near the edge of the property I have not opened since the last war.

Carrying armfuls of swords and shields, I rap on the door of the quartering house. Klaus answers. Wordlessly, he takes in the load in my arms. His smile dies, replaced by a grave frown I remember from the worst of our times together and hoped not to see again.

"Hop to," he barks without needing an instruction from me. "There's a raid afoot."

I STUDY THE LINE OF TWENTY-FIVE MEN, EVERYONE IN THE QUARTERING house who knows how to wield a sword or shield. A part of me is glad fewer young men need the skill; another worries that half-numbers will not be enough to protect my nascent crop. The buckler strapped to my arm and pistol on my hip seem insufficient against Opechancanough, whom I know to be extremely clever from before the former Powhatan leader died. The battles fought with him at the head were the most lethal, the natives using their familiar terrain to brutal advantage.

One look back at the house, to where I can see Sarah watching from our bedroom window, makes my decision for me. I unbelt my pistol and offer it to Klaus.

"Too frightened?" His attempt at a teasing smile is a wan ghost of its usual self. "Or thinking you should recant your order to incapacitate rather than kill?"

"Sarah is frightened." I look into my friend's eyes, the first friend I made in the wake of losing everything. "And, in honor of the love I hold for her, I must be cautious."

Now, Klaus offers me something far closer to a true smile. "You love her?"

"More than I thought I might ever love another," I admit.

"Ha!" He claps me on the shoulder then takes the gun and horn of powder. "All right, then, go hide in the house with the other women. I'll defend your land for you."

"I know you shall." I walk back to the house then around it and into the forest. As the greenery swallows me, I begin to hear the whispers of Powhatan footfalls. Even for my ears, they are nearly imperceptible.

My human ears, that is. I slough off my shield, my clothes, and shift into my wolf form. My tongue lolls out of my mouth, and I crouch. I promised Sarah I would keep myself safe, keep our future safe. This is the best way I can do that.

Still, my fur prickles uneasily. These shall be the first human eyes to see this form since I fled Moorhurst alone. I fight for my family now, as I did then.

Every rustle of the forest is intensified. I hear the Powhatan party approach and remain frozen. Should they spy me before I am ready, all is lost. They spread out, climb trees, ready tomahawks and bows.

One hollers a war cry, and hell returns to Jamestown. Klaus fires a shot. Henrik charges the tree line, swinging wildly in a way that forces me to question whether he has truly handled a blade before. The others follow suit, variably at ease with their weapons. Arrows rain down from the treetops. Henrik spins, falls.

I lunge. Using the tree cover to disguise myself just as they do, I explode from a bush at the one I suspect gave the war cry. Colors are lost on my lupine eyes, so I cannot search his clothing to confirm. I can, however, barrel into him with all my weight before he can breach cover with an axe held high.

He grunts as we land in the dirt. No deaths, Sarah said. I slam one paw onto his wrist holding the tomahawk and lean forward until his fingers release. He sneers at me and says something in their rolling tongue. I flip his blade away with my nose and club the man with another paw, claws hidden in soft sheaths. His head snaps to the side, unconscious.

In my distraction, several of the others have broken the tree line to engage my men. Metal clashes off metal and wood. I leap off the unconscious man and charge free. One of the archers shouts something I cannot understand, and another Powhatan turns from fighting Klaus to see me. His eyes grow wide as I snarl.

Fear, surely, does not break Sarah's rule.

An arrow lances into my flank. I whine, snap the shaft with my teeth to keep it from driving deeper, and spit it into the grass. The Powhatan who noticed me has gathered the attention of two others, three of the seven on the field now circling me with weapons defensively out. I circle just the same. One favors his left leg. Another keeps looking to the first for instructions. These are simple weaknesses to take advantage of, especially if they expect no more than an animal.

They all inhale as one, a cue so clear they might have told me they intend to strike. I move a heartbeat before they do. Father's voice hums in my mind's ear; *Think like a man, bite like a wolf.*

I dodge left, then right, confusing the target of my body. When the one with the lame leg hesitates, I swipe out with another softened foot. The back of a knee is vulnerable on any man, whether they wear leathers or plate; on this man, it is so weak that a single impact sends him to the grass with a soft scream.

The next charges me with a tomahawk. I throw my weight into him, knocking him down, and catch the third's forearm between my teeth. Blood gushes over my tongue, salty and sickening as his scream, but bone does not crunch. He may scar, but he shall live.

One of the archers shouts again. The Powhatan language is strange to my ear, unlike the handful of European ones Mother insisted we learn in school, but a few words, I have deemed vital enough to learn.

When the word *wolf* leaves the archer's lips, I know they have realized I am not what I seem. My fur prickles. I brace, prepared to run if they focus all attention on me—or if they should decide that, against a thing such as me, allying with my own men might better suit their cause.

Instead, the Powhatans help their fallen brethren to their feet and retreat into the woods, watching me all the while. Confusion braids the tension in the air. My men wonder why a random wolf attack worries the Powhatans so, why the wolf only attacked Powhatans.

The Powhatans, I fear, wonder just what exactly they share these woods with.

But there shall be no answers from my lips. I turn and bolt for the trees once more, away from the angle of their retreat, before Klaus or another of my men can decide I now present the largest threat and turn on me. My clothes await me, and with a little preternatural speed, I am climbing the wall up to Sarah's open window before Klaus has deemed the situation safe enough to holster my pistol.

Her cold hands encircle my wrists, and she pulls me the last few inches, her strength rising to meet my own. I tumble inside and wince. The arrowhead remains in my thigh, throbbing faintly.

"Oh!" She claps her hands over her mouth, then rushes to her dresser and withdraws a small pouch.

"Apologies." I start to sit up with a grimace.

"What were you thinking?" Her tone is as iron as her hand on my shoulder, pushing me down as she rolls me over. I dare not resist. After all, the floor hides my smile.

She sets the pouch down beside my head, and I feel cool fingers at the waist of my trousers. They soothe the burning ache of the injury even as my gut heats with her touch. She slides the fabric down my hips, carefully avoiding the embedded flint. My whole back is bared to the air when she shoves my shirt aside, and I cannot find it in my heart to mind. Months of fear and worry disappear with her gentle, soothing noises. I know now that there is no threat in Virginia that we cannot face together. That she will keep herself safe and that I will do the same for her.

"I must pull the rest out." She presses a strap of leather against my lips to muffle my scream. Downstairs, I hear Klaus and the others parade into the kitchen, victorious. Henrik's weak voice loosens another knot in my chest.

"Now."

A burst of brilliant pain sends me writhing. Hot blood oozes from the now-open wound. But just as soon as I think I might rather have fallen unconscious than faced this, Sarah's hands are there, smoothing cool cream and bandaging just tightly enough that I no longer fear my leg may tumble off the joint.

"You know," she says, "it was truly spectacular, watching you fight as a wolf. I have never seen anything so… powerful."

There is a rich, heady want in her words. She releases the iron grasp holding me down, and I twist to look at her. Eyes as deep as the ocean beckon me closer, beg me to drown in their depths.

We have survived. We shall survive. I catch Sarah in my arms, pull her to my lips. Victory dances between us just as brightly as it does in the kitchen. Soon, I will ask to hear of her day. Later, one of the men will come pounding up the stairs with news of their success. For now, I care for nothing more than her breathy, contented sigh and discovering just how well her bandage might stay.

WHAT REMAINS

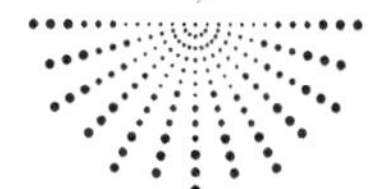

Sarah

WHEN RAFE AND I AT LAST LEAVE OUR BEDROOM, WE SPEND THE evening drinking and feasting with the rest of the plantation. Henrik tells the story of the arrow in his shoulder perhaps a dozen times, and each time it gets closer to a fatal blow. Everyone indulges him, still worried over his pallor and the severe face Dinah made upon leaving his sickbed. She promises me she believes he will heal, but I saw it written on her face. Henrik's condition is the only question mark lingering over most of Bluebonnet.

That is, until I tell Rafe the true story of my morning, after we return to bed that night. He snarls at Elizabeth's behavior so that I think he might leap from bed and go after her himself. When I confess what she did to me, that she is the reason I am like this, I am forced to hold him down.

"Your own sister?" he growls. "She is truly what I expect of a vampire. Whatever soul she had left this mortal coil when she was transformed, I am certain."

I cannot quite find it in myself to disagree. I very nearly cannot find it in myself to utter the truth of William, merely due to the tears that boil behind my eyes the moment I think of him. Kind, unjealous Rafe holds me until I weep myself into slumber.

The next morning, I squeeze my eyes shut a moment longer, pretending he might be beside me instead of already in the fields. It is surprisingly difficult to face my first day truly without my sister, even as my body aches with injuries she dealt me. The mattress shifts, and the warmth of the blankets slowly filter into my notice. I open one eye.

There lies Rafe, rumpled with sleep and smiling softly at me. My heart country-dances through my chest, and I throw an impulsive arm around him.

He grimaces. "Apologies. I heal quickly, but not quite as quickly as you, it seems."

"No, I apologize." I do not withdraw my arm. Releasing him seems impossible. "I shall have to be gentler with my delicate flower."

His laughter, round and rumbling, fills our bedroom. I hope desperately that might be the first sound our child hears.

RAFE TUCKS MY ARM THROUGH HIS AS WE APPROACH JAMESTOWN TO SEE how others fared in the attack. I swallow hard. Even with him beside me, my welcome in the fort has always been chilly at the best of times.

Mr. Spraggins alone stands at the gate, and my spirit sinks. I did not warn them in time. What violence has been perpetrated by Elizabeth's choices? How many lives has she truly ended?

"Mr. Stone!" Mr. Spraggins leans forward, peering under his helmet. "And if it isn't the hero of Jamestown, Mistress Stone! How fares Bluebonnet?"

"Hero?" The word stutters off my tongue, foreign and strange.

"I'd say so." His answering grin is bright, if tired. "Sir Thomas managed to get word to Governor Yeardley fast enough that we scraped by with only a few casualties, including Mr. Cole. When those ba—that is, Powhatans–saw the governor's army coming, they couldn't run fast enough."

"Oh." I sway slightly against Rafe, unsteady on my feet. No deaths. All five hundred-odd lives in the fort, saved. More than I could have imagined in another lifetime.

"She is too glad everything worked out." Rafe smiles down at me. "The gate, if you would not mind? I think seeing the proof might steady her nerves further."

"I will ring the church bells to signal her arrival myself, if you like." Spraggins opens a single door of the massive gate and bows as I pass by him.

My head whirls. They were ready. Preparations saved lives—English and Powhatan, though I don't know that Matatishe would see that exactly as I do. I step inside, and it is as if I am seeing Jamestown for the very first time. Mosquitoes buzz in thick clouds, mud squelches underfoot, but everywhere I turn, a smile awaits me. Mr. Warren bows deeply. Ms. Winnifred, whom I have hardly seen since her wedding, offers me a curtsy and a few mumbled thanks. Father Buck rushes over to us and begins praying. I do not mind that the words are as acid dripped in my ears—they are prayers of safety and of gratitude. Only a creature far more monstrous than myself could turn them away.

I look up at Rafe, wonderstruck. He struts next to me as if he were a rooster fresh from bedding the best hen, desperately proud. I can barely hide my giggle.

"What?" he asks. "You deserve every drop. Perhaps I shall come into town more often if I can hear them rave over my wife, the savior of Jamestown."

A wilder laugh bursts from my lips. My actions brought Elizabe—

No. They did not. I did not kill William. It is her actions, and hers alone, that have dragged us all here. Were it not for Elizabeth, I would be married in London by now.

What an odd thought. There might have been a Lady Sarah Wentworth who was blissfully happy, enjoying the London circuit on William's arm. Perhaps that is the woman who died the night I was transformed. I cannot imagine a life, a smile, without Rafe now. I cannot imagine myself without Jamestown.

I can, however, grieve William as a woman rather than as a monster. I can look upon these now-familiar streets and think how he would have loved them. All of Jamestown would have delighted him, though only for a visit. He lacked any sort of adventuresome spirit. He would have been a steady presence, after my childhood with Father. I think if I had ever set foot here, as the Sarah I am now or the one I was then, I would not have been able to leave. There is something in me which belongs here.

"Mister and Mistress Stone." Sir Thomas sweeps into a bow, Mistress Forrest curtsying at his side. "Jamestown owes you a boon of thanks."

"You owe me nothing," I say. Any debt the town may have owed has been repaid thousandfold today.

He inclines his head. "How keeps Bluebonnet? Were you able to make your own preparations as well?"

"We had a small handful of casualties, but nothing that should affect more than the season," Rafe says. "What of other plantations?"

Mistress Forrest frowns, and Sir Thomas squeezes her hand.

"Reports have been trickling in. It seems a handful of outlying plantations have been ravaged and burned, including"—he cuts his eyes at me—"Thistledawn."

"Burned?" I cover my mouth in shock.

He nods. "Many of the staff fled before the attack, blessedly though strangely, and I am afraid we have heard nothing from either Mr. Moore or your sister."

Had a party of Powhatans come across either, they would have been the ones in danger. Still, I cast my eyes to the ground and pray I look adequately shocked. If neither Elizabeth nor George ever emerge from the woods, I am not certain I shall mind. Thistledawn can lay in ruin; all that I care for is that the slaves it held go free.

"I hate to be the bearer of bad news on such a lovely day." He bows to me again, awkwardly but not unkindly, and the two of them move off.

Rafe looks at me. I look up at him, at the home I've made in his gaze.

"It is no more than they deserve," I whisper.

He grins.

MONTHS LATER, I STRUGGLE TO BEND OVER MY SWOLLEN BELLY TO PICK a patch of delicious-looking mushrooms from the base of a cypress. A friendly oak offers me a pillar of support from which to try. Matatishe was right—the colors of a Virginia autumn are so vibrant they shame England. Fiery reds and oranges flicker in the branches, spotted here and there with pure butter yellows that made me laugh the first I saw them. I have taken one of each home and pressed them, reminders of my very first autumn here. The last Rafe and I shall ever have on our own.

A branch breaks in the distance, and I snap my head up. I can now tell the fall of a human foot from that of an animal, and I do not believe that to have been an animal step. Relations with the Powhatans continue to worsen, but Matatishe says she does not believe another attack is imminent. And she shall warn me. The deaths of her people were also vastly limited from those before by my actions, a fact which she values especially with Manteo still so recently gone.

But it is Elizabeth who steps from the brush. Even as I recognize her, my mind rebels against the idea. George returned a week after the Powhatan attack, and I have heard he's begun rebuilding Thistledawn, though he stays in the fort for now. I passed him a message about how to maintain his diet shortly after, and we have not spoken since. Still, no one has so much as heard from Elizabeth—until now.

The woman in front of me reminds me of nothing so much as Emmeline, her rag doll which she left outside for a winter. Her dress is filthy, caked in three shades of mud and a red stain I can smell is old blood. Her precious golden hair hangs in mats around her face, jabbed through here and there with twigs and leaves. Hunger hollows her cheeks and darkens her eyes. There is a strange looseness to her limbs, as if the stitches holding her together are weakening.

"Sarah." Her voice rattles from her throat, and she holds her hands out pleadingly. "My sister."

I eye her warily. "Where have you been?"

Her laugh has lost all its bell-like clarity. "Everywhere, but I wish to come home. George will not have me."

A clever move.

"Might I stay with you? Simply until I find another husband." She takes another step closer.

"No." I speak before the word even fully takes shape in my mind. She is my sister; I cannot kill her. But winter approaches. Bluebonnet would suffer from the loss of animals, and my soul would suffer from the other deaths Elizabeth drags in her wake like the strings of a marionette.

Tears well in her eyes, and I step back, abandoning my supportive oak and feeling the weight of my child settle once more on my aching ankles. She may look weak, but I shall not make the error of underestimating her again.

Her gaze drops instantly to my stomach.

"You're pregnant," she says the words like an accusation. "How?"

I curl my arms protectively around the little life I have so dutifully grown these last months. I love my baby already. The babe prefers the blood of wolves to any other, grows restless at night, and kicks whenever Rafe laughs. I know my child as well as I know myself. Staring at Elizabeth now, the difference between us becomes stark. Had she fallen pregnant, it would have satisfied neither her nor George. Their baby would have been another trophy, a French settee, rather than a soul they were entrusted to love and serve.

"Perhaps I am not as inhuman as you believed," I say.

"How dare you?" Elizabeth's face freezes over, a brittle mask of rage. "I made you what you—"

Her words break off on a squeak, and I smell sun-warmed fur. I needn't turn to know what has occurred. A wolf the size of Father's prized stallion and dark as a night without stars has stepped from the brush behind me. His emerald eyes glow, as always, and hot breath gusts over my shoulder, promising he has opened his mouth to reveal the curved and dangerous points of his teeth.

"Sarah," Elizabeth whispers, as if I do not know.

I lay a hand upon my husband's shoulder and smile. "There is more to the world than you think, sister. Unless you would like to learn what I have, I would suggest you leave."

She swallows audibly. Her icy eyes dart from Rafe to my stomach to my intractable expression. Elizabeth has always been fond of turning her back on me, a habit I did not notice until the depth of her callousness was revealed. This time, perhaps the last time, she backs away from me into the forest. I stroke Rafe's silken ears and offer the trees one wish.

Keep her away from me. However you must, do not let her touch my life. She shall ruin it, and I shall be forced to act.

The trees rustle in response.

EPILOGUE

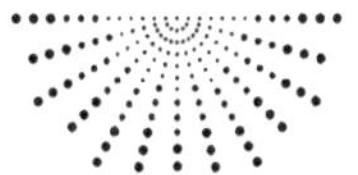

Rafe

EARLY SPRING SUN, THOUGH WAN AND WATERY, STILL SENDS SARAH cringing inside her bonnet as we stride the path to Jamestown. I adjust the angle, hiding another inch of skin, and she smiles at me.

Crispin whines and shakes a tiny fist at me for stealing the sun he has already fallen in love with.

"Hush," Sarah says gently, stroking his silken cheek. "Mama needs the shade, and so do you. You burn faster than any other baby I've ever seen."

My chest fills to bursting. My wife and my boy, such a beautiful picture that I wish I had a painter's touch. Perhaps I'll hire the next who sails in. More art lines the walls of Bluebonnet than once did. I mentioned noticing it at Thistledawn, and Sarah confessed she'd thought the same with a laugh. I cannot tell whether that or my small son's blue eyes, the same shade as his mother's, are what truly brighten the place, but even winter was a delight. Sarah revealed herself to be a dab hand at the fiddle, and we danced the season away.

Crispin loves music almost as much as he loves my ever less rare laughter, yet another trait that reminds me of my brother.

Sarah suggested the name. I thought a good, strong choice like John would suit, but the moment she said it, I knew. My Crispin shall have a hair more common sense than my brother but at least as much heart and spirit. I cannot take back what happened in Moorhurst. I cannot roll back time and try it all again. But I can—and will—sculpt a new, better generation with Sarah at my side.

Cole stands next to a new man at the gate, Anselm Quinn, hired to replace Spraggins after I offered him a position at Bluebonnet. It's a temporary role for Cole as well; Governor Yeardley will be taking him up to the governor's manse just as soon as Quinn is trained up for a much-deserved easy life.

"Do not start him talking," Cole grumbles as we approach. "He's the worst for babies."

"Well, are you not pleased to see the colony blossom before our very eyes?" Quinn waggles metal-clad fingers at Crispin, who screws up his face in anticipation of tears.

Cole is clever enough to begin opening the gate, forcing Quinn away. Sarah bounces our son. Crispin's tantrums come infrequently, but we have noticed he has particularly sensitive ears.

His capabilities—what he truly is—remain thus far a mystery, but Sarah and I are committed to showing him the safest life regardless. He certainly takes human food, and he seems more hirsute than a number of infants I've seen, but he burns like kindling. Sarah also claims his teeth to be particularly sharp, evidenced by small puncture wounds around her breast. But, as she always says, he is first and foremost our son.

We walk into Jamestown, and the parade of admirers begins. He is a handsome boy. My black hair suits Sarah's eyes, and he is as perfectly plump as one can imagine an infant. We crawl down the street, fielding compliments, presents, and attention. Sarah and I exchange the occasional look. We avoided coming into town for so long after his birth knowing this would occur. New life in Jamestown is always an event. When either of us tire, we shall make an excuse and depart, but simply knowing that makes the creep down the road vastly pleasanter.

"Why is the south gate open?" I ask as it comes into view.

Mr. Sheffield glances over his shoulder at the expanse of brackish river beyond. "Ah, a new ship is coming in today. According to rumor, there shall be an influx of colonists."

"Would you like to see a ship?" Sarah asks Crispin.

He gurgles brightly in response, and everyone laughs, including myself. It is easier, knowing how dear it is to the two I love most in the world. I tuck my arm through Sarah's and lead her toward the gate she started her new life through, nearly a year ago.

A three-masted ship bobs in the ocean, and a trio of flat-bottomed boats already row down the river. On the dock, a small party waits to welcome them.

"Look at the rowboats, Cris—" Sarah's words die on her tongue. Her heartbeat speeds. She leans forward, squints slightly. Every speck of color drains from her cheeks, and she looks up at me. "Run."

Thank you for reading! Book 2 will be out soon!

ALSO BY ID JOHNSON

Stand Alone Titles

All I Want for Christmas is Pooch

(sweet contemporary romance)

Christmas Memory

(sweet contemporary romance)

The Doll Maker's Daughter at Christmas

(clean romance/historical)

Pretty Little Monster

(young adult/suspense)

The Journey to Normal: Our Family's Life with Autism *(nonfiction)*

Found by the Alpha (fantasy romance)

Love Throughout Time

(time travel romance)

Back to Titanic

Back to Gettysburg

Back to Bunker Hill

Back to the Highlands

Back to Port Royal

Back to the Spanish Inquisition (coming Sept 2025)

Silverwood Academy

(paranormal romance)

Vampire Hunter

World Builder

Realm Jumper

Celestial Springs

(psychological thriller/literary fiction/women's fiction)

<u>Beneath the Inconstant Moon</u>

<u>The First Mrs. Edwards</u>

<u>Leaving Ginny</u>

The Motherhood

(dystopian romance)

<u>Rain's Rebellion</u>

<u>Rain's Run</u>

<u>Rain's Return</u>

Ashes and Rose Petals

(contemporary romance/retelling of Romeo and Juliet and Cinderella)

<u>Girl in the Attic</u>

<u>Girl From the Tomb</u>

<u>Girl On the Beach</u>

Nashville Country Dreams

(contemporary romance)

<u>Meant to Marry Me</u>

<u>Lead Me Home</u>

<u>You Are the Reason</u>

Forever Love series

(clean romance/historical)

<u>Cordia's Will: A Civil War Story of Love and Loss</u>

<u>Cordia's Hope: A Story of Love on the Frontier</u>

The Clandestine Saga series

(paranormal romance)

<u>Transformation</u>

<u>Resurrection</u>

<u>Repercussion</u>

<u>Absolution</u>

<u>Illumination</u>

<u>Destruction</u>

<u>Annihilation</u>

<u>Obliteration</u>

<u>Termination</u>

A Vampire Hunter's Tale (based on The Clandestine Saga)

(paranormal/alternate history)

<u>Aaron</u>

<u>Jamie</u>

<u>Elliott</u>

<u>Christian</u>

The Chronicles of Cassidy (based on The Clandestine Saga)

(young adult paranormal)

<u>So You Think Your Sister's a Vampire Hunter?</u>

<u>Who Wants to Be a Vampire Hunter?</u>

<u>How Not to Be a Vampire Hunter</u>

<u>My Life As a Teenage Vampire Hunter</u>

<u>Vampire Hunting Isn't for Morons</u>

<u>Vampires Bite and Other Life Lessons</u>

<u>Gone Guardian</u>

<u>Death Does Not Become Her</u>

Blood of the Vampire Hunter (based on The Clandestine Saga)

(paranormal romance)

<u>Night Slayer</u>

Shadow Stalker

Queen Catcher

Mother Hunter

Father Finder

Ghosts of Southampton series

(historical romance)

Prelude

Titanic

Residuum

Lusitania

Heartwarming Holidays Sweet Romance series

(Christian/clean romance)

Melody's Christmas

Christmas Cocoa

Winter Woods

Waiting On Love

Shamrock Hearts

A Blossoming Spring Romance

Firecracker!

Falling in Love

Thankful for You

Melody's Christmas Wedding

The New Year's Date

Charles Town Brides (based on Heartwarming Holidays Sweet Romance)

(Christian/clean romance)

From This Moment

Can't Help Falling in Love

It's Your Love

When You Say Nothing At All

My Girl

Unchained Melody

I Only Have Eyes For You

At Last

The Very Thought of You

Reaper's Hollow

(paranormal/urban fantasy)

Ruin's Lot

Ruin's Promise

Ruin's Legacy

When Kings Collide

(steamy historical romance)

Princess of Silence

Princess of Hearts

Collections

Ghosts of Southampton Books 0-2

Reaper's Hollow Books 1-3

The Clandestine Saga Books 1-3

The Chronicles of Cassidy Books 1-4

Celestial Springs Collection

Heartwarming Holidays Sweet Romance Books 1-3

Heartwarming Holidays Sweet Romance Books 4-7

Websites: https://books2read.com/ap/xX7ZD8/ID-Johnson

For updates, visit www.authoridjohnson.blogspot.com

Follow on Twitter @authoridjohnson

Find me on Facebook at www.facebook.com/IDJohnsonAuthor

Instagram: @authoridjohnson

Follow me on Bookbub: https://www.bookbub.com/authors/id-johnson

www.ingramcontent.com/pod-product-compliance
Lightning Source LLC
Chambersburg PA
CBHW060307310726
48976CB00007B/2244